A
CAPTAIN
and a CORSET

MARY WINE

ALSO AVAILABLE FROM MARY WINE AND SOURCEBOOKS CASABLANCA

ISBN-13: 978-1-4022-6483-2

9 781402 264832

50699

EAN

Praise for *A Lady Can Never Be Too Curious*

"The pages spark with manners and mayhem. Wine has created a world readers will want to return to, especially after a conclusion that leaves many questions unanswered."

—*Publishers Weekly*

"The chemistry between the two main characters is off the charts."

—*Fresh Fiction*

"This story grabbed me right at the beginning and I had great fun seeing the world the author created."

—*Long and Short Reviews*

"Love scenes were very hot and steamy."

—*Paranormal & Romantic Suspense*

"Steampunk fans will happily embrace the altered history offered by this escape into 1840 Great Britain as Wine steps away from her Scottish series."

—*Booklist*

"This fast-paced, unique Steampunk story has introduced me to a whole new world that I can't wait to read more of… A wonderful story. Wine is making a distinct mark in Steampunk."

—*Night Owl Reviews*

"I'm really starting to get into the Steampunk genre, and this book has made me fall in love a little more."

—*RomFan Reviews*

Praise for Mary Wine

"Mary Wine brings history to life with major sizzle factor."

"The writing, as always, is fantastic, and the dialogue will make you wither and melt... Mary Wine is an author you can trust to deliver."

"Wine knows her strengths and plays into them as she lures readers into a fast-paced tale."

"Mary Wine always does an excellent historical... exceptionally well researched and extremely authentic."

"Mary Wine's writing is absolutely stellar."

"Mary Wine has a definite knack for pacing."

Also by Mary Wine

A CAPTAIN
and a CORSET

MARY WINE

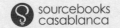

sourcebooks
casablanca

Published by Sourcebooks Casablanca, an imprint of Sourcebooks, Inc.
P.O. Box 4410, Naperville, Illinois 60567-4410
(630) 961-3900
Fax: (630) 961-2168
www.sourcebooks.com

Printed and bound in the United States of America
VP 10 9 8 7 6 5 4 3 2 1

This one is for David Neil. Thanks for listening. It's a talent you are a master of and I spend a lot of time trying to perfect. I hope you always know what a treasure your friendship is.

One

London, 1843

"BECOMING FRUSTRATED WILL NOT SOLVE THIS. QUITE the opposite actually."

Sophia Stevenson resisted the urge to wipe her forehead on her sleeve and had to bite her lip when she realized just how unladylike the impulse was. Of course, there was very little about her current circumstance that was ladylike at all. Perspiration was trickling down the sides of her face and she was wearing a pair of cycling pantaloons in the presence of a man. Her aunts would have brain seizures if they knew.

"You need to focus, Miss Stevenson."

Bion Donkova's tone was both condescending and irritating. It was completely unjust that the man appeared so composed while she struggled to maintain even a hint of civility. His dark eyes were full of expectation too, irritating her further. He'd already decided that she would fail and she longed to swing the wrench at his square-cut jaw.

But she wasn't raised to be a quitter. The way Bion

watched her, like a school headmaster, stirred up her fighting spirit. She wouldn't back down from the challenge he'd placed before her. Nor would she waste her time on a temper tantrum.

Sophia tightened her grip on the large wrench and stretched her arm into the huge engine in front of her. Steam hissed, singeing the skin just above the protective leather glove she wore. The hot water coated the leather, making it harder to control the wrench. Oh... but she would control it!

In spite of the steam, she leaned forward so that she could see the small pipe the water was escaping from. The inside of the engine was hot and the water boiled the moment it hit the metal components that made it up. The round, purple lenses of her glasses fogged over, but she gave a little jerk of her head to shake them down her nose a bit. She peered over the rims and spotted the problem area. She fitted the wrench around the gasket and started to tighten it.

Just one more turn...

The water began to dribble, the steam decreasing until it stopped completely. She'd expected to feel relief; instead, she marveled at her own success.

A sense of accomplishment filled her, lightening her mood until she withdrew from the engine and came face-to-face with Bion Donkova.

She noticed too much about him—or more pointedly, how she felt about him—which was quite inappropriate for a young lady. But the teachings of her childhood didn't seem to stop her gaze from wandering.

His square jaw appealed to her—so did the way she

had to tip her head back to make eye contact with him because of his greater height. His wide shoulder span was not at all in fashion, but she discovered that her gaze lingered on it and the thick bulges of muscle beneath his uniform coat.

But the man was frowning at her, his expression dark and unyielding. She should have been used to such after half a year, but lately she had been irritated more and more by his glowering. Instead of putting the wrench away, she hesitated and shot a hard look back into his dark eyes. Something inside her snapped, like a leather riding whip, insisting that she show him she would stand her ground instead of scurrying off like some mouse under the guise of replacing the wrench.

His eyes narrowed, taking in her challenge. He stepped closer, and for just a moment, something twisted in her belly. The intensity exceeded anything she'd felt before. Her breath froze, suspending her inside the moment for what felt like an hour before she stepped back, uncertainty smothering her pride. A lady did not allow a gentleman so close, except for during a dance when there were chaperones. Society was one hundred percent unforgiving of promiscuity.

She pushed her glasses back into position, grateful for the colored glass shielding her from his scrutiny. For some reason, it felt as though he could see right into her thoughts. Which was ridiculous, of course. But her knees felt weak.

"The entire point of the glasses is to protect your vision," Bion critiqued her. "No matter what crisis befalls the ship you are on, you need to remember that your ability to see Dimension Gates is irreplaceable. Allow your eyes to be damaged and the ship is lost just as surely as if this emergency with the engine was never solved."

"I understand the importance of being able to guide a ship through a Dimension Gate."

Those gates were like tunnels through dimensions that allowed an airship to take a shortcut across the globe. They were a marvel she'd never known about until her encounter with a Root Ball had transformed her eyes so she might see them.

"I wonder at times," Bion growled.

"You needn't," she snapped.

Sophia placed the wrench back in the small metal clamp that held it next to the engine and closed the hatch before taking off the leather gauntlet.

Oh, how she wanted to throw it at his feet…

The impulse was intense and she realized she was grinding her teeth. What was wrong with her? Bion Donkova was certainly not the first man to glower down at her while pointing out how she fell short of his expectations. For all that they lived in the Enlightened Age, men still considered themselves superior to women. At least in the society beyond the walls of the Illuminists' Solitary Chamber, they did.

"My expectations are high only because the consequences of failure are equally high," Bion continued.

For just a moment, his voice held a note of something she might have labeled concern. But that idea fled as she looked at the stone mask his face was set into. There was nothing caring in the grim set of his lips or the hard set of his jaw. But there was a flicker of something in his dark eyes which appeared very personal.

Which was ridiculous, of course. The man was her training officer. It was his duty, not his choice.

Life among the secretive Illuminist Order was supposed to be different than the Victorian world outside the walls of the Solitary Chamber. Here, a woman had the same rights as a man—as long as she was willing to earn her way. It was like a dream come true really, because outside, in the rest of London, there were plenty of women working their years away without the promise of respect. They would toil and be reminded that women should keep to their place. That it was a man's world. Among the Illuminists, she might have position and respect, even freedom to make her own choices. So she would meet the expectations of her training officer, even if he irritated her almost beyond her control.

That idea restored Sophia's confidence. She hung the glove from a peg next to the wrench, so it would be ready for the next person who had to deal with the engine, and took a deep breath. "Since it is your intention to simulate an emergency, Captain Donkova, you must accept that some risk is unavoidable. I doubt I will be of much assistance if I am preoccupied with my own discomfort. I do believe you were trying to impress upon me the idea of prioritizing."

He didn't care for her words, or maybe it was her tone, or perhaps the reason a muscle twitched along his jaw was due to her formal mode of address. Captain Bion Donkova had dark hair to go with his dark eyes, which paired rather well with his disgruntled expression. His arms were crossed over his chest, hiding his gold Illuminist Order pin.

Yet she knew it was there, pinned securely and prominently to his maroon uniform coat. There was a row of buttons running down the front of the coat and it ended at his hips like any maritime captain's uniform. But Bion was captain of an airship, a marvelous invention, the mechanics of which the Illuminist Order kept secret from the rest of the world. Like a great many other things the Order had. No one entered their world of wonders without wearing one of their membership pins.

"You should accept that everything I ask you to do has purpose, Miss Stevenson," he stated.

"I completed the requirement, thereby proving that I have achieved the skills I am expected to master," she countered.

"Your demeanor contradicts your statement," he argued, stepping closer. "I can see it in your eyes."

She stiffened and raised her chin. "Looking into my eyes is not part of your responsibility to train me, Captain." She didn't care for how irritated she sounded. The man brought out the worst in her. Why couldn't she simply ignore him? "So… good day."

She turned to leave, but he reached out and caught her upper arm. It was almost unnatural the way he moved so quickly—or without any regard for properness.

He shouldn't touch her…

She gasped and tried to shake off his hold. "I have asked you before, Captain Donkova, to maintain a decent distance between us. Your forwardness is quite vulgar."

But it is also exciting.

No, it was not!

"Stop handling me as if you were some dockside bully."

Her insult should have irritated him. Instead, his lips curled into a cocksure grin making him appear for all the world as if she had indeed challenged him by tossing the gauntlet at the tips of his polished boots.

"I suggest you be more mindful of what charges you level at me, Miss Stevenson." He pulled her closer and she was momentarily breathless again. "I do consider myself a man of action and might decide to lend truth to your accusations."

She snarled at him. The sound was soft but he heard it. For a moment, something that fascinated her flickered in his dark eyes. Excitement twisted through her belly as she became intensely aware of how warm his hand was on her arm, its heat burning through her jacket sleeve. She was being flooded with awareness. Tiny details about his features suddenly assaulted her thoughts. Part of her wanted to lean closer, discarding every bit of sense she had in order to discover how much more intensely she might feel. But his gaze dropped to her lips and she jerked back, a warning bell ringing insistently inside her mind.

This was dangerous… *He* was dangerous.

And she was somehow susceptible to him.

Which was completely unacceptable.

She drew herself up as prim and proper as her aunts had taught her to be. "No matter what authority the Illuminist Order grants you over me, it does not give you the right to be familiar with my person. I'm a respectable woman." She was agitated, and her Irish brogue began to surface in spite of years of practice to banish it. "And ye'll be remembering that fact, sir."

He released her and she turned her back on him— which was more for her own benefit than any slight intended against him. Not as if he'd notice; the brute was too thick-skinned for her barbs. No, she needed to be free from him so she might collect her thoughts. Sophia hurried across the mock deck of the training facility. The low ceiling and narrow corridor simulated the conditions on board airships for those learning to maintain and run the engines that powered the huge, sky-faring vessels. She hurried down a section of steps that was so steep it was practically a ladder, but her lack of a petticoat allowed her to traverse it easily. There were no skirts allowed in the engine room or, in this case, the engine room training area. She wore a pair of trousers with only a maroon uniform jacket to cover her corset.

She hurried through a doorway and struggled to compose herself as she entered one of the hallways used by Illuminist students. There were men and women of all ages. The four-block complex, known as a Solitary Chamber, was much more than a single chamber. It was a sprawling complex that was in fact a small city.

Sophia reached up to finger the silver pin on her jacket. It had a compass above the main Illuminist insignia, embedded with its tiny Deep Earth Crystal. The crystal would complete the electrical current at many of the doorways, allowing her to pass. She felt the current as she went under the large archways that led to the Novices' quarters. For an entire year, she'd wear the silver pin and there would be many arches she couldn't pass through until she took her Oath of Allegiance. The Illuminists guarded their secrets well.

She sighed once the door to her own room was closed but frowned and twisted to lean her forehead against it. The solid oak panel didn't give her the reassurance she sought because she knew very well that Bion Donkova had the authority to enter her chamber anytime he felt it necessary.

Which was too often.

He was her training officer and in many ways her judge. Inspecting her rooms was just another test she had to face on her way to becoming a full member of the Order. But she shivered because it was just so completely inappropriate. Her own father had stopped entering her bedroom years ago, in accordance with society's demand for demure and modest behavior. She'd started wearing steel-boned corsets and double petticoats the moment her body developed curves, but Bion could enter her room without even knocking.

Shocking.

Scandalous.

But society considered all Illuminists beneath them. Still, she found it hard to adjust to the idea of the airship captain inside her personal rooms.

The fact that he'd had to give up his post in order to train her didn't give her much satisfaction. She couldn't quite feel grateful, and it was getting harder to ignore how much she wished him to leave her to her future.

You'd miss him…

I would not!

She forced herself to straighten and seek out a bath. The lights came on as she entered the parlor but they came on at a normal level, which was too bright for her sensitive eyes, even with her protective glasses. The Illuminist Order pin she wore engaged the lights built into panels along the walls without her needing to touch them. She squinted and hurried to turn several of them off. Deep Earth Crystals illuminated when stones of opposite gender were close. Inside each wall mounting was a male crystal. Her pin contained a female specimen. It was quite a convenience—there was none of the soot or smoke emitted by kerosene or gas lamps. No danger of fire either. Part of her longed for her father's home, with its lack of Illuminist technology, but she couldn't return to normal society.

The light level lowered, and her eyes stopped aching. She paused in front of a mirror and pulled the glasses off her face. Once she had had blue eyes as clear as a summer sky. Now there were specks of amber in them, the result of her encounter with a Root Ball, a very rare cluster of seed crystals that surrounded a new Deep Earth Crystal. When a Root Ball was exposed to water, it vaporized and the steam could alter the human eye.

For a moment, she recalled the moment when her best friend, Janette Aston, had found the Root Ball. The sun had been blistering their faces as a man named Grainger held a gun on them. Janette was a Pure Spirit. She could hear Deep Earth Crystals but had never known of them until she boldly tried to enter the Solitary Lodge one afternoon last year. Somehow, they'd both ended up on the Hawaiian Islands and it had altered Sophia's life forever.

That steam had stimulated growth in the rods of her retinas, so that her eyesight was much keener—and more sensitive.

Are you sure you are not thinking about your feelings for Bion Donkova?

She scoffed at her thoughts, rejecting such foolishness.

The airship captain had been with her in the Kingdom of Hawaii when Janette had found the Root Ball.

You're not being very kind… to wish him on his way and away from you…

Her cheeks heated with a touch of shame because her frustration was unkind. Bion had cared for her after the damned Root Ball had vaporized and she hadn't known better than to look at it. She hadn't known anything about Deep Earth Crystals or the power they could produce. The man had carried her when her knees buckled from the pain and he hadn't deserted her as she'd recovered. It hadn't been his duty to make sure she was comfortable; truly she ought to be more thankful.

Had it really only been half a year ago?

It seemed much, much longer. Janette was married and in love with her husband, and happily wore her gold Illuminist member pin now, which was fortunate, since Janette was a Pure Spirit, which meant she could hear Deep Earth Crystals—her mother had even been an Illuminist without her daughter ever knowing. Wouldn't the matrons have a delightful time spreading that rumor?

They likely were, since Janette was an Illuminist

now and her mother often visited while wearing a pin of the Order. It was very likely all their names were being tarred and feathered for daring to associate with an Order that violated womanhood by stripping innocence away. Sophia had heard such lamentations many a day during tea. It had never concerned her greatly, but now it seemed fate had ensured that she discover what the Secret Order was about.

Her eyes were changed irreversibly. The dark glasses that were necessary to prevent pain from assaulting her in the bright light of day marked her as an Illuminist. She knew she didn't have to join the Order, but Bion had been quick to tell her that she would not be safe back in her father's care. She'd wanted to argue—still did—but to what end? Should she return home and hide in the back room forever and risk one of her father's well-to-do clients noticing her glasses? Her sisters would not fare well if that happened.

Besides, what sort of life was it to live in the back room of a tailor shop? She adored working with fabric, but what use was a pretty dress if she had nowhere to wear it? No ball to attend where she might waltz in her silk petticoats, and no afternoon tea with friends where they might laugh together?

Enough pity!

That was the most useful thought she'd had all day. Well, at least since leaving Bion. The man was arrogant, but he knew the world she'd been tossed into. In a way, she'd been shanghaied. One afternoon stroll had ended with her being dragged into a carriage and taken away from her life forever. Never once in her sheltered life had she ever thought someone might use her to force her best friend to do something illegal. Of course, it was only a crime among the Illuminist Order to harvest Deep Earth Crystals for the Helikeians, but Janette had been on her way to joining the Order. The Helikeians didn't share the Illuminists' views on leaving the rest of the world alone. Their greatest wish was to gain enough Deep Earth Crystal to equip an army to conquer the world. The Illuminists had held them off for centuries, as they clung to their ideals of honor and dedication to learning. Now, Sophia's life was a series of challenges that she must conquer, or else she risked losing more.

Shanghaiing was the true word for it. It was more than sin and vice that kept the upper crust of society inside their closed carriages and their section of town. There were tales of men and women taken from dark alleys to become slaves aboard the vessels heading for the Orient. Sophia wasn't fool enough to think there were no dangers in the world; she knew some of them were just across the street from her own doorstep. But she hadn't realized there were two forces facing off that might easily wipe out everything Britain might muster to defend herself with. She paused, looking at the silver pin in a mirror. How much more was there to learn? Or fear?

It is for your protection, Miss Stevenson.

Bion's deep voice rose from her memory clear as a church bell.

Or just possibly it was more about keeping her in the possession of the Illuminist Order. Soon, she would be a Navigator. The fleet of airships the Order used to transport their goods and their members traveled

through dimension gates. Only a Navigator could
see the seams and guide the ship to the correct place.
With her eyes altered, she was as rare a commodity
as her friend Janette. Navigators were either born of
two Navigator parents or created by being exposed to
a Root Ball. Bion was protecting her, but he was also
ensuring that she did not tip the scales by working
with the Helikeians.

Not that she was tempted. No, she'd witnessed just
what manner of fiends the men of the Helikeian cause
were while she was in their keeping.

Sophia gave in to the urge to groan out loud.
She was sick unto death of hearing about how she
needed watching, guarding, and protecting, even if
there was logic to support it. Little girls truly were
the silliest creatures on the planet for wishing to be
princesses. The royal family had to retreat behind
their estate walls for any privacy and she understood
how they felt. Fine possessions did not quench the
yearning for freedom.

Not a bit.

❧

Soft applause filled the mock engine room. Guardian
Lykos Claxton appeared near the edge of the training
stage, slowly clapping his hands. Bion clasped the rail
and glared at him.

"It's not a good day to try my patience," Bion
warned. His tone made it clear he wasn't toying.

Lykos cocked his head to one side, a lock of his
fair hair moving across his forehead as he did so. "I
am not the one straining your rather notable reserves

of restraint. The culprit just left, attired in a very nice set of trousers. I fear she was somewhat uncomfortable being seen wearing trousers in public."

Bion growled softly before using his grip on the rail to assist him in jumping over it. He landed on the floor in a perfect stance; knees bent enough to absorb the shock and hands ready to deal with any threat.

Lykos lifted his hands in mock surrender. "By all means, train her as you see fit. I simply wanted to thank you for amusing me so greatly."

Bion straightened. "I warned you, Guardian…"

Lykos shook his head. "I understand you are looking for an outlet for all that turmoil our newest foundling seems to inspire inside you, but I assure you, I am not your man tonight."

Bion sent his fist into his opposite palm, the sound popping loudly across the room. "I believe you will serve quite nicely."

"I might argue on behalf of my comrade, but I discover myself agreeing with you, Captain," Guardian Darius Lawley interrupted from the doorway. He was formally attired in a brown suit that complemented his black hair and eyes. Settled in his ear was a control with several copper and brass gears that would allow him to open any door throughout the Solitary Chamber. It covered most of his ear, and when he pressed it, the door behind him closed.

"Lykos has a misplaced sense of humor at times," Darius continued. "But the ladies do enjoy his fair features."

Lykos made a face. "I have no use for 'ladies' of any sort. Tempting your wife away from the ever-so-proper

Society beyond our Order improved her immensely. The upper crust's ideal of what a woman should be is ridiculous. A lady has limbs instead of arms and a gentleman never bothers his wife with his base needs, nor can a lady be seen while in the family way, for the very sight of her rounded belly might be too much for another lady's delicate sensibilities. The lady must also not be burdened with higher learning, for it will harden her mothering instincts." Lykos shook his head. "Drivel. They spend their lives inventing rules of conduct that lack any benefit instead of expanding their minds."

"But it led to the current situation with Miss Stevenson. She was raised to be a lady yet finds herself among us—the uncivilized Illuminists. A situation bound to cause friction as she adjusts," Bion remarked dryly. "I thought you and your wife were assigned to the Hawaiian Islands, Guardian Lawley."

Darius nodded. "I had the pleasure of escorting Grainger here for trial."

"That bastard is still breathing?" Bion demanded.

"A fact I find irritating as well," Lykos agreed. "I thought the doctor predicted he would die from his head injury. You really should have done a better job of cracking the man's skull, Captain Donkova."

"An oversight I will be happy to remedy," Bion assured them.

"The law is clear. The man will have his trial and his sentence will be carried out in a civilized manner, else we are no better than he is." Darius offered them a chilling look. "The man lingered near death for weeks but managed to recover, which leaves us the task of

convicting him. Since Miss Stevenson is still in a delicate state, it was determined we would come to her."

Bion snorted. "Do yourself a favor and refrain from
mentioning your opinion of her current state. Miss
Stevenson will be quite willing to correct you on the
matter of how she views her strength."

Darius grinned. "My wife described her as a redhead
masquerading as a blonde. By the look on your face,
Janette's assessment appears accurate."

"I have the situation well in hand," Bion responded.
No one missed the warning in his tone. "Her training
is progressing well."

"All the more reason to be finished with the cause
of her transformation. There will be an official inquiry
tomorrow. Both of you have been summoned by
the Marshals."

Bion nodded, then left the engine training room.
His expression was controlled and devoid of any hints
of his true feelings, but inside, he was elated. It was
a savage sort of enjoyment, but one he didn't try to
control. Compatriot Grainger was a Helikeian. Their
Order was as old as the Illuminists', but they were very
different. Helikeians would use Deep Earth Crystals
and their power to build weapons for the purpose
of global domination. For a solid millennia, the two
orders had been clashing. Bion was certainly going to
enjoy standing up before a Marshal to help Grainger
get the conviction he so richly deserved.

To be sure, a part of him would rather know that
the man had died from the blow to the head Bion had
inflicted out on that Hawaiian lava flow. Bion snarled
softly, the memory of that day still branded into his mind.

Even now, he was furious with himself. Janette Lawley was a Pure Spirit, and it had been his duty to keep her from falling into Helikeian hands. Still, he should have prevented the event that had torn Sophia away from her family.

Guilt was a bitch that chewed on him relentlessly. So much so that he had requested to be Sophia's personal advisor during her training. The posting had been approved reluctantly because his own skills as a captain were exceptional and the Order needed him back in the air fleet.

But the Order would have to wait. Becoming a Navigator was something Illuminists waited years, often decades, for. It was something many trained for but never gained the opportunity to achieve. Root Balls were rare and competition for access to them was fierce. No member of the Order ever endured the agony of the transformation without being completely willing and eager. Only the elite were selected for transformation.

Except Sophia Stevenson. She was unprepared, ignorant of the process taking place inside her. Which was his failing.

The sting of that knowledge was intense, but he didn't try to squelch it. Pain sometimes taught a deeper lesson than anything else. There was no way he would allow her to fall into the hands of a less accomplished training officer than himself.

Not a single chance in hell.

❧

Sophia shut the book she'd been trying to read. She had classes to prepare for, but her mind was restless.

She made her way into the bathroom, still amazed by the conveniences offered by the Illuminists' society. Her father had proudly installed piped-in water a few years before to the delight of the entire family. But here in the smallest, humblest rooms of the Solitary Chamber, she might have a hot bath without heating a kettle.

What did it matter that she might take a hot bath without stoking up the fire if she could not hear her father telling his favorite hunting story at the supper table once more?

She shook off her melancholy, ordering herself to concentrate on more practical matters. More positive ones.

She had rights among the Illuminists, rights her sisters would never enjoy in high society, with its ideas of what place a woman should stand in.

Like being able to kiss Bion Donkova if you like…

She most certainly did not like that idea.

How would you know? You've never been kissed.

Well, at least not by a man, she hadn't. There had been Jonathon Saddler, who had kissed her in the Brimmers garden during a ball last spring. Somehow, she doubted Bion would hesitate when he leaned toward her or that his kiss would be anything like the soft salutation Jonathon had bestowed on her before stiffening and hurrying her back to the safety of the matrons' watchful eyes.

There were no matrons inside the Illuminist society. In fact, among her rights was the one to take a lover without repercussions. Sophia laughed, certain her mother's ghost was going to appear any second to reprimand her for even thinking such a thing.

But you've taken it a step further with thinking about how Bion might kiss you.

Sophia ground her teeth, not sure if she was exasperated or frustrated. She honestly wasn't sure anymore. The first few months she had been a Novice had not seemed so difficult. She'd had classes to attend, like at a university, the difference being that among the Illuminists, females might study any subject from anatomy to the zodiac. Heat teased her cheeks when she recalled the one anatomy class she'd attended. She had expected a lecture and arrived to find the classroom full of scale models as well as two live ones.

She unbuttoned her maroon coat and caught a glimpse of herself in the small mirror set above the sink. There was also a full-length one near the bathtub, but she'd draped a sheet over it, not wanting to see her entire body unclothed. Such was wicked, depraved, wanton…

Or at least that was what the matrons had whispered.

She drew in a deep breath and forced herself to look at her reflection in the mirror as she shrugged out of her coat. Her shoulders were smooth and sprinkled with tiny freckles. As far back as she could recall, her mother had insisted she wear a wide-brimmed hat to keep her face free of freckles to avoid being thought lowbred. In fact, everything she did was in an effort to avoid gossip and rumors. Her behavior had been constantly critiqued so that she might mend her ways before society labeled her something that might bring shame to the family.

Yet now, all of it was useless. The Illuminists were looked down upon by society, like the unfortunates who worked in the brothels or the Jews who kept to their own sections of town. Once a person began wearing the gold pin of the Illuminist Order, they were not received by the most respected members of society. There were exceptions—those who benefited from the Illuminist technology too much to look down their noses at them.

She turned the knob to fill the tub with water—it was nice, with a high back like a little slipper shoe. It was coated in white enamel and the water coming from the tap was the clearest she had ever seen. She cupped her hand beneath it, marveling at the pristine clearness. Only country homes—and the Illuminists—had such good water. According to one of her professors, they used a filtration system, but she'd not yet studied it. She did know how to use the twin levers attached to either side of the water pipe. She lifted them, and as she did so, the crystals in each lever began to react to one another. They formed a current and steam began to gently rise from the water coming from the tap. Once more she cupped the water, smiling at the temperature. A hot bath. So easily. There were advantages to being an Illuminist, no doubt about it.

She fussed with the busk closure on the front of her corset. The undergarment bothered her because she was used to making her own, which fit her perfectly. But every possession she had was lost to her now.

Another little dictate she'd learned from Bion Donkova. In all fairness, she shouldn't be cross with him because Novices were not allowed contact with anyone outside the Order during their first year, but once more her temper flickered at just the idea of the man.

Maybe she should be concerned about her reaction to him. It was definitely volatile—as though there were something inside her straining against her hold on it. Her aunts would have labeled it "base," uncivilized urges best squelched before they caused her to fall from grace. Doing so made her a lady, setting her above the common woman.

She'd been reared on such ideals, but the wonders of the Illuminist world surrounding her made it hard to hold on to such dictates. Science made sense, while her aunts' sayings rarely did.

Her aunts were right about one thing: the feelings Bion unleashed inside her were proving uncontrollable.

Stepping into the tub, she sighed as the warm water covered her skin and warmed her toes. But once she was settled, the image of Bion returned. When it came to the man appearing in her thoughts, she seemed to have little discipline. He was so meticulous, in his maroon uniform with its gleaming buttons. He never appeared with even a single dull button, nor did his chin ever have a hint of stubble. Bion didn't follow fashion, with its preference for sideburns and mustaches. His square-cut jaw was scraped clean and added to the polished image he presented.

But she'd seen another side of him—a savage side.

Heat teased her cheeks and it wasn't due to the hot water. No, it was far worse than that. Young ladies did not blush at the memory of men behaving badly. In fact, ladies did not see the sort of struggles she'd witnessed. That sort of thing was kept well on the other side of parlor doors. Yet, she was not sorry she had seen it. Somehow, it felt personal, her knowledge of Bion's true character. She liked the way it made her feel, even the way it rattled her composure, because there had been too much order in her life.

There. She'd confessed to her unladylike yearnings.

Sophia picked up a bar of soap and began to bathe. Her cheeks remained hot because Bion lingered in her thoughts, and tonight, it felt strangely intimate. As though the man were somehow aware of her fascination. Which was ridiculous of course. He was far too busy trying to mold her into his ideal of a Navigator. The man didn't suffer from her lack of focus.

Yet even after finishing her bath and drying herself, she still glanced over her shoulder, looking around the room before pressing the controls for the lights. They dimmed before leaving her room in darkness. Sometimes, it felt like the man was her personal shadow. Now that it was dark, she might admit to being comforted by that fact. At least a bit, deep down, where uncertainty was still lodged inside her despite her best efforts to face her new life without faltering. No matter how frustrating the man was, it was still nice to go to sleep knowing her world would not be completely full of strangers in the morning. Bion Donkova was bound to be there.

But she still wasn't sure if that pleased her or not.

❧

The secured Novice wing of the dormitory was quiet. Bion stopped and looked at the logbook sitting neatly near the archways that held a collection of male Deep Earth Crystals. The only person who might cross the arch without an Illuminist pin was a Pure Spirit.

There were still two Guardians posted to add more security to those Novices sleeping beyond the gate. Each coming and going was noted clearly on the creamy parchment of the log. He flipped open his pocket watch to compare the current time with the one printed next to Sophia's entry.

She wouldn't care to know how often he checked up on her. Seeing if she returned to her rooms directly after a training session or that she answered him truthfully when he asked where she'd gone the night before.

No, she wouldn't be pleased at all, but he was. Their fledgling Navigator was everything the others on the waiting list for a Root Ball had proven they were. She had integrity and grit, but all that knowledge did was frustrate him.

He didn't need to like her.

"I'm a respectable woman…"

Her words rose from his memory, offering him the perfect evidence to back up his opinion. No, liking her was something which would lead him down a path neither of them would like. For all that she was a Navigator, Miss Sophia Stevenson had been raised by upper society. He was uncouth in her eyes. A savage.

His lips twitched up and he walked through the arch to hide his lapse of control from the Guardians. Personally, he enjoyed knowing he wasn't a gentleman. In his world, he had earned his place and didn't long for the blessing of the matrons. What he was, he'd earned, not been born into. He didn't judge his fellow humans by the circumstances of their birth. In the Illuminist world, a man could make his own fortune.

He stopped outside her door. Temptation urged him to reach for the handle and forego the brass knocker, the savage inside him delighting at the idea of surprising her.

He paused, his fingers closing into a fist.

He had the authority to enter her chambers, but the right was given to him to ensure she was not conducting treason, not to placate his own cravings. But there were instances lately when he was forgetting just why he was entering her chambers—or more pointedly, he was searching for an excuse to see her, so had no other reason.

Duty was something he'd devoted his life to. Tonight wouldn't see him discarding those ideals in favor of following his impulses, whatever the hell they were... Sophia Stevenson was his trainee. Nothing more.

"Wake up, sleepyhead."

Sophia opened her eyes instantly. "Janette?" She sat up to see her best friend pulling the curtains open.

"Janette, do not—"

Her warning came too late. The morning sun brightened the room, sending pain shooting through Sophia's eyes. She jerked and closed her eyes, rolling over and reaching for her glasses, but they were not on the bedside table. Accidently, she knocked the lamp and heard it crash to the floor.

"Oh, Sophia, I'm terribly sorry. I forgot." Janette yanked the curtains closed but did so too hard and the rod they were strung on came right off the wall. The rod and curtains joined the lamp on the floor, the polished wood surface accentuating the noise.

Sophia struggled to her knees, gasping when she heard hurried footfalls a mere second before the door to her bedroom burst open. She barely had time to grab the bedding to shield herself when she found herself face-to-face with Bion Donkova, with Darius Lawley a half step behind him. Both men were attired in suits, but at that moment they looked anything but civilized.

"We're fine," Janette offered apologetically. "I just forgot about her eyes being sensitive."

"I am well enough, thank you." The polite term felt awkward as Sophia's cheeks burned scarlet. She remained clutching the bedding to her chin, squinting her eyes in the bright light.

Darius turned his back and retreated from the room, like a gentleman.

"I'll find your glasses," Janette said on her way out of the door.

"Your glasses should be placed on your nightstand." Bion frowned at her.

His tone matched the formal picture he presented in his uniform coat buttoned to his collar. In contrast, her flimsy chemise was teasing the tops of her thighs beneath the bedding. The tops of her breasts were barely hidden by the sheet because her corset pushed them up to the edge of the chemise. The reprimand on his face did not fit with the impropriety of the moment.

For Christ's sake, if a man was looming over her bed while she was indisposed… shouldn't he be enamored of her? Or at the very least somewhat interested in charming her? But then again, it was Bion. Nothing about her pleased him.

"If your glasses were in the correct place, you would not have alarmed other members of the crew," he admonished.

"We are not aboard one of your ships, Captain, and I certainly will not be taking advice from you on how I keep myself in my bedroom." She rose up on her knees, the need to face him head-on burning through any protest her common sense might have made. "And I am not dressed, sir!"

"I've seen you in less."

Her eyes widened, the deep tone of his voice setting off a ripple of excitement racing along her skin. Her mouth dropped open and satisfaction flickered in his dark eyes, the remains of her composure shredded. Bion Donkova had fast reflexes, but today she was faster. Her hand connected with his face, delivering a slap that resounded loudly in the morning air.

She expected him to be furious; instead, the man growled. The sound sent her back, the sheer maleness of it making her shiver. Challenge appeared in his eyes and his lips curved up into an arrogant smirk. For a moment, he looked very much like a pirate, the sort of man accustomed to being ruthless in the pursuit of what he craved.

He gripped the footrail of her bed and leaned forward. "But if you can't tolerate the threat to your modesty, feel free to cry out. I'm sure Guardian Lawley will be happy to rescue you before you fall victim to a fit of vapors."

Her temper boiled. If it were possible for steam to

rise from her ears, it would have. But her pride refused to let his challenge pass. With a soft hiss, she forced herself to release the bedding and climb out of bed. The urge to tug her chemise up to cover more of her breasts was also squelched as she lifted her chin and shot him a scorching look.

"I can handle your gutter behavior quite well. Look as you will. All that proves is how much you deserve my contempt."

She intended to walk past him, but he captured her wrist, his larger hand closing all the way around her limb. It wasn't the first time he'd manhandled her, but for some reason she was acutely aware of how much strength he had today. Tension curled through her belly, teasing her with a flicker of heat she'd never experienced before. It was dark and tempting and almost irresistible. *Almost*.

"Release me."

He chuckled, amusement still flickering in his eyes. His grip tightened a mere fraction, almost as if he might disregard her demand.

Pirate... ruthless and without boundaries. Why had she never realized just what sort of nature he had hidden beneath his formal exterior and endless lectures about duty?

She was trembling, the realization of which cut through her outrage like a rapier. Something in his gaze made it look as if he was reading her thoughts, which was impossible. But she felt it nonetheless.

He pulled her closer, until they were mere inches apart. "I do believe I might just enjoy your attempts to handle my gutter behavior, Miss Stevenson."

His voice was low and edged with warning. What flared up in the depths of his dark eyes made her shiver. He felt it, that telltale reaction through his grip on her wrist. He smoothed his thumb across the tender skin of her inner wrist before lifting her hand and boldly pressing a kiss against the same spot.

It was nothing like the kiss Jonathon Saddler had given her. This was scorching hot and it stole her breath. Her heart began to race, feeling as if it were straining to break free of her chest. Every bit of self-control she had seemed to be slipping through her fingers like sand, leaving her without anything to hold on to.

With a savage jerk, she twisted her wrist, angling to break his grip at the weakest spot, as she'd learn in her Asian fighting classes. He straightened instantly, his larger body adopting a polished fighting stance to prove he knew far more about the Eastern arts than she did. Something lit his eyes, but she shied away from taking a closer look at it. A warning rose up from her mind, telling her to beware of learning more about this side of his nature. Or her reaction to it.

She hurried around him, brushing past a startled Janette and slamming shut the bathroom door, betraying just how unsettled she was. What horrified her most was the way she collapsed onto the closed lid of the toilet, her legs trembling too much to support her. She shook her head, hugging her wrist to her chest. She could not—would not—be affected by him so deeply.

≈∾

The grand hall of the Solitary Chamber was impressive. Its ceiling rose a full two stories and was constructed with elegant arches. The molding would have put Buckingham Palace to shame with its intricate details. The center was carpeted with thick, burgundy carpet. The windows stretched up to the ceiling, with foot-wide panes of glass and velvet curtains edged with tassels framing them. The cost in velvet was enough to make her tailor's brain reel, but when Sophia added in the pressed chenille wallpaper, the opulence was astounding.

But she couldn't enjoy the moment. Instead of taking the time to appreciate all the detail of the inner sanctum of the Solitary Chamber, Sophia had to battle to maintain her self-control. At the end of the hall, standing near the raised portion of the floor, were three Marshals, or judges. The scales of justice graced their Illuminist pins, whereas Bion's had a compass denoting his career path among the air fleet. Guardian Lawley was waiting as well, his pin displaying crossed swords to proclaim his position as a constable.

For all appearances, they looked like men she had lived among her entire life. They were dressed in wool trousers with pin-tucked shirts and cravats worn over vests with watch pockets and jackets constructed of tweed.

After all the warnings she'd endured about how unnatural the Illuminist Order was, she discovered herself agreeing with many of the ways they operated, such as allowing women to testify at a trial. It seemed quite logical; after all, she had been the one abducted.

Satisfaction warmed her, burning away her self-doubt and the last of the strange reaction she'd had to Bion. Now she was consumed by the need for justice.

Grainger had been the one behind her abduction. His ruffians had grabbed her right off the street; Grainger had ripped her mother's cameo off her neck, setting his trap in motion. He'd taken such delight in her suffering and gleefully tormented her by reiterating his plans to torture her if Janette did not arrive to do his bidding once she received Sophia's cameo.

Oh yes, she was going to enjoy the right of an Illuminist member to testify regardless of her gender. Among the Illuminists, being female did not mean she had fewer rights. It was like something out of a little girl's dream world, and yet, it was solid reality for those willing to pledge themselves to the secretive Order. She looked over at the man who had so easily put a bullet through her leg in his quest to harvest Deep Earth Crystals.

Grainger was still just as repulsive as she recalled. *Compatriot* Grainger, actually. Among the Helikeians, they referred to one another as Compatriots.

Sophia didn't chastise herself for staring at the man. It was almost necessary in a way, because her life had changed so drastically the moment she had met him. Her gaze lowered to his wrists and the silver handcuffs keeping him prisoner. He'd used rope to make her just as helpless and put a burlap sack over her head before stuffing her into a pit.

The fear she'd suffered still felt too fresh. It rose up from her memory, thick and choking.

She shook it off, looking away from the man. But she ended up locking gazes with Bion. His dark eyes were too keen and, she felt, appeared as though he could read her thoughts as plainly as the morning news circular. She was clasping her hands so tightly, her fingernails dug into her palms. Janette stood nearby with her husband, Darius, at her side. He had a hand gently resting on the small of her back. It should have slightly shocked her, such an intimate touch displayed so publicly. Instead, Sophia discovered herself glad for her friend, but that same emotion only highlighted just how alone she felt.

Well, there was nothing for it. Honestly, that wasn't something that had changed since being abducted either. She had no suitor missing her.

"This trial will be called to order."

She looked back at the Marshals, fighting against the tide of emotions seeing Grainger was unleashing.

Later. Yes, later she might take the time to nurse her personal hurts. For the moment, she would be strong and steady. The Marshal standing in the center lifted a gavel and pounded it onto the desk in front of him. The sound reminded her of the crack of gunpowder right before a bullet had torn through her leg, and she flinched. Grainger had been so pleased with his ability to harm her out on that lava flow. She lost the battle to not look at him again.

The man was grinning at her. The Marshal began to read the charges against him, but all the formal-sounding voice did was solicit a flicker of achievement in Grainger's eyes, leaving no doubt that he believed completely in the Helikeian cause.

"Mr. Grainger. You stand accused of being a Helikeian and, in the service of that order, you committed the crime of abducting Miss Sophia Stevenson. Furthermore, you planned to harvest Deep

Earth Crystals after forcing the compliance of Mrs. Lawley." The Marshal peered over the edge of his spectacles at Grainger. "Do you have any defense to render to this court?"

"Of course I do," Grainger insisted. "But you are too ignorant to understand the purity of the Helikeian Order. You accept any member, taking in the strays and lowbred. It weakens you. Soon, we will crush you and the ridiculous governments allowed to flourish like mold on the face of the Earth. The Pure Spirit Mrs. Lawley is rightfully ours. Our actions created her; it was our cunning that separated her bloodline from your Order. She belongs to us." He suddenly shot a look at Sophia that curled her toes. "Just as you belong to us because I had a hand in your creation."

"I do not." Formal hearing or not, Sophia didn't think she could have held her tongue if the queen herself were present. "Nor shall I ever."

Grainger's eyes brightened with anticipation. "You will."

Icy dread tingled up the nape of her neck. It spread quickly, traveling across her skin and leaving her fighting the urge to tremble—she would not. Not here, not while Bion watched.

"Enough!" The Marshal pounded the gavel again.

"It is not enough!" Grainger snarled. "Only after we have reduced you to rubble will it be enough! You do not hold any power over me! I will prevail. I am superior to you, my very blood more pure!"

"Remove the accused!" the Marshal ordered.

"With pleasure," Bion bit out. It wasn't his place or his duty, but no one stopped him from gripping

Grainger's arm and pulling him around to face the back of the hall.

Grainger surprised them all by laughing. It was a high-pitched sound that hinted at lunacy. Bion towered over him, but Grainger drew himself up like a nobleman being propositioned by a street whore.

"Remove your inferior hands from my person! I come from a pure bloodline that has served the Helikeian Order for hundreds of years. No one here is my equal. We shall prevail!"

Bion dragged Grainger from the hall and the Marshal shook his head. The Guardians positioned at the back of the hall snapped into action and took Grainger through the doors.

"The man is insane," the Marshal announced. "Quite out of his mind I'd say."

"He was in his right mind well enough when he held a gun on my wife and forced her to harvest Deep Earth Crystals." Darius Lawley spoke up. "He should be shot for treason or attempted murder at the least."

The Marshal stared back at him with a bland expression. "We are not savages. We do not execute the mentally unstable. We shall leave barbaric behavior to the unenlightened beyond our Order and the Helikeians. Judgment will be suspended until a physician declares the accused able of facing the accusations lodged against him."

The Marshal lifted his gavel and pounded it against the desk twice. The sound was piercing, ripping a hole in Sophia's peace of mind. "But… what does that mean?"

"It means we'll have the privilege of keeping Grainger under lock and key while his comrades enjoy the fact that he is still among the living in spite of his crimes," Bion muttered from across the hall.

"This is not an airship, Captain Donkova," the Marshal admonished. "Justice does not need to be so black and white here. Unlike the close confines of an airship, we have the facilities to care for the criminally insane."

Bion closed the distance between them, his stride determined. "So we will waste resources on curing the man before we condemn him?" Bion's tone left no doubt that he wasn't really asking a question. It was dry and condescending, earning him a dark look from the Marshal.

"We shall conduct ourselves as civilized men, ones who do not seek vengeance, but instead focus on maintaining justice."

The Marshal struck the desk again, harder and sharper this time. All three stood and exited the hall. The level of intensity went with them, leaving Sophia feeling disappointed. She turned and left, her emotions swirling in a turbulent cyclone.

Did she want Grainger dead? She honestly didn't know. Part of her was relieved to not have to lend her testimony toward condemning a man. But that left her wondering if she was a coward, one of the many who demand justice but are unwilling to stand up and face those they wanted punished.

One thing was certain and that was that she avoided making eye contact with Bion Donkova as she passed him. She could feel his dark gaze on her, but she kept her attention on the door, proving without a doubt that she was a coward.

❧

"You're on dangerously thin ice, Captain."

Bion slowly grinned at Darius. "A place where, I assure you, I'm quite comfortable, Guardian Lawley."

Darius chuckled softly, taking a moment to notice that his wife was heading out of the sanctum in pursuit of her friend.

"It is a facet of my personality you have already encountered." Darius jerked his attention away from Janette's exit and stared at Bion. "I was willing to let you and others believe me a traitor," Bion continued. "I knew you and your team might kill me before any explanation could be rendered, so kindly spare me the lecture I see brewing in your eyes. I do not live my life on safe ground, not when there are Helikeians to expose. Our own laws allow them to infiltrate our ranks. Unmasking them will not be simple or done on safe ground."

"We are not talking about Helikeians, but of your personal involvement with your trainee," Darius advised. "I have treaded on that thin ice; it's a perilous journey between duty and distraction. Miss Stevenson might well be worth the risk, but you need to be careful how many rules you challenge along the way."

Bion shook his head. "You mistake the situation, Guardian. Miss Stevenson is my responsibility; the only distraction is her propensity to challenge my authority. I continue to hope she will mature past such behavior."

Guardian Lawley surprised him by grinning. Bion couldn't claim to know the man well, but what experience he did have with Lawley had been facing a man with iron control. The amusement on his face was a stark contrast to the man he'd dealt with in the Hawaiian Islands.

"Do enlighten me, Captain. Exactly when did it become standard practice to instruct Navigator Novices over the footrails of their beds with the sort of personal remarks I heard this morning?"

"There is little privacy aboard airships. Miss Stevenson is best prepared if she learns that now," Bion remarked calmly, but heat was rising beneath his collar. Guardian Lawley merely continued to grin, making it plain he wasn't swayed by Bion's response— excuse, really.

Bion turned and left the sanctum. Frustration was sitting heavily on his back, the lack of satisfaction from the hearing making him edgy. Grainger deserved death. The man was a bastard of the worst sort, one without remorse or compassion for those he had injured. The man hadn't hesitated when he'd put a bullet through Sophia's leg and Bion was certain he would happily continue his service to the Helikeians if freedom was his once more.

Damned Helikeians. They were as old as the Illuminist Order and could trace their roots back to the ancient civilizations that had given them their foundation in knowledge. Long after the Greeks had been conquered, their devotion to science, logic, and learning was still being cultivated by the two Orders. The difference was, the Illuminists had long ago cast off prejudice. Membership was open to anyone willing to pledge themselves to the Order. That didn't come without a cost, for society shunned anyone wearing an Illuminist pin on their person. But loyalty was the price expected to enter the world of the Illuminists.

The Helikeians had split off centuries before, when they began to favor arrogance over tolerance and power over knowledge. Now, they dreamed of conquering the world and disposing of anyone they judged inferior, "purifying the bloodlines," as they called it. They would stop at nothing to gain the upper hand over the Illuminists.

Sophia was just a commodity in their eyes.

Bion felt the sting of that fact like a new tattoo. She was too naive to understand, too much a product of her upbringing beyond the walls of the Illuminist world. It fell to him to ensure she did not fall into Helikeian hands. If she did, it would be his duty to neutralize her, by ending her life if that was the only means available to him.

From the moment he'd been accepted as a junior cadet in the airship corps at the tender age of sixteen, his life had been dedicated to duty. Each year and rank along his path to Captain had only seen him facing deeper personal commitments. There was no reason training a Novice Navigator should test him so greatly. Or frustrate him like Sophia did.

Yet another challenge of her society upbringing—an Illuminist woman didn't have any difficulty embracing passion. If she hadn't been raised by puritan Victorian society, he just might try his hand at kissing her. Becoming lovers would certainly be a better use for the sparks that flew between them.

He bet she'd slap him again.

But all that knowledge did was make him think about trying it.

✧

Asian fighting was something Sophia found fascinating. It was a technique from the Far East that the Illuminist Order offered classes in. As far back as she could recall, she'd been told how ladies should be sheltered by the men of the house. Only fallen women resorted to defending themselves. It was uncivilized and unladylike.

Yet among the Illuminists, learning to defend yourself wasn't frowned upon. In fact, all members were encouraged to learn some form of self-defense to strengthen the security of the Order.

Bion's idea of encouraging her had been to bluntly order her to begin taking classes.

At least she didn't resent this order. Her training included a form of kicking and punching that made pugilists look like fools. The men in the local pub punching one another in the face until one fell wouldn't last a full minute with one of the masters of the Asian fighting arts. They used their bodies in amazing ways, teaching her to deliver a blow that would drop a man despite her smaller size.

Her master was from China, but he was unlike any of the Chinese people she had seen scurrying down the streets with their heads lowered. He held himself with pride. Outside the Solitary Chamber, her father's elite customers would look down their noses at him, declaring him a street urchin. How wrong they were. He was a master of an art she was in awe of.

She arrived for class and began to stretch like the other students. Her uniform consisted of a baggy pair of pants that ended at her ankles and a tunic top. There was nothing else to the uniform, so she'd taken to wearing a camisole beneath it to support her breasts. A corset was out of the question because the fighting form required twisting and bending.

At least the preparation for class was something she knew how to do. Her father had sent her and her sister off to ballet class for many years to ensure they learned to move gracefully. Her father would certainly be surprised to see how she was using her flexibility now.

For just a moment, she indulged herself and let her father's face remain in the center of her thoughts. But a moment later, Grainger's face rose from her memories to torment her with just how she had been separated from her family. She shook her head to clear her thoughts. The master instructor wasn't just accomplished in the art he taught; the man could spot anyone daydreaming in his class.

And he had very creative ways of helping his students recover their focus.

But her attention wandered once again when Bion entered the room. He stopped at the edge of the hardwood floor that made up the instruction area and bowed respectfully toward the master. He was wearing the same clothing she was, but he didn't need his uniform to look like a captain. The man simply did not blend in with the rest of the students. He looked far too confident.

Suspicion tingled along her nape as she watched

him move to the front of the room and bow to the master once more. The class was called to order, saving her from her curiosity. Students lined up according to rank, leaving her at the back of the room. Bion remained in the front row as they began their first exercise. The pace of the class was demanding, and it required all of her attention. It suited her mood and she applied herself vigorously to the hour of training. Maybe exhaustion would help her sleep in spite of her confrontation with Grainger. Her uniform became saturated with perspiration and her hair was wet with it when it came time to bow and end the class.

"Miss Stevenson, remain for the second hour of instruction."

The master's command stunned her because only advanced students were invited to the next class, where the basic moves she was practicing were applied to a live opponent. But no one argued with the master.

"Yes, sir," she replied with a quick bow. She fought the urge to look over at Bion. The master was not a man influenced by others often, but she had to admit that she had no idea what manner of relationship Bion had with him.

She tried to shake off her feelings, because once again she was far too close to pitying herself, which wouldn't do. Maybe she was separated from her family until her novitiate ended, but she would not disgrace them by failing to face a challenge head-on. That was the Stevenson way, the Irish blood in them. She could hear her father's booming voice rising up from her memory as he lectured her brothers about never forgetting that the Stevensons were strong enough to weather any storm. She leveled her chin before facing the master.

"Today, we shall put to test what you have learned."

She bowed, not really understanding, although her belly was balled up with apprehension.

"You have been learning how to shift your weight and use knowledge to defeat your opponent."

Bion moved closer, making her struggle to keep her eyes on the master. Heat radiated from him, the kind that you could detect even after the fire had been reduced to ashes, the bricks of the fireplace warming your hands for hours.

He warms your temper, sure enough.

"Today, I wish to challenge you with more than practicing against an imaginary opponent," the Master continued.

She lost the battle to keep her gaze away from Bion and cut a quick look at him. His expression might be unreadable, but there was satisfaction in his eyes.

"Captain Donkova will assist you by being your attacker."

Her temper was heating up.

"Attempt to prevent him from breaking your balance."

She needed to focus, but it was proving difficult. Curse the man…

Bion bowed to her before spreading his feet and arms. He was set to lunge at her, and in another second, he did. She remembered what to do but did it too slowly to prevent him from locking his arms around her.

"You'd better fight me off, because I'm not going to play the gentleman and let you go," he whispered next to her ear. His warm breath set off a tiny response that rippled down her neck. The unexpected feeling propelled her into action. She rammed her knee into his groin.

He sucked in his breath, his hold loosening, and she turned, ducking under his arm while holding on to his other wrist and using the hold to pull his arm across her body. She ended up behind him, with his arm locked.

"Well done," the Master praised.

That was her cue to release him, but she paused a moment with him in her grasp, rebelling against the rules. It was an intense little impulse that flared up in response to knowing that she had him at her mercy.

Bion didn't care for being bested by her. When she faced him once again, she could see the determination in his eyes. His controlled expression was slipping just a bit, his lips thinned as he bowed and took another aggressive stance. He wasn't going to show her any mercy.

She didn't want any. That feeling came from the same place her impulse to keep him pinned had—deep down in the part of her nature she'd always locked away because it was in conflict with every ideal her life had been full of... up until now. Now, being a lady didn't matter, defeating Bion did.

And she wanted to.

It was a furious need, one that had her taking a fighting stance and moving slowly to make sure he didn't push her into a corner.

Surprise appeared in his eyes a split second before he attacked once more. They grappled, struggling to gain advantage over the other. Bion cursed under his breath when she broke out of his first attempt to capture her. She wasn't sure how she did it. It wasn't a matter of thinking but of responding.

She caught a glimpse of his white teeth as he grinned before he hunched over and launched himself at her. He caught her firmly around the waist and drove her backward onto the floor with his full weight.

"Your knee won't be much use now, my little Novice."

"I am not yours in any sense… of… the… word." Her last word came out as a wheeze because the man was on top of her. She struggled to draw breath while battling against panic.

It was just there, the fear, the unmistakable taste of helplessness left over from when she'd been Grainger's prisoner. It rose up like a demon from hell, terrifying her with its grasping claws. She bucked, surprising Bion with her strength, but she was past noticing him. Her heart was pounding so hard, it felt as if it might burst and sweat beaded on her skin as she struggled to free herself.

The master clapped his hands a single time and Bion released her instantly. For a moment, she lay on the polished wood floor feeling exposed. It was as if the air was too cool now that Bion wasn't on top of her.

She rolled over, her cheeks burning scarlet as shame tore through her. The emotional surge left her trembling, her muscles threatening to fail her. Tears escaped from her eyes, but her face was slick with perspiration so they didn't leave trails—except across her mind each one burned, increasing her humiliation. The remaining minutes of the class were a torment. The moment she was dismissed, she fled.

❦

"I'm surprised Master Lee allowed that."

Bion stiffened and his eyes narrowed when Guardian Decima Talaska smiled. She was a veteran Guardian Hunter; her specialty was hunting down traitors, but he didn't enjoy knowing she'd snuck up on him.

"Master Lee understands my training methods," Bion responded. "It's part of the Asian mind-set to train harder when faced with difficult circumstances." His tone was designed to end the conversation, but Decima stepped into his path.

"What is your hurry, Captain? I am quite convinced your trainee is on her way back to her quarters."

Decima gave her Asian fighting uniform a tug so that the crisp cotton snapped. "Since you appear to be in the mood to grapple with a smaller operant, I believe I can use the practice."

Bion shook his head. "My goal was to impress upon Miss Stevenson the reality of what she might someday have to face."

"Interesting." Decima drawled softly. "According to her file, she has performed very well in her time here. I saw nothing to indicate such a harsh lesson might be needed. In fact, her first encounter with our Order was nothing short of brutal. The fact that she has already begun Asian fighting training shows her respect for the need to defend herself."

"I don't need to defend my methods to you, Guardian," Bion insisted. "She is not the first Navigator I have trained."

"Yet she is the first Novice you have attempted to guide through her transition."

Bion shook his head. "That makes little difference."

Decima abandoned her teasing demeanor. Her features hardened and he found himself facing the side of her that made her so successful as a Hunter. The woman had a spine of solid steel.

"A Novice needs guidance. Something your little grappling lesson lacked completely. In fact, I'm almost sure she'll have nightmares tonight."

"I doubt it." But his gut twisted as he failed to believe his own words.

"I saw her face when she left; you didn't." Decima's words sliced into him. "So if you're finished tormenting your trainee, I'll be happy to give you a target with enough training to make you work for your victory."

The master was calling the next class to order. Bion looked at the door until a soft scoff from Decima drew him back into class. It was only after they were beginning that he noticed the flicker of amusement in her green eyes. He shook his head slightly as he admitted defeat. Guardian Decima had played him perfectly, and there was a lesson in being so predictable.

Just as there was one in her words about guidance. But what stuck in his mind long after class and into the evening was her warning about Sophia suffering nightmares.

That twisted his gut.

❧

The Solitary Chamber encompassed an entire four-block section of town and Sophia didn't even know how far the structures extended belowground. In fact, she'd seen only a very small percentage of the inside of the Illuminist community. Once a prospective member passed the entrance exam, they studied for an entire year as a Novice. Her membership pin was silver, not gold like the full members.

There was also a crystal in the center of it. The crystal would complete the circuit and allow her into sections of the chambers where only those who had taken their Oath of Allegiance might go. The Illuminist Order had many fine comforts, but learning about the science behind those amazing things would cost a member loyalty.

Death was the penalty for treason. The Illuminists only shared their knowledge with those willing to pledge themselves to the idea of utilizing all their effort toward greater learning.

She hurried down the hallways, making her way to the wing of Novices' dormitories. She reached the wing of rooms assigned to her. First she passed two Guardians standing at the gates. One pressed on the device fitted over his ear and the gates' current was completed so that she could pass through to the rooms assigned to her. Her rooms were little comfort; every noise made her flinch.

Enough already!

Scolding herself didn't improve the situation. Her belly rumbled because she hadn't stopped at the common kitchen for food. Bathing made her skin feel normal again. But she still felt Bion's hands on her...

No, you do not! You will not and that's the end of it!

A few pieces of bread sat on the table in the small center room. It wasn't much of a parlor, but she didn't have many friends to invite over so it didn't matter. There were several stacks of books on the table now and a napkin folded around the bread. She sat and chewed on one slice. She thought tea sounded divine, but it would keep her awake, so she resisted the urge and washed the bread down with water. The water itself was a marvel. She held up the glass and looked at it, still astounded by the purity.

Right across the street from the Solitary Chamber in her father's tailor shop, which was located in the best portion of town, the water was not nearly as good. The family had lived on the second floor since her mother died. In a way, she'd been glad her father had moved them, for she couldn't stomach the home she'd lived in for the first ten years of her life because everywhere she looked she saw her mother.

And now, she saw Grainger.

She shuddered and the water sloshed over the rim of the glass. She put it down and wiped her fingers on the edge of her chemise. The room was dark except for the lamp nearest the bed. Reaching for the controls to extinguish the light gave her another pause, but she ordered herself to do it. She was not afraid of the dark.

Only of Bion's touch…

No! Not even that. Once in bed, she forced herself to recite Bible verses until she fell asleep. But even with such divine mental occupation, her rest was not peaceful. She kicked at the bedding, thrashing as Grainger's face filled her dreams. There was the gun, and she felt her flesh being torn by the bullet once again.

We created you... She tried to run, only to discover her body pinned to the ground.

You belong to us... Grainger's voice was louder and closer and more hideous than she recalled. It was like pure evil, if such a thing might have a tone. She strained against the man holding her down, finally jerking up and gaining her freedom. But only for a moment because she collided with another hard body.

"Sweet Sophia, you seem to need assistance."

Sophia was still caught between sleep and reality. Not really awake, the sound of his voice was soothing. She dug her fingers into his clothing as another shiver shook her. Bion was just another piece of her dream.

"It was a dream." He wrapped her tightly in his embrace, ending her struggles as she shivered.

The fear had retreated mostly, but it was still there, lingering near enough for her to feel it. Bion's voice confirmed that Grainger wasn't there and for the moment, that was all her exhausted mind could absorb. She gave a little sigh as his scent filled her senses. Even through the wool of his coat she could detect the familiar smell. She wasn't thinking, wasn't concerned with the frustrations that he so often elicited from her.

She snuggled closer, seeking immersion in his embrace. His hand moved slowly along her back, soothing her with a long stroke and then another that sent delight through her. Who might have thought that such a simple touch might be so enjoyable?

Somewhere in the back of her exhausted mind, there was a reason why she shouldn't continue to rest against him, a logic that would have her struggling out of his embrace if she weren't so sleepy. But all that mattered was that she trusted him to keep Grainger away.

Bion Donkova didn't know how to fail. For the moment, she was content to be his primary duty.

~∞~

Bion was frozen in shock. It took him a moment to realize Sophia Stevenson had reduced him to indecision with nothing more than a soft sigh. But what a sound it was! Feminine, delicate… *needy*. Damn, he didn't need to think of her wanting him.

It wasn't the first time he'd been pressed against her, but this time was so vastly different. He sat for several long moments, just savoring the feeling of her breath against his neck. Her heart was beating against his chest, slowing down as she relaxed into a deeper sleep.

He gently cradled her upper body and lowered her to the surface of her bed. She frowned and made another needy sound as she turned one way and then the other. Her lips pushed into a pout as she twisted again. He smoothed the hair off her face and she sighed again, turning toward him… seeking him.

Ah hell. He should leave. She would be furious—there was no doubt about that. But that thought made it even easier for him to kick off his boots and lie down beside her. He had a fascination with her temper, possibly an unhealthy one, but it was wrapping its roots around him more and more with every encounter.

It was far too simple, too enjoyable to gather her

against his side. And he liked the contented sound she made as she nuzzled against his chest… *far too much*.

But he was fairly sure he'd attempt to kill any man who tried to make him leave.

Bloody hell.

Two

SOPHIA SMILED, SURPRISED HER NOSE WASN'T COLD FOR a change. In fact, she was toasty warm from head to toe and her body was humming with contentment. She stretched one leg and then another before rubbing her nose against her pillow one final time before forcing herself to rise. How tempting it was to be lazy.

She frowned when the fabric tickled her nose, feeling rougher than she recalled her sheeting should be. She stroked her pillow, only to discover it to be the same texture as wool. Now that she was waking up, it smelled also like wool and something else, something from her dreams…

Her eyes flew open and she lifted her head. She blinked and then blinked again, but the sight of Bion Donkova lying on his back in the center of her bed didn't dissipate. Her chemise was twisted up to the top of her thighs while Bion had an arm locked very familiarly along her back. She looked at his lower body and heard him chuckle once she'd discovered that he was indeed wearing all his clothing.

"I save my seductions for females who are wide awake," he said.

She jerked upward and then stood up, frantically trying to recall how the man had arrived in her bed. Bion stretched, cocking his head from side to side until his neck popped. She backed away from him, completely alarmed by the lazy look on his face—relaxed, actually. The man was at ease, comfortable even, and her cheeks burned scarlet. He'd slept in her bed!

They'd slept together!

"What are ye doing in me bed?" she demanded.

He sat up, pausing as he began to pull his boots on. "Your Irish comes out when you're agitated," he noted.

"Agitated?" She nearly choked on the word and her hands propped onto her hips. "Ye're right about that, Bion Donkova. Now explain to me how ye came to be here."

He stood up, but his unruly hair and disheveled appearance prevented him from impressing her as he usually did. Instead, she felt drawn toward this unexpected peek at what the man looked like when he wasn't buttoned and polished in his uniform. It was surprising and mesmerizing, threatening to draw her closer to him.

It was like nothing she had ever experienced. Ladies did not receive gentlemen in their… unmentionables!

Of course, Bion wasn't a gentleman and had never professed to be interested in behaving like one.

"You were having nightmares." He brushed his hair back with his hand, restoring some of his normal poise. "The night Guardian summoned me to investigate the cries he heard coming from your room, since he knew you retired alone."

"And why is it he didn't simply look into the matter himself?" she asked suspiciously.

He surprised her by answering with a grin. One of his dark eyebrows arched mockingly. "Because, Miss Stevenson, I consider you my priority and what manner of gentleman would I be to turn my back on you when you settled so very contentedly into my embrace?"

She sputtered but he held up a hand to silence her. "And I thoroughly enjoyed the evening." His dark gaze dropped to the cleavage on display above the edge of her corset. "Thoroughly."

He performed a half bow before turning to leave the room. His boot heels clicked along the polished floorboards of the outer room and she heard the door open and close.

Her mouth dropped open, but what made her eyes widen was the sudden rush of clarity that engulfed her. Memory returned with vigor, illuminating the events of the night before until she rubbed at her forehead to try and erase them. She had accepted his embrace—actually enjoyed it. She was going to hell, straight to the flames of damnation where the wicked paid for their sins, that place where fallen women ended up because they lacked discipline.

Except that among the Illuminists, taking a lover was not forbidden. She shivered, gooseflesh rising along her bare arms. She rubbed them, trembling as her memory teased her with just how much she had enjoyed Bion stroking her last night. It was a fleeting recollection, like a disjointed portion of a dream that she couldn't recall the ending to. All she was certain of was the feeling of being held in his embrace.

It had been bliss.

❧

A good challenge was better than any luxury. Grainger focused on this thought, seeing the words in his mind while refusing to notice the chill of the floor he sat on. Of course, there was a bed very nearby, one with clean sheets and thick blankets that would no doubt drive the ache from his frozen toes. But he was better than that, better than the trap they had so neatly prepared for him.

He would face the challenge of continuing to dupe his captors. The mentally ill did not mind the cold or the lack of civilized clothing, so he must pretend nothing bothered him as well. Those were small discomforts that he had the mental discipline to endure while focusing his attention on his goal.

He discarded his clothing, conquering the protest from his pride. Modesty meant nothing compared to the possibility of escaping and earning the esteem of his Helikeian compatriots. Great men often had to go beyond the lengths others were willing to endure in order to claim victory.

Yes, escape. Such would be a grand accomplish-ment. Yet it would not come easily. He let himself drool when the Guardians came round to check on him. They shook their heads and muttered about how broken his mind was before locking the door on his cell once again.

Fools.

His mind was sound and sharp, and every day he was absorbing facts about his surroundings. The opportunity would come. He concentrated on that fact as the day stretched into the evening. His belly knotted with hunger but he ignored the meals offered, only played with the food delivered to him near sunset. Making two holes in the slice of bread, he placed it over his face like a mask.

"No one knows who I am now!" he shouted. "I shall be disguised as I walk away!"

"All right, send for a doctor," one of the Guardians conceded. "I believe he is mad. I can hear his belly rumbling like a starving hound's and all he's doing is playing with the food."

It took no effort to collapse onto the floor in a fit of amusement. Grainger let his laughter grow louder and louder as he sensed himself moving closer to victory.

He didn't know yet how he would escape, but avoiding execution was the first step. Deceiving his captors into thinking him a broken fool was the second, for then they would soon relax their guard.

Then? Well, he'd be waiting for the opportunity while the fools thinking him locked away were busy judging him insane.

He sniffed and suffered a cramp from hunger that left sweat beaded on his forehead.

He was Helikeian, his bloodline pure and unpolluted by weakness. The Illuminists allowed too many into their ranks. They were like mongrel dogs, products that were defective from birth. The only solution was extermination, so that they could not pass their tainted blood on to another generation.

Someday soon, the Helikeians would wipe all degenerates off the face of the planet and there would be only one master race.

The Helikeian.

❧

Rumors clearly moved as quickly through Illuminists as they did among the social elite beyond the walls of the Solitary Chamber. By teatime, Sophia was thoroughly frustrated with just how easily she blushed.

Because you spent the night in Bion's embrace.

Maybe so, but that was all she'd done.

At least the afternoon allowed her to retreat to the vast library the Solitary Chamber afforded its students. Most of the people in it were Novices like herself. She headed for one of the alcoves hidden in the arches that supported the wall. Here she might turn down the light and be more comfortable, a very nice accommodation made for Navigators.

You mean a convenient place for you to hide from Bion.

She scoffed at her own thoughts and removed her glasses. Bion would seek her out no matter where she went if that was his desire.

Are you hoping that will be the case?

She ground her teeth and had to swallow a grumble. She had gone her entire adult life without dwelling upon matters of intimacy. Why couldn't she dismiss them now?

Because ye spent the night in Bion's embrace…

She was still innocent, for heaven's sake.

Are you frustrated that he was there or that you did not learn more about what passes between lovers?

She knew what happened when the wicks were turned down. At least, she had a basic understanding of the mechanics. But she had to admit that she'd had no clue as to just how easily her emotions might overwhelm her. Every little sensation was magnified. Her head ached and she rubbed her temples now that she was removed from the curious looks she'd felt aimed at her throughout the day.

"You will become more at ease with it," a female voice assured her. "Abandoning that slumped shoulders and downcast eyes posture you have adopted will likely speed things along."

Sophia looked up, realizing she'd been doing exactly what Decima Talaska had accused her of. Sophia straightened her back and looked the veteran Illuminist straight in the eye. Guardian Decima moved into the alcove and studied her.

"Well done," Decima remarked playfully. "I was concerned."

Sophia laughed, earning a flutter of eyelashes from Decima. The female Guardian had emerald green eyes and looked delicate, but she carried herself with more confidence than any woman Sophia had ever met.

"You doubt me?" Decima purred softly.

"Not precisely," Sophia answered slowly, while trying to decide just what it was about the other woman that fascinated her. "I believe it is more a matter of wondering just what your remedy might be if I confessed to needing assistance."

Decima laughed, a low sound that was oddly

knowledgeable. Her gold Illuminist pin was secured to the lapel of her vest. Once, on a night that seemed very long ago, Sophia had seen Decima in a ball gown at the Brimmer spring party, but she never wore even a skirt inside the Solitary Chamber walls. She favored cycling pantaloons and only put on a skirt when she was heading outside. She was a Hunter, a classification of Guardian who searched for members of the Order who had broken their Oaths of Allegiance.

"You doubt I would offer you a kindly shoulder to whimper on?" Decima's eyes narrowed thoughtfully for a moment. "A wise judgment of my character. You have promise."

"That isn't meant to imply that I find you lacking in feminine graces," Sophia offered.

Decima locked her hands behind her back and sent her a stiff look. "I will have you know, dearest Sophia, that I take great pains to ensure that every feminine grace is banished from my behavior."

"You haven't succeeded," Sophia declared solemnly.

Decima stiffened. "I'm suddenly tempted to wrinkle my nose at you."

"Which is my sister Cora's favorite response to any argument I ever made to her." Sophia smiled as her sister's face came to mind, but it was bittersweet because she missed her terribly. "Mind you, our mother was always quick to warn Cora that she'd have droopy skin if she didn't stop."

"Ah yes, the importance of maintaining appearances. Something you were raised to be obedient to."

There was a note of judgment in Decima's voice that irritated Sophia. "It's no more ridiculous than you insisting on banishing feminine graces. Aren't you maintaining appearances as well? Ensuring that you are taken seriously as a Guardian when your gender threatens to set you apart? We aren't so different."

Decima's expression hardened but there was a hint of vulnerability in her eyes.

"Well spoken." Bion's voice came from just outside the entrance to the alcove. With the light behind him, his silhouette glowed as he entered. "Guardian Decima likes to think herself very far removed from her own gender."

Decima faced off with Bion, embodying the supreme confidence Sophia admired in her. There was no quivering, no hint of unsteadiness. She didn't even seem to notice the fact that her head barely reached Bion's shoulders.

"We all have our weaknesses," Decima purred. "Captain Donkova likes to believe himself so accomplished, but he is as fallible as the rest of us." Bion frowned but Decima held up a delicate finger to quiet him. She cast her gaze toward Sophia. "Which accounts for his attempts to smother you with his devotion to your training."

Bion suddenly grinned. "I assure you, Guardian, I was very careful to avoid smothering her last night. Novices' beds are rather small when there are two in them."

Decima shook her head. "If you wanted me to depart, attempting to shock me is rather a predictable method to employ. Somehow, I expected more originality from you, Captain, but it isn't the first time you've disappointed me."

There was a note of reprimand in her tone that made Sophia curious. Bion's eyes narrowed in response. Decima turned and left without another look back at Sophia. It was a kindness, one Sophia wasn't ignorant of. Her temper flared to life as she struggled to control the rise of emotions Bion's suggestive statement had aroused in her. *Aroused.*

"Of all the presumptuous statements," she exploded.

Bion cocked his head at an angle and crossed his arms over his chest. The pose made him look impossibly large, the sleeves of his uniform straining as his biceps bulged. She wanted to stop noticing things like that.

"You really are no gentleman."

His amused expression ignited her temper further. She just couldn't squelch the urge to stick her finger out at him and move closer. "Only a knave would allow himself to be thought my lover when you haven't even stolen a kiss."

She jabbed him in the center of his chest, her finger still pressing the maroon wool of his uniform when he struck. He unfolded his arms in a flash, sweeping her arm aside in a fluid motion, then completing a full circle around her waist and clamping her against his body. He flattened his hands against her back, pressing her forward so that there wasn't an inch of space between them before his mouth smothered her gasp. She really had never been kissed before.

Bion swept every last doubt from her mind with a firm conquest of her mouth. His lips were hotter than she had ever imagined. The contact was alarming and she pushed against his chest, but he cupped the nape of her neck and continued his assault. Yet it wasn't crushing; he tenderly teased her lips with his, tasting her and sending a flood of sensation through her.

Her body filled with pleasure as excitement tore through her belly with a fierceness that stunned her. Bion took full advantage of her paralysis, tilting his head so that their lips might fit together more completely. The delicate skin was suddenly alive with sensation that overwhelmed every thought she had, sweeping it away and leaving her nothing but the impulses he so often inspired in her.

She kissed him back—slowly, tentatively as she tried to mimic his motions. She flattened her hands against his chest and stretched up onto her toes to press her lips against his more firmly. There was no debate about the wisdom of it; only need fueled her actions. He groaned softly, his chest rumbling beneath her fingertips. He tightened his grip on her neck and the kiss became harder. He pressed her lips apart, seeking a deeper taste of her. She shuddered. Too many points of contact were flooding her with sensation simultaneously. It was overwhelming, the sheer volume of it too much for her to handle. He was suddenly too strong, too hard, and too demanding. The intensity of the moment threatened to rip away every last layer of her free will, leaving her at the mercy of her responses to him.

She shoved against him, interrupting their kiss with the amount of strength she used.

"Release me."

She'd gained a few inches of space, but he didn't release her completely. For a frozen moment, she stared into Bion's eyes and witnessed a side of his personality she'd only seen glimpses of before. It sent shivers down her spine and tantalized her at the same time. A twist of anticipation went through her belly as she stared into his dark eyes. There was a hunger there, an insatiable, burning need that kept her breathless. Like some sort of promise that she felt deep inside, where the only rules were the ones made by her feelings.

"As you like," he muttered at last. "But I warned you not to label me something unless you want me to embody it." His eyes narrowed. "I prefer action, and I believe you do too."

She stumbled back when he released her. Once she regained her balance, she advanced on him once more before realizing what she was doing. One of his dark eyebrows arched and he held his arms wide, beckoning her closer with his fingers.

"By all means, step up, madam. I will be happy to meet your challenge. Now that I've stolen a kiss and you have so boldly returned it, shall we proceed to lending truth to the gossip that we are lovers? It would certainly be a better use for all the anger you like to aim at me."

Her cheeks burned scarlet, but she had to battle against the urge to do exactly what he suggested. There was an insane twist of need prodding her to punch the man square in the center of his chest. It was practically impossible to control. "We shall not," she choked out.

"Hmm, now that is disappointing," he grumbled suggestively. "Especially when your lips are still glistening from the kiss you so passionately demanded I take from you. Normally I would correct you on your terminology, but in this case, I believe I enjoy your saying I stole it. And your challenge makes you an accessory to the crime." His voice deepened dangerously. "We might make fine lovers. I could promise you an end to your nightmares."

He reached out and stroked her cheek. It was a tender touch, surprising her with just how seductive he could be.

Temptation needled her. For a moment, she was caught in its grasp, her reason for refusing lost somewhere in the back of her mind. The hesitation drew his attention, his eyes flickering with anticipation. He reached for her, and she recoiled, sure her faltering self-discipline was about to crumble.

She drew in a deep breath and swallowed roughly.

"I am not impressed with your attempts to lay the blame for this… impropriety at my feet. You should never have allowed it to be said that we are lovers. I have a right to be irritated by such a thing. It is misplaced of you to think I am challenging you in some personal manner." She'd spat the last word at him before she realized how inappropriate it was to even say such a thing. "You are only making excuses for yourself, like some sort of… well…"

"Well, what, Miss Stevenson?" He took one lazy step toward her, his eyes daring her to stand her ground.

"Like a pirate," she sputtered before her nerve snapped and she retreated from his imposing form. "Your pin might be that of a captain, but you have all the makings of a marauding, arrogant pirate." There.

She'd insulted him as any decent lady should. She nodded but wasn't honestly sure if she was trying to impress him or herself with her words.

His lips curved into a mocking grin, and he lifted his hand to his lips and blew her a kiss. "I will do my best to live up to your expectations of me... sweet Sophia."

"Why are you calling me 'sweet'?"

"Pirates don't use formal forms of address, not with delectable morsels of womanhood such as you. They tend to take what they crave."

He caught a handful of her skirt and held her steady as he stole another kiss from her. This time the kiss was hard and demanding. The heat burning her cheeks suddenly flowed through her body like molten lava. Her lips tingled and the sensation rippled down her body. There wasn't a spot it didn't touch, not a single patch of skin that wasn't envious of the touch her lips enjoyed. Longing erupted inside her, making her thirsty for more contact between them.

She felt as though she was falling and what bothered her was just how little control she seemed to have over her descent. When Bion pulled away, her breath was raspy. His lips curved into a smug grin that infuriated her.

She slapped him, the sound drawing curious looks from those in the center of the library. The dim light offered her sanctuary from their gaze but not from the soft chuckle Bion offered in response.

"You..."

One dark eyebrow rose, his eyes narrowing with challenge. She bit back her words, stunned by just how much effort it took to do so. Her skirt flared out

as she turned and hurried away. The only problem
was, she was running from herself.

❧

"He is clearly suffering from delusions," Dr. Hallas
decided. "He shall need to be removed to the treat-
ment rooms on the other side of the Solitary Chamber,
so my staff can attend to him properly."

The guards looked at one another before one spoke
up. "But he's accused of treason and was placed here
to ensure he doesn't escape."

"My good man, this fellow is in no condition to
escape." The doctor went to the door of the cell and
opened it. He stood back and looked at Grainger.
"You may leave, Mr. Grainger."

Grainger continued to hop about the cell like a
giant toad. The slice of bread with its twin holes was
stuck to his face as he frolicked.

"You see, gentlemen, he is completely immersed
in his delusions. He has no desire to escape." The
doctor lifted his chin and walked out of the cell. "I
will send two of my staff members with a wheelchair
for him."

Grainger found his control tested. He could taste
victory, even if the exact means were still not fully
clear. He hopped again and faced the solid walls of
his cell. There was only a single, small window in the
door, making escape very unlikely. But he would soon
be moving, and the ignorant Illuminists imprisoning
him would never know that they were being manipu-
lated by his superior intellect.

Not until it was too late.

"You look ready to kill," Janette Lawley said as she sat down next to Sophia in the common dining area. It was fashioned like a great hall from a century past, when the majority of a castle's population ate together. In this case, it helped reduce the risk of fire in the dormitory wings by removing the need for Novices to cook.

"I don't suppose I need you to explain," Janette added as Sophia continued to glare at her through her purple-tinted glasses.

"Good," Sophia snapped. She stiffened when she realized how tart she sounded. "Forgive me, Janette. It has been a trying day."

"Only the day?"

Sophia returned to glaring at her friend.

Janette waved her hand. "Don't think me unkind, Sophia. I recall very well just how vexing these Illuminist men can be. But it will all right itself, you'll see."

Sophia lowered her fork. There really was no point in pretending she could eat. "I am truly happy for you, Janette, but when did you begin believing rumors? You used to be much more interesting."

Janette laughed. "True. Didn't we make a solemn promise to one another to never believe gossip?"

"When we were about eight years old." Sophia smiled with the memory. "I recall that we even set out the lace napkins to ensure we both remembered how important the occasion was."

"That's right," Janette agreed. "Which means you shall have to share all the details of your evening with Captain Donkova with me. Otherwise, I shall be left with nothing but gossip." Janette smiled and dipped her spoon into her bowl and lifted a steaming measure of soup up to her lips. The white steam twisted around her nose for a moment before she turned a ghastly shade of gray and the spoon clattered back into the bowl, splattering soup onto the table.

"Oh, dear... how clumsy of me." She dabbed at the table but couldn't seem to look at the soup. She pushed it away at last, looking as if she was fighting off nausea.

"What's the matter?"

Janette smiled, and her cheeks colored as her eyes glittered with happiness. "I'm pregnant."

Sophia nearly choked on her own soup. Janette laughed at the look on her face, which earned her a pout from Sophia. "You said that word just to be shocking, Janette Aston."

"Janette Aston Lawley, which makes my announcement quite acceptable," she argued.

"I don't care if you are married and an Illuminist; that word is uncouth." But Sophia laughed softly in spite of her reprimand. "It does not belong in an open dining hall."

Janette leaned forward. "Perhaps not, but since we don't have to worry about our fathers banishing us to some drafty castle in the Highlands anymore, there isn't any reason to tailor our speech to please the gossiping horde that we used to have to accommodate before coming here."

But I also don't get to hear my sisters teasing me over the breakfast table.

Sophia tried to brush the thought aside but Janette knew her far too well. Her friend gasped and looked stricken.

"I'm so sorry, Sophia. That was terribly mean of me to forget you are separated from your family."

"I am quite adjusted to the situation," Sophia spoke softly, doing her best to mask the sting. "It isn't as if it is forever."

Janette wasn't fooled. She leaned across the table. "It will be better, now that you've taken a lover."

"I have not... taken a lover." She struggled to keep her voice down. "And I assure you, if I were to do anything of the sort, it certainly wouldn't be Bion Donkova. I am forced to deal with his arrogant, commanding attitude enough during the day, thank you very much."

"You forgot to mention handsome."

"He is but—" Sophia froze as Janette smirked with victory.

"But what?" Janette inquired far too innocently.

"But," Sophia announced, "he is not my lover."

Oh, but you've been thinking about what it would be like all day.

Sophia picked up her fork, intent on finishing her supper so she might escape. Janette rolled her eyes before selecting something else on her dinner plate and sniffing at it.

⁓

Walking along the corridors that led to the secured Novice wing felt twice as long tonight. Anticipation was twisting through Sophia, growing stronger with every step. Somehow, her rooms had ceased to be a sanctuary from Bion's irritating persona and become the very place she couldn't escape him. In fact, her rooms were now the most dangerous place to be with the man because they might have complete privacy—coupled with her lack of self-discipline. She shuffled her steps.

The two men standing guard at the entrance noticed her and she straightened her back and picked up her feet. They nodded to her and one reached for his earpiece and opened the secured gate that led to her dormitory wing. But her cheeks colored because they knew Bion had spent the night with her. The fact that they didn't consider it a mark upon her reputation didn't ease her discomfort as she continued down to her door and opened it slowly.

Her hesitation annoyed her. She was not afraid of the man.

Only the way he makes you lose control.

That was a shameful truth.

But an exciting one too.

She sent the door closed with a sigh. Her thoughts were far too unruly. The day had been demanding and she needed to sleep, but she knew it was going to be another restless night. Inside the entry room, the light level was lower. She pulled her glasses off, enjoying the moment of freedom from them. Her desk had two books on it that she needed to read, but her mind was too restless to concentrate. She left her glasses on top of them and sought out the bathroom. Maybe a bath would calm her.

Maybe taking Bion as your lover will…

Enough!

⤝⤞

"She doesn't need you at the moment, Captain," Darius Lawley said over the rim of his brandy glass.

"Well, I might argue that point," Lykos Claxton interjected with a cocky smirk.

"But you won't," Darius countered.

Lykos frowned. "You're no fun at all since you married." He leaned forward and pushed the brandy glass Bion had left untouched closer to him. "Go on, I'm curious what you might do if you loosened up a bit."

"How is it you are still among the living?" Bion growled.

Darius chuckled and offered Bion a toast. "It seems we have something in common, Captain. We both fail to understand Guardian Lykos's propensity to agitate us."

"I am neither married nor hypnotized by someone I am unwilling to admit my attraction to, which leaves me the pleasure of watching the pair of you," Lykos announced dramatically.

"I am so pleased to hear that," Decima purred softly.

Lykos stiffened, his eyes narrowing as he turned to look at her. "Taking brandy with the men tonight, Guardian? I might claim to be surprised, but then again, I am well aware of your everlasting struggle to ignore your gender and ensure we notice your efforts."

Decima softened her expression, becoming a radiant vision. She relaxed her formal posture and became alluring in an instant. With a delicate hand, she reached for the brandy snifter sitting in front of Lykos, but she didn't pick it up. Instead, she traced the rim of it with the tip of one slim finger.

"I would never be so predictable, Guardian Claxton."

She turned and left, but Lykos's gaze was fixed on her departing figure.

"Not mesmerized my ass," Darius muttered, gaining a soft, menacing chuckle from Bion. Darius lifted his brandy in a silent toast to the captain.

Bion surprised them by sitting down and reaching for the crystal decanter sitting in the middle of the table. "Being on land has some advantages," he said as he poured a measure of the strong beverage into a snifter. "I can never indulge myself when aboard ship."

It wasn't a duty he lamented, even if part of him was amused by the idea of acting like a pirate. The men around him were ones dedicated to duty. It was not an easy road, but the truest rewards came from achieving what many found too demanding. He lifted the glass to his nose and inhaled. No, he didn't regret anything. Not even stealing that kiss from Sophia Stevenson. That had been his pleasure.

And hers too.

For a moment he allowed himself to recall the way she'd kissed him. Tentatively, but she'd still responded with far more passion than he'd expected. That was the detail he really needed to forget. He took another sip of the brandy and then another as he tried to let the strong beverage erase the memory of just how well her body fit against his.

Instead, all the brandy did was strip aside his reasons for not seeking her out.

So he lifted his glass toward Lykos, smiling when the man filled it again. He'd never been a slave to drinking, but for the moment, the snifter was keeping him in his chair.

It felt like a monumental achievement.

❧

"Come, my friend, we have a fine carriage for you."

Grainger cocked his head to one side and looked at the orderlies. They had on white coats and were smiling at him. The wheelchair was a wide one but what alarmed him were the thick leather straps secured to each armrest and on the footrest too. He smiled at them and clapped his hands together.

"He's a cheery one," one of the men said.

"Aye, lucky for him too, since I heard he was going to face execution for his crimes," the other remarked. "I suppose the fear was too much for the bloke."

Grainger hopped in a small circle, needing a moment to hide his expression. He did not fear an Illuminist. But like any beasts of burden, he had to outsmart them when he was surrounded.

"Come on… we're going on a little walkabout," the orderly cooed.

Grainger clapped again and hopped toward the chair. It shimmied as he climbed into it and clapped some more.

"All right then, let's go."

"Shouldn't I secure him?"

The orderly behind the chair began pushing it. "Don't bother. He's harmless. He might have survived that knock on the head, but it left him simple. It's in his file from Hawaii too. The man hasn't made sense since he opened his eyes. If you ask me, they should have just left him there, where it was warm enough for him to run about half clothed."

Grainger didn't have to fake his smile. It was bright and full of victory but the two fools so easily assisting him out of the prison area were clueless. They wouldn't last a day as Helikeians. Failure wasn't tolerated among his elite Order. In fact, any member who proved inferior would be eliminated so that his blood could not be passed on.

There were guards at the end of the hallway, where a large arch went from one side of the hallway to the other. Inside it were Deep Earth Crystals, and one of the guards depressed his ear control device to complete the current so that the orderlies might proceed through. Grainger hummed and moved his head from side to side as they left the prison wing behind them.

"Must be nice to be so cheerful," the orderly pushing the chair remarked.

"I'll be right happy if he continues to do what we ask without giving us fits like some of the other patients," his companion responded.

Grainger continued to smile, enjoying the feeling of impending freedom. He clapped his hands, almost giddy with the knowledge that he wasn't strapped to the chair.

Such trusting fools. He was going to enjoy killing them.

❧

Sophia punched her pillow, but the action didn't relieve much of her frustration. She was so tired her head ached, and yet she couldn't seem to sleep for more than half an hour without waking.

You're just waiting on that man's next visit.

She grumbled and sat up. The bedding was kicked to the foot of the bed, so it was simple to swing her legs over the edge. The floor was cool against her bare feet when she suddenly realized there was something in the air. Looking through the open bedroom door, she stared at the darkness of the other room, trying to decide what it was she saw. It was like fog, only composed of light rather than moisture. She stepped toward it, drawn forward in fascination. She could see the residue of light drifting through the darkness; she could actually see the particles as tiny pinpoints of light. The room was dark, and yet, it wasn't. It was as though she could see all the layers that made up the darkness.

"You see the light flow now... excellent."

Sophia froze, her muscles tightening as alarm raced through her. She recognized the voice; she still heard it in her nightmares. Worse still was the certain knowledge that Grainger was standing in the corner of her room.

"What a trophy you shall be," he cooed like he might over a newly acquired racehorse. "My crowning achievement."

He was more than a shadow now. She could see him disturbing the flow of light. Fear gripped her, but rather than paralyzing her, it sent her into motion. She lifted her knee and sent her foot toward his jaw. There was a snap and the solid connection of flesh against flesh.

"Get out!" She struggled to move away from the bed so that she might have more room to defend herself, but Grainger wasn't a Novice when it came to fighting arts. He pressed forward, rubbing his jaw. So she jumped up onto the bed and walked right across its soft surface.

"I mean it, get out!" She didn't wait for him but instead made a dash for the door. Grainger caught her in the outer room, locking his arms around her body like a trap. She struggled, filling her lungs to scream, but he clamped a hand over her mouth.

She cupped her fist in one hand and twisted her entire body to send her elbow back into her captor. He howled and his hold broke, but she'd made it only two paces before she tripped over something lying on the floor. Horror gagged her as she realized it was a man. She floundered as she tried to regain her footing but gasped when something looped around her neck and jerked her back. It was a brutal hold that kept her from filling her lungs. They burned as Grainger snickered next to her ear. The last thing she saw was the bodies of the two men who normally guarded the entrance to the secured wing. Blood coated the side of one of their faces and both were as still as death. One had been stripped of his suit and lay naked on the carpet. Seeing a nude male wasn't what horrified her. What crushed her composure at last was the fact that she could not dislodge whatever he was holding her with, and the certain knowledge that he had what he needed to walk out without being noticed. Her vision began to darken and she slumped forward, no longer able to fight.

Grainger maintained his hold a little longer, just to make sure she wasn't employing a new tactic in her struggle. When he released the dressing robe tie, she fell over and lay still on the floor. He made sure she was still breathing, smiling when her chest lifted. But he cursed because his jaw was aching. He grabbed her wrist and hoisted her up and over his shoulder. The wheelchair was just inside the doorway and he dumped her into it. He froze for a moment, the sight of her bare legs making him pause. He turned and went toward the small wardrobe standing in the bedroom. He opened the curtains just a few inches to allow some moonlight in. He yanked a skirt off its hanger and grabbed a coat as well. He had no idea if they matched and didn't much care.

Victory was so close he could taste it. He dropped the skirt over her head and lifted her body up so it would fall down to her waist. He ended up pulling each of her arms free but the garment settled into place well enough. She was light enough that the task didn't prove too difficult and soon the coat was buttoned in place over her corset and chemise. He smiled as he buckled the leather straps, securing her wrists and ankles to the chair. He would not be the one feeling their bite. No, he was far too intelligent for that.

Grainger straightened his vest and made sure the small ear device was nestled in place before he opened the door and pushed the wheelchair out into the hallway. It was well after midnight and the other Novices were all asleep. He walked right through the gate, the lack of guards still undiscovered.

Yes, victory was his, and it was every bit as sweet as he'd anticipated it would be.

⤚⤙

"You hold your brandy well," Lykos remarked as he sat down at the small table Bion lingered at. The rest of the dining hall was only half full now.

"Why so disappointed?" Bion asked as he contemplated finding his bed, then discarded the idea because it would entail moving—something he was loathe to do at the moment. It would be far too tempting to walk toward Sophia's room rather than his own. "Hoping to win a few rounds of cards?"

Lykos shrugged. "Or learn a few interesting things when your lips loosened."

Bion finished off the last of the brandy in his snifter. "My mother often put more than this snifter holds in the supper stew. She used to say it kept the blood flowing. Russia is not as warm as Britain."

"I forgot you hailed from the frozen expanses. It explains your fascination with living among the clouds."

Bion grinned. "You have me correctly figured on that account, Guardian."

"But only that account?" Lykos inquired. "Is that what your tone is meant to imply?"

Bion nodded, his eyes narrowing. "Forgive me, Guardian, but I find myself more comfortable knowing you cannot deduce every detail of my personality."

"Some Guardians might accuse you of having dark secrets since you want to guard them so carefully."

"And my mother would have labeled you as nosy as the old matchmaker in the village we lived in."

Lykos lifted his snifter and inhaled the scent of the liquor before answering. "Nosy… yes, but it keeps me alive."

"My secrets serve me the same way," Bion responded. "It's best to be unpredictable with the number of pirates roaming the skies. Any traitor sailing with me will discover it difficult to plan my downfall."

Airships were only as secure as their crews. Since it was much faster to transport Deep Earth Crystals via airship, piracy had become a serious threat. It was another reason the society around them had so little information about the struggle being fought between the Illuminists and Helikeian Orders. Much of it was happening far above their heads.

This was the reason Grainger was so desperate to get his hands on Sophia. With only two ways to produce a Navigator, they were very rare. Sophia had no idea how many coveted her situation.

Misfortune actually.

Bion's Novice Navigator was neither accomplished nor content with her new skills. He'd never thought to pity anyone who beat the odds and gained the opportunity to hold a Root Ball in their hands. Everything she was experiencing, he'd spent the majority of his life in pursuit of. He stiffened, remembering that he hadn't had to cut himself off from his family as Sophia did. Joining the after-dinner brandy party had only been an excuse to get a closer look at Darius Lawley and learn the secret to his new bride's contentment. Janette Aston was happily wearing her Illuminist pin, and Bion wanted to know why.

His lips twitched slightly with amusement and Lykos raised an inquisitive eyebrow. "I was simply contemplating just what my trainee might think of my fascination with discovering the secret of Mrs. Lawley's conversion to our Order."

Lykos slowly smiled. "My patience is rewarded at last." He sat up, abandoning his lazy sprawl. "That statement unmasks you, Captain."

"I doubt it."

Lykos shook his head. "Don't. Without a doubt, there is more to your relationship with your trainee. No man who has devoted so much of his time toward the goal of becoming what she is would entertain any thought about her happiness. Not unless he was thinking with his tender feelings."

"My tender feelings are far harder than you might realize," Bion informed him. "I was raised in an unforgiving land and the harsher conditions of the air fleet suit me well. I have no use for those who whine about the unjustness of circumstances. Miss Stevenson has been granted a gift. A very rare one, even if it is also a challenge."

"You rather enjoy watching someone such as Miss Stevenson rising above what fate has tried to crush her with, don't you?"

Bion chuckled softly, a flicker of heat entering his eyes. "That is a fact, Guardian."

"It is—" Lykos paused, looking past Bion at someone entering the hall. His expression hardened instantly and Bion was on his feet a second later.

"Captain Donkova, Head Guardian Pavola has been searching for you but you were not in your rooms."

"I know where I was, man."

The young Guardian swallowed nervously, betraying his inexperience. Bion clamped down on the urge to snap at the man.

"It seems the suspected traitor Grainger was not insane."

"There was nothing suspected about it; the man is a traitor," Bion snarled. Lykos reached out, gripped a hand around his arm to silence him.

"Where is the man now?"

The young Guardian stammered. "He was… transferred to… to the medical… wing but it seems… the staff underestimated his condition."

"How badly?" Bion demanded.

"He killed the two orderlies charged with moving him from the prison wing and… it seems… he also took the two Guardians standing watch over the secured Novice—"

Bion lost control of his temper and grabbed the front of the man's jacket. "Where is my trainee?" he snarled savagely.

The man paled. "Gone."

           ∝

The sweet smell of fresh air—Grainger paused for a moment to savor it. The city streets were quiet in the dark hours, but he wasn't foolish enough to believe them deserted. There was a whole different class of people who preferred the darkness to the light of day. Even in the better parts of town, the shadows would be harboring creatures; really, they were more base than anything that might be called human.

He pushed the wheelchair, keeping his chin level as he went. The night breeze blew some dry leaves across the road and footsteps echoed from down one of the alleys he passed, but no one stepped out to stop him. Grainger passed the tailor shop and moved past the millinery store and other merchants. Two more blocks and he came to the door he sought.

Wouldn't the Illuminists like to know that there

was a devoted Helikeian living so very close to their Solitary Chamber?

He laughed softly as he reached for the door knocker. The sound echoed through the silent city street, but no one moved their curtains aside to look down at him. Of course not; it was far healthier to ignore those who came calling at such hours. A small panel opened and a doorman peered at him through the iron grate secured over it.

"I have just escaped and do not have my pin."

The man remained silent and looked at the slumped form of Sophia. "This is a Navigator. Open the door, Compatriot. I am delivering a prize worthy of reward."

The door opened and Grainger pushed the chair inside. Behind him, the doorman shut it softly, concealing their location completely.

❧

Bion was a man who prided himself on his control. But when provoked, he was capable of pure, undiluted savagery. It wasn't civilized or polite, but when it came to snatching victory out of the jaws of bastards like Grainger, that facet of his personality served him well.

Tonight, he let it loose, covering the distance between the dining hall and Sophia's room in record time. Only Lykos kept pace and the Guardians inside the small chambers moved out of his way. The signs of a struggle were clear. Bion followed the overturned furniture, kneeling to inspect the dark splotches of blood on the floor.

"I do believe the rougher aspects of your personality

might come in very handy very soon," Lykos said softly, kneeling next to him.

Bion locked gazes with him, surprised by the fierce determination in the fair-faced Guardian's stare. Lykos Claxton was a wolf, cleverly donning the fleece of a sheep to dupe those around them.

"My plan exactly."

"I believe I should be part of any planning," Guardian Pavola interrupted from across the room.

Bion stood and fixed the head of security with a deadly look. "I was opposed to lodging Miss Stevenson here, and I believe my argument has unfortunately been proven valid. She should have been in the air, where this could not have happened. Retrieving her will be my duty."

"Your position may indeed be correct, but that does not endow you with the ability to brush aside the law," Pavola answered. "We have Hunters for this sort of situation."

"Your Hunters are not anywhere near suited for this." Bion stepped closer, forcing Pavola to look up at him. "Grainger is no doubt hurrying out of the city while we stand here arguing. Once he has her aboard an airship, retrieving her will become nearly impossible. Every second you waste discussing the necessary course of action increases the odds of the Helikeians utilizing her for their own means."

There was already an unstable situation in the skies. Utilizing the dimensional gates was the only way to escape the pirates roaming the trade routes. It was the Illuminists' most critical advantage and now Sophia just might tip those scales back into the favor of the Helikeians.

Guardian Pavola stiffened. "Your insolence is misplaced, Captain Donkova. What makes the Illuminist Order strong is our dedication to rules and structure. Otherwise, we would be nothing more than outlaws."

Bion slowly grinned, but it wasn't a cheerful expression. Pavola stepped back in response.

"Oh, there are times for lawlessness," Bion offered softly. "Now more than ever. I promise you one thing, Guardian, I am your man."

And he was going to find Sophia or die trying.

She needed to wake up. Sophia knew it but couldn't seem to break free of sleep's hold. She struggled, straining to open her eyes, but they felt glued shut. Thrashing from one side to the other seemed of little help. All she managed to do was half open her eyes.

"Hurry up with that chloroform."

Horror kept her eyes partially open, but her straining only allowed her to see a white cloth coming toward her face. She smelled the noxious fumes and tried to hold her breath.

"Resist all you like. I do enjoy a good fight."

She was regaining her wits and opened her eyes all the way. Grainger stood over her, pressing the cloth to her face. Her skin crawled with revulsion and her lungs were burning. Her captor clasped the nape of her neck, and her hands were still strapped to the armrests of the wheelchair. The need to breathe broke through her resistance. She inhaled and the chemicals began to do their work. Her vision blurred and another few breaths sent her back into darkness.

"And I will enjoy seeing you put to work for the Helikeian cause."

Grainger smiled, watching Sophia slump once more against the back of the wheelchair. He stood there for several long moments, making sure she was disabled. He wanted to take advantage of the fine house he was in, bathe and make himself presentable, but delivering his prize was much more important.

"Is the carriage ready?"

"Yes, Compatriot."

Grainger enjoyed the sound of the title "Compatriot." It had been too long since he'd heard the word spoken with the proper respect. The Illuminists had tried to humiliate him by sneering as they spoke his title, but he was the victor now.

"Send word to Dr. Nerval that I have recovered the Navigator. Since he was the man who discovered the Pure Spirit Janette Aston, he will be happy to hear the Navigator is now in our hands."

"Yes, Compatriot. I will send the telegram myself."

Even Dr. Nerval would have to acknowledge his achievements. The doctor was an esteemed member of the Helikeian Community, his bloodline almost royal. It would be good to have the approval of such a man. Grainger rubbed his hands together.

"Let us go." Three words had rarely given him such satisfaction before. Now, as he pushed the wheelchair through the house toward the back door, he was filled with a sense of accomplishment.

Yes... he was the superior man. Soon, every member of the Helikeian Order would see proof of his standing among them, for he was certain to be decorated with the Sapphire Phalanx for his achievement. It was the highest award within the Helikeian Order. Once he wore the pin, no one would question him. Not ever.

All he had to do was deliver his prize to the airship station. The doorman opened the back door and a carriage waited there. The house was owned by a doctor, giving him the perfect excuse to order the vehicle brought around at such an hour. They loaded his prize and set off without a single look from the residences nearby.

❦

"Not going to ask what I'm doing?" Bion asked Lykos.

Bion didn't stop what he was doing to turn and look at Lykos, nor did he care that the other man had followed him into his private rooms. Bion reached up, onto the top of his wardrobe, and lifted a case. Once it was sitting on a small table, he opened it to reveal a stack of neatly folded garments.

"I'm more of a visual man," Lykos remarked nonchalantly. "A man's actions often say more than his words."

"True."

"Of course, I would be delighted to hear your plan if you are in the mood to share it with me?" Lykos drawled.

"I'm not."

Bion stripped off his maroon uniform coat and tossed it across the footrail of his bed. His pants and polished boots landed nearby and he reached for the first item in the case. He pulled on a pair of sturdy pants with leather-reinforced inner thighs. The shirt was less formal than the one he'd worn beneath his uniform. He didn't bother buttoning it all the way, leaving the top gaping open. A leather vest was next, worn in several places and constructed with numerous pockets. Over that he secured a weapons harness with a holster that hung beneath his left arm and two scabbards for knifes. He reached into the case and removed a pistol that gleamed from recent polishing. Bion checked the Deep Earth Crystal secured in the firing pin before sliding it into his holster. A pair of worn, knee-high boots came next. He finished off his look with a sturdy, dark blue wool over-jacket. It was the sort of thing a Naval man might wear, unless you took a closer look and noticed the additional pockets for glasses and other Illuminist paraphernalia.

"You have achieved a rather disreputable look, Captain."

Bion wasn't quite finished. He picked up a scarf and knotted it around his head. Once the ends fell down his back, Lykos chuckled.

"You lack only the gold hoop earring to be taken for a pirate from a century ago," Lykos observed. "Mind you, another man might question just why you have all the necessary accouterments to achieve such a look."

Bion grinned. "I know my enemy because there are times it is very beneficial to blend in." He pulled a hat off the hatstand in the corner and tugged it down low. "Which is why I can tell you with all confidence that I will retrieve my trainee. Or die trying."

Bion shot Lykos a hard look. For a moment,

the two men found solace in each other's company because they were brethren.

"I can promise you this much, Guardian. The Marshals will not get another opportunity to deal with him."

Three

"YOU PRESENT YOURSELF AS IF YOU EXPECT SOME manner of great reward."

The room was quiet as a tomb. Sophia watched the three men seated at the end of it as they contemplated Grainger with narrowed eyes. Each one sat in a throne-like chair that reminded her of something Henry VIII might have used. The backs were carved with crests of some sort but the room was only partially lit, so she couldn't make out the detail.

She could make out the shackles clamped around her wrists well enough. Each band was two inches wide and there was a chain running between them.

"I have brought you a Navigator," Grainger insisted. "One I created. Such a feat is most certainly worthy of notice."

"Her eyes may be altered, but she is not fully trained," one of the men observed. "Therefore, you have brought us an unusable trainee."

"She is not untrained."

"She is not fully accomplished in the art of distinguishing interdimension gates," the man in the center chair replied. "Did you believe we have not been keeping abreast of her progress? I assure you, we have. It is true that you helped to create her, and for that, you may continue to serve within our ranks. But there will be no reward until she becomes a Navigator."

"Bastards," Sophia muttered, but the gag tied around her mouth muffled her curse. She really wished she knew a few more.

The man sitting in the center chair shifted his attention to her. His thin lips curved slightly, the expression nauseating her. There was something about him that made her skin feel dirty. He stood up and his polished shoes made sharp sounds on the gleaming wooden floor as he approached her. She strained against the leather strap binding her, but it didn't give even a tiny bit.

The man waited for her to expend her strength, enjoyment flickering in his eyes as he watched her flail. He leaned down and peered into her eyes. "She has potential, but as you know, Compatriot Grainger, only success is rewarded among our ranks. The Soiled Dove is due to dock this evening. Captain Aetos will be expecting you."

Grainger stiffened, rage twisted his features, but he kept his lips pressed firmly together in spite of the way his face turned red.

He offered a half bow. "She will be everything you expect. I swear it."

The man standing near her turned, his hands locking formally behind him as he walked back toward Grainger. "Captain Aetos will be taking on supplies and no doubt a few more crew, since some choose death over serving the Helikeian Order. You will need to find someone who can train her, since the Soiled Dove doesn't boast a Navigator."

The two men still sitting in their chairs chuckled softly, making it plain they didn't think Grainger could accomplish the task being put to him.

"I understand my task and I will prevail."

There was a confidence in his tone that chilled her blood, because every man in the room appeared very pleased by it. In their eyes, she was a thing without rights. A shiver made its way down her spine and Bion's warnings rose from her memory.

"Men will kill to own you…"

The ones watching her certainly thought they could own her.

❧

"It is a shame we must take to the skies so soon."

Grainger was standing in front of a mirror, inspecting his newly shaved face. He turned his head one way and then the other before sniffing with approval.

"We'll have to endure the rougher conditions of living aboard a ship." He adjusted his silk cravat. "Still, I intend to enjoy civilized attire while I might—something I shall not forget the Illuminists denied me."

Satisfied that his vest was sitting perfectly, he turned to consider Sophia. "I should leave you bound to that chair, as your brethren did to me."

Sophia narrowed her eyes, the only insult she might offer with the gag still in place.

"But I suppose I cannot begin to educate you on

the merits of the Helikeian Order if I treat you as the Illuminists would."

He waved his hand and someone behind her began loosening the gag. Some of her hair was caught in the knot and was yanked out of her head before the thing came loose. The pain was miniscule compared with the relief of finally being able to close her mouth. Her tongue was dry as a bolt of wool.

"You may bathe, but be assured that there is no escape from this house. Attempt it and you will be secured to that chair until nightfall."

Two burly men finished unbuckling the straps which bound her, then withdrew to the doorway. They never looked directly at her. Each wore a gold pin with the crest of the Helikeian Order on it.

For all that she had heard of the Illuminist enemy, being faced with men who believed as deeply in the Helikeian cause as Bion did in the Illuminist one was startling.

She stood up and shakily moved toward the bathroom at the other end of the room. It really wasn't a choice, unless she wanted to soil herself. At least it had a sturdy door with a latch, but once she'd secured it, she realized just how small it was compared to the two men guarding her.

They'd kick the door in with little effort.

Well, she had privacy—for the moment at least. Tears stung her eyes. She wiped them away and turned on the water to the bathtub to cover any sound she might make. She didn't have time to cry. Hadn't had the time, really, for a very long time. More tears eased down her cheeks in spite of her resolve to maintain her composure. She decided to focus on the task at hand, which brought Bion to mind. In order to ignore the rogue, she'd quite often focused on the task at hand.

Maybe that had been a foolish waste of an opportunity.

She looked around the bathroom, seeking any form of escape, but there was none—only the door she'd entered through. Dread knotted her belly as she undressed and stepped into the bath. She might well have lost her opportunity to choose her first lover.

A day ago, she'd have chastised herself for thinking about Bion in such a way, but it was amazing the way opinion changed when freedom of choice no longer rested in her hands. She'd always expected to be formally courted and won by a man her father would happily shake hands with before granting them his blessing.

Bion was a devilish rouge who stormed her defenses; he wasn't the courting type.

But she had trembled in his embrace. For a moment, she allowed herself to relive the experience. Never once had she believed a kiss might affect her so deeply. It was frightening in its intensity but wildly enticing for the very same reason. There was something deep inside her that blossomed at the idea of being so completely out of control.

She trembled as she realized the harsh reality facing her. Cooperating with her captors would place her on Bion's enemy list. The man was ferocious when it came to battling the Helikeians.

Yet she had no idea how to escape, and that unleashed a flood of despair that left her sitting on the side of the tub long after her hair had dried.

❦

"Mind where you're leading me. We'll end up shang-haied for sure."

A waterfront prostitute flung the words at her would-be customer when he tried to tug her down a dark alley. The man shrugged and pressed her against the wall right where they were. There was a rustle as her skirts were raised, but she didn't protest.

Bion peered out from beneath the brim of his hat, missing none of the details of the scene before him. In this section of town, a man was wise to keep his guard up. But all around him, men were eagerly spending their pay on cheap liquor. As their wits dulled, prostitutes moved closer to relieve the men of more of their coin.

Tonight, Bion sought the women employed by the boarding masters. They didn't demand coin first, but took their intoxicated victims down the alleys to where they might be sold into service aboard airships. It wasn't always women who lured the unsuspecting men to their doom. Crooked barkeepers or boarding-house owners all joined the enterprise.

There was a shortage of men willing to labor aboard ships and risk dying before setting foot on land again.

Helikeians were just as desperate for labor for their sky vessels as the seafaring community was for their ships. The men who made up the crews of the Helikeian airships faced brutal masters and the added bonus of being told the only way out was death. The Order had no intention of allowing men to escape and warn the general population of the ships sailing the skies. They were little more than pirates that stole men for their crews as easily as they did cargo from defeated ships.

"Here now, love, come have a drink with me."

Bion turned to look at a woman who had one foot propped on the top of a small barrel. Her skirt was hiked to afford him a generous view of her calf and knee.

"I'll not bore you; you have my word on that," she said.

"Is that so?" Bion stepped closer to her, pressing up against her body as he laid his hand over her left breast.

"Here now." She laughed as she pushed him away. "The least you can do is buy me a drink before we get on to what you like."

Bion folded his arms over his chest, grinning. There was the unmistakable presence of a pin beneath her bodice collar. Illuminists wore their pins with pride. Only Helikeians stooped to deception by hiding their pins. The female winked at him but all she managed to do was inspire disgust. Every man serving beneath his authority on ship did so with pride. There were recruits eagerly awaiting their turn to be airborne.

Sophia was the one exception to that.

Bion followed the woman down the alley, the sway of her hips less than arousing.

"Here we are… Peter pours the best Irish whiskey in town." She beckoned him further down the alley, far past where anyone on the street might be able to see them.

"Just a bit more," she continued. "It's more private-like back here. No one to disturb us."

Peter, the barkeep she led him to, had greasy hair and splotches on his shirt. His establishment wasn't much better. The tables were rough and several were missing chunks due to fights. The chairs were mismatched and the customers sitting in them less than refined. Several had untouched drinks in front of them and cards in their hands that they weren't paying attention to.

It was a den of thieves, no mistake about it.

"Just get off ship?" the woman cooed to him as she delivered a glass full of dark whiskey.

Bion lifted the glass but paused before taking a sip. "Just stepped back onto the ground." He tossed back the drink and chuckled at the way the woman's eyes slanted with satisfaction. She sashayed back toward the bar to fetch another for him.

Bion leaned back in the chair, giving his company the illusion that he was primed to enjoy the nighttime pleasures. Someone began to beat the keys of the worn piano, filling the space with a rather out-of-tune polka. The drink was overly strong, but they were going to have to feed him a great deal more to render him senseless. Science was a wonderful tool, especially when it came to outsmarting his enemy. Swallowing a half pound of butter hadn't been pleasant, but the fat would coat his insides and make it much harder for the liquor to be absorbed.

"You're thirsty," his escort remarked as she delivered another glass. She sat on the edge of the table, making sure that her skirt flipped aside to allow him a look at her thigh. "How long were you at sea?"

"Wasn't at sea," Bion offered. He grinned and leaned back in the chair, letting her believe he was falling under the influence of the alcohol Peter was serving up.

She leaned forward so he was treated to a view of her cleavage. "Didn't you say you were newly off ship, love?"

Bion shook his head, smiling like a besotted fool. The liquor was laced with something but his tolerance was higher than they gave him credit for. "I did and so I am, but I wasn't at sea," he drawled.

She leaned closer, peering into his eyes. Her smile faded as she realized his eyes weren't streaked with amber. He wasn't a Navigator.

"Now don't you worry…" He sat forward and patted her knee. "Maybe my eyes are normal sort of eyes, but I know how to navigate."

She smiled. He was treading on dangerous ground. It took more effort than he'd anticipated remaining in the chair. Every instinct he had was firing off, warning him to evade the trap being so neatly closed around him. Instead, he forced himself to seal his own doom by uttering a few more incriminating sentences.

"You know, there is nothing quite like a sunset… among the clouds."

He was taking a huge risk, but it was the only plan he'd been able to concoct given the short amount of time. Grainger wouldn't risk leaving Sophia on the ground for very long. Every moment she resided within the city was an opportunity for an Illuminist Hunter to locate her. They'd get her on board an airship as quickly as possible. The only thing they would have to wait for was dusk to conceal them. Bion glanced around the makeshift bar. It was a trap set up to fill slots on an airship. Unless he missed his guess, the barkeep and his cohorts would be gone by midnight. He couldn't dismiss the possibility that he wasn't going to be lucky enough to end up on the same vessel as Sophia. It gnawed on his insides as he tapped his toe in time with the offbeat piano.

But a bad plan was better than no plan.

❦

Her belly growled low and long, the sound clear in the silent room. The man guarding her kept his eyes on the tray sitting on the table. The tea was long cold as was the soup, but it still looked delicious.

Missing a meal won't hurt you. Sophia turned her back on the table, trying to listen to her own advice. There was only one reason why the guard would be so interested in making sure she ate. The food or the tea had to be laced with something designed to steal her senses. But it was proving more difficult than she'd anticipated, ignoring her hunger—and her fear.

She worried the edge of her jacket as she contemplated the closed draperies covering the window. Thick, heavy velvet with tassel trim, they kept even a tiny sliver of sunlight from entering the room. They also made sure no one caught a glimpse of her from the outside.

Where was she? How far away from the Solitary Chamber? *From Bion?*

She was suddenly endowed with a new appreciation for the man's vigilance. In fact, she missed it horribly at the moment. Her belly rumbled again, and there was a soft sound from the man behind her. He reached into his vest pocket and withdrew a small key. He fit it into the lock on the door and left.

Her relief was short-lived because he returned only a few moments later. She felt her mouth go dry as he set a dark bottle on a small table and gathered up a length of cloth in his hand. He kept his head back as he tipped the bottle into the cloth, then set it aside. The look in his eyes when he shifted his attention to her chilled her blood.

But she lifted her arms and curled her fingers into tight fists. She wouldn't be any lamb waiting for the slaughter. Her skills in Asian fighting might be weak, but she was going to put them to the test.

By every drop of Irish blood she had, she would not go down without a fight.

※

"How much did you give him?"

Bion moved away from a kick delivered to his belly. He had to squelch the urge to roll all the way over and gain his feet.

"A fair amount," Peter groused. "Look at him. He's a big one, and I didn't want to risk losing him. He claimed he knew how to navigate and that's what you told me you wanted. So pay up or I'll sell him to the dockyard."

Bion cracked open an eye. He got a glimpse of worn boots before he looked up further to see five men looking down at him. They were all watching him, so he flashed them a bright smile.

"Where'd the pretty one go?" He sat up, remembering to let his head wobble just a little. "Nothing personal and all… but where's the honey gone?"

"I heard you can navigate."

Bion struggled to his feet, making a good show of being intoxicated. In truth, he only had a pounding headache. Who might have thought he'd ever find himself grateful for butter?

"I've been learning about it," he declared as he swayed. "Me last captain put me to work on the bridge… he did."

"How much did you learn?" The man asking the question was obviously the leader. The men near him kept a sharp eye on him and one hand beneath the open edges of their vests, where their pistols were hidden from the local constables, no doubt. The man in the middle peered into Bion's eyes.

"Well now, I'm not a Navigator myself but I've been training them that have the gift. Just getting those amber streaks in the eyes doesn't mean you know how to use the skill. It takes a man like me to guide 'em." Bion slurred his speech and added a hiccup. "Now where'd the lady go?"

"She left you in my keeping."

Bion swayed again. " Why would she do something like that? We were going to get to know each other."

"Because you'll be working for me from now on."

"Now see here," Peter argued. "He's not yours. You haven't paid for him. I could get a lot for him down on the dock, what with the way he's on his feet after all I gave him."

"I'm buying," the man in the center said. "But if he's lying, I'll toss him overboard and be back to take my money out of your hide for setting me up."

One of the men handed over a wad of folded bills.

"See now," Bion stammered, "what's this business?

You can't be buying a man just like that. I've got me a ship, made me mark on the roster. I just came looking for a pretty girl before—"

"Now you have a new ship"—one of the men pulled out his pistol, aiming it at Bion's heart—"and a Navigator for you to train. Unless you want to admit you were lying?"

Bion shuffled back a step only to run into Peter's thugs. A moment later, pain split his skull as someone clubbed him from behind. There was no fending off the blackness; it jerked him away from consciousness in a blinding flash.

❧

"This is a rash plan."

"I think our good captain will agree with you—once he wakes up, that is," Lykos whispered softly to Decima. He stroked her side with a delicate motion, chuckling when she made a disgruntled sound. In the dark alley, he pulled her closer and buried his head in her hair.

"Do remember to play the part, my dear. You are, after all, a veteran Hunter and should know how to blend in to your surroundings."

"And you are an experienced Guardian. Do try not to sound so pleased," Decima whispered against his neck. "It is a sure sign of a lack of professionalism."

Lykos chuckled and pressed a kiss against her temple. He kept his gaze on Bion's slumped form and the men doing their best to lift him, but it was a struggle. Lykos had to admit that his attention was trying to wander to the sweet opportunity attempting to wiggle out of his embrace.

"You are correct." But Lykos tightened his embrace for a fraction of a moment before he forced himself to return to duty. "Frustratingly so."

Decima opened her lips to argue or perhaps chastise him, but he pressed his mouth against hers, sealing whatever she'd intended to hurl at him beneath a hard kiss. It wasn't as passionate as he would have liked, more of a declaration of his intentions once time permitted him the luxury of giving in to his impulses.

She hissed at him when he relaxed his hold, pushing against him until he released her completely. In the dingy alley she was even more stunning, despite the tattered dress she wore.

"Until later," he offered with a slight inclination of his head.

She turned her back on him, using their duty like some fortress that would offer her protection. Some day very soon, he was going to enjoy storming her defenses.

❧

Bion rolled over and landed facedown on the floor.

His elbows smarted, but it was nothing compared to the way the back of his skull felt. Cracking an eye open, he realized he'd been lying in a hammock.

"On your feet."

Bion was happy to comply, but the man standing over him wasn't very pleased when he ended up looking up into Bion's furious glare. Bion rolled his shoulders and his neck popped as he stared down into the smaller man's face. "Who clubbed me? You?"

"No." The man swallowed roughly. "Captain Aetos wanted to see you now that we're off the ground."

There was a dull hissing sound and the deck beneath his feet vibrated a tiny amount. Bion knew the feel of a ship—he was more at home in the sky than on the surface of the Earth—but this was not an Illuminist ship. The air was stale because the hatches that would have allowed a breeze in were closed shut. Not far ahead, a trapdoor opened to the deck above, sunlight pouring down over the ladder leading up, out of the hold.

"This way. It isn't wise to keep the captain waiting. He's right fond of tossing men overboard when he doesn't have any use for them—or those that just piss him off. He tosses those over the rail too. Don't say I didn't warn you."

Bion grinned at the crewman's back. It was a savage expression and he didn't bother to control it. He climbed out of the hold, sweeping the deck with a critical glance on his way to the captain's cabin at the back of the ship. The crewman rapped on the door and pushed it open when someone hollered inside.

But the crewman stayed outside, holding the door open for Bion. There was a look in the man's eyes that confirmed Captain Aetos was everything Bion expected of an airship pirate. He maintained order on the vessel like countless other lawless men had done through the ages, through merciless savagery.

"About time you rolled out of your rack." Captain Aetos had just finished grooming, the scent of soap lingering in the cabin. He was inspecting his short beard in a small mirror. "I don't suffer lazy dogs aboard the Soiled Dove."

"Never met a captain who did."

Aetos put the mirror down on a desk that had several charts unrolled on its top. "And I don't care for arrogant men among my crew either."

Bion folded his arms over his chest in response. Aetos rose, standing eye to eye with Bion. "If you have a problem with my authority, speak plainly."

"Can't really do that just yet, since I haven't heard what it is you are expecting of me. Where are we bound?"

A gleam of anticipation flickered in the captain's eyes. "You're an opportunistic one."

Bion inclined his head.

Aetos laughed softly. "I like that in a man." He tapped the charts on his desktop. "Since you aren't demanding to know what manner of vessel this is, you've proven yourself a man of his word. You did just get off ship and you weren't at sea."

"Sounds like I said a little too much."

"Better sold to me than a whaling ship."

Bion wasn't willing to agree so quickly. "I like a good opportunity but not when it comes with a billy club across me skull."

Aetos didn't even blink. "I needed a man who could train a Navigator, and I don't need any complications from the Illuminist authorities." His eyes narrowed. "What captain did you sail with?"

Bion truly hated the man in that moment. For the innocent sailor caught in his net, there wouldn't be a hope of answering the question correctly. It was clear the crew member cowering outside the cabin door had reason to fear Aetos.

"Kyros."

Aetos grinned, the expression more victorious than pleased. "What position did you hold?"

"I was his first officer."

The captain shifted, moving his right hand toward the butt of the pistol strapped to his hip.

"Kyros was a Helikeian and I knew it," Bion admitted. "But I wasn't there for any order's benefit. I was there to get my hands on a Root Ball." Bion stepped forward and boldly looked at the charts. "So when are you going to get around to telling me what sort of venture this is?"

"You just might have been worth what I paid for you."

Bion looked up, locking gazes with the captain. "I look out for myself first. If you don't like it, toss me off your ship because I won't be changing."

Aetos's face darkened, but he held back his first comment. Bion didn't move his attention away. He continued to stare at the man, making it clear that he wouldn't be backing down. It was a risk, one that might just end with him free-falling through the clouds, but there was no way he was going to behave like the crewman cowering outside the door.

"If you get the Navigator working, I just might be able to put that Root Ball in your hands."

"I know my craft and I don't take anyone interfering in my methods," Bion shot back.

"With the exception of myself, I agree." Aetos nodded. "But no one stays on this ship without producing results."

"In that case, you'd better introduce me to this Navigator."

Someone threw water on her and Sophia jumped. The air was cool and she shivered as the cold water soaked her hair and bodice. She wiped it out of her eyes.

Someone laughed and then several others joined in. She opened her eyes and stared into the faces of the roughest lot of men she'd ever set eyes on. They were every bit as repulsive as the gossips had speculated ungentlemanly men might be. Some sported unkempt beards—a clean-scraped chin was nowhere in sight. Their clothing was mismatched, many with collars open halfway down their chests. They were clustered around her, some straining onto their toes to see over the shoulders of the ones in front of them. What chilled her further was the number of pistols stuck into belts and waistbands.

"Well now, this is a bit of finery."

Sophia struggled to her feet to face the man addressing her. The rest of the group seemed to be waiting on him. They leered at her but looked toward him before saying anything.

"I do believe I owe you a bit of thanks, Compatriot Grainger."

She spun around, searching for her nemesis and felt her legs protest. Several spots hurt and one ankle felt twisted. Memory rushed back, reminding her of the struggle she'd had with the burly guard. She smiled slowly, happy to know she hadn't gone down without a fight.

"She is a prize," Grainger informed them, but there was a note of disgust in his tone that pleased Sophia. "My prize."

"No, Compatriot. I am captain of the Soiled Dove. If she's my Navigator, she's my prize and a member of my crew from here forward."

Sophia turned to look at the captain. He was a large man, and obviously not one concerned with appearances. His dark hair was long and held back from his face. Unlike a good many of his crew, his beard was trimmed and clean. His shirt was open to his chest and the shirtsleeves rolled up to expose his forearms. The skin of his lower arms was tanned from the sun, proving that he was quite at ease half dressed.

"I am Captain Aetos," he offered as he stepped closer and peered into her eyes. His were a brilliant shade of blue, and Sophia looked away from them.

He instantly grabbed a handful of her wet bodice and jerked her close.

"Let me see your eyes."

Sophia sent an icy glare at him, then she very precisely peeled his hand off her using one of the techniques Bion had insisted she learn in Asian fighting class.

"You're going to be stubborn," the captain declared as he let her move a few paces away from him. There really was nowhere to go and a hiss from behind her drew her attention. She gasped when she turned her head. Two large exhaust pipes stuck out behind the deck she stood on. She was actually on an airship, built for carrying cargo in its holds. Hovering above the deck she was on were three rectangular balloons attached to the ship by heavy netting.

"Look your fill. You'll have plenty of time to memorize every detail of the Soiled Dove," Captain

Aetos informed her softly to the delight of his gathered crew members. "You belong to me now."

"She does not!" Grainger interjected, earning a scowl from the captain. "I created her—"

"Lock your jaw, Compatriot." The captain's voice took on the sting of a leather whip. "Keep forgetting who is captain of this vessel and I will have you tossed over the rail, no matter our altitude."

There were a few snickers in response from the crew, proving the captain was a man of his word. There was a solid-looking railing running along the edges of the deck, but it rose only about a meter. Tossing someone over wouldn't prove too difficult. Sophia's throat went dry as she realized there were clouds floating past and beneath them.

Grainger sniffed and thrust his chin out. His features twisted in an odd manner before he yanked a polished knife out of his sleeve. "I created her and I shall control her. You will not take away my triumph!"

The tension was so tight in the air around her, she could practically taste it. She shuffled back, away from Grainger. His head snapped around in her direction and he reached toward her, his hand looking so much like a talon that she recoiled from it. The sunlight flashed off the knife blade, turning her stomach. He would spill her blood, she was absolutely sure of it. Someone grabbed her wrist, jerking her away from Grainger.

Sophia stumbled and looked up in time to see Grainger being thrown over the railing of the airship. His scream faded rapidly until only the hissing of steam could be heard.

"You there, stand steady." Captain Aetos pointed

at the man who had tossed Grainger overboard. He was every bit as large as Aetos and turned to face the rest of the crew.

Sophia clamped her teeth down so hard she tasted blood from her lower lip. Maybe she was still caught in the hold of the chloroform because she was certain the man she faced was Bion Donkova.

It couldn't be. She was snapping under the pressure, her mind taking refuge in delusions. She was as mad as Grainger.

"I warned you that I give the orders aboard this vessel. That includes deciding who stays aboard," Aetos informed Bion.

Bion shrugged and folded his arms across his chest. The pose was branded into her memory, sending a rush of relief through her that was squelched a moment later when she realized that Aetos was narrowing his eyes. The captain wasn't angry over the death that had just occurred; he was furious at the thought of his authority being usurped.

Bion might just follow Grainger.

"You told me my duty was to keep the Navigator working at her station and I warned you that I look out for myself first. If she's my ticket to a Root Ball, I'll have an issue with any man who threatens her."

"That doesn't grant you permission to throw anyone off this vessel," Aetos growled.

The captain's razor-edged tone didn't seem to bother Bion. He stood straight and unwavering, as the rest of the crew waited to see if there would be another man tossed overboard. Some of them appeared eager for the entertainment. Sophia's belly twisted again.

"To my way of thinking, it does," Bion answered. "I'm only working for you so long as I get my payment. Anyone who pulls a knife on the method of my earning that payment is someone I consider a threat, and I never let a threat go unanswered."

Surprise registered on the faces of many of the crew. They looked toward their captain, waiting to see what he'd decide. The deck was silent except for the soft hissing of steam.

Aetos suddenly chuckled and slapped Bion on the shoulder. "You have a pirate's heart, my good man. You should thank sweet Lucy for picking you out of the crowd for my crew. You're right at home." His tone suddenly hardened. "Providing you can do what you said you could. I want her working on the bridge." Aetos shifted his gaze to Sophia. "Beat her, seduce her—I don't care. As long as I see results. I'm going to enjoy surprising those Illuminist cargo ships. The profits will be high."

The crew cheered, showing off their missing teeth as they smiled.

"Navigators don't work like that. It takes time for their sight to come all the way in. She looks pretty young. I doubt she has full dimension sight," Bion warned. "Besides, I don't see a crystal array on the bow either. Her sight is worthless without the array to open the seams between dimensions."

The crew quieted, casting worried looks back at Aetos again. Tension knotted the muscles along Sophia's neck as she realized the game Bion was playing.

Aetos cursed low and long. Her cheeks heated at the profanity. She had to admit that the curses she'd heard previously were nothing compared to what her current situation might offer. The stain brightening her cheeks drew his attention.

Captain Aetos laughed. "I haven't seen a female blush in a very long time—not since I buggered my best friend's cousin in the hen house while her mother thought I was pitching hay." He waved his hand. "Get back to your posts. I already have to waste one man on this fledgling Navigator. The rest of you will earn your keep or get off my ship!"

The crew jumped and scurried back to their positions. Some climbed the netting that secured the large balloons above them. They held binoculars to their eyes as they scanned the skies around them.

"Find out what she can do," Aetos ordered. "I don't suffer useless members of my crew. And leave getting an array to me." He turned and surveyed his crew at their posts and paused to look back at Bion. "You did well enough today. Grainger was a damned nuisance, one we're well rid of. You might live past dawn after all. She gets the small cabin on the port side since her eyes are delicate. You can share it with her—maybe she'll decide she likes ruffians."

"I do not," Sophia blurted out. "And I shall not keep close quarters with any gentleman."

"Well now, it seems we have an understanding," the captain responded happily, flashing a grin at her. "No gentleman shall invade your privacy because there isn't a single gentleman on this vessel."

The crew hooted with laughter, more than one of them making obscene gestures that burned into her mind.

"Your vulgarities are revolting," she protested. But she couldn't ignore the fact that she was very much at the man's mercy. Bion might be near, but he was also stranded on the Soiled Dove. Panic clawed at her, refusing to be banished no matter how hard she tried.

Aetos frowned at her. "I liked you better when you were biting your lip out of fear." He moved toward her and stopped only a single step away. "If keeping you terrified keeps your mouth from annoying me with useless chatter... that can be arranged, Miss Stevenson. You're a member of my crew, just as the fellow who just tossed a man overboard in your defense is. Up here, it's in everyone's best interest to remember your crewmate is your best friend"—his eyes narrowed dangerously—"your only friend. I'm captain of this vessel and I'll use any means at my disposal to win the prize. The Illuminists are moving Deep Earth Crystals through the dimension gates and you will help me chase them down. Your only choice is how much motivation you will require to perform to my specifications. I promise you, my worst is far more revolting than having one gentleman invading your privacy. Now get back to your cabin. You'll find glasses there to protect your eyes."

"She'll perform," Bion promised. "I do my job so long as I get paid." He reached out and closed his hand around her upper arm and pulled her away from the captain.

She should have been relieved—and she was a little—but the problem plaguing her was that she wasn't sure who was more dangerous—Aetos or Bion.

She had a feeling she was about to find out.

❦

"You're damned lucky I was able to find you."

Sophia turned around in the tiny cabin Bion escorted her to. "I know that," she snapped, then she shivered, her body refusing to maintain any sort of composure now that there was a solid door shielding her from the outside world.

"I warned you there would be men willing to kill in their quest to own you." He shook his head and moved the tattered curtain away from the tiny window the cabin offered.

"It isn't as if I ran off," she replied. "My dorm door was firmly shut, in accordance with the rules, I assure you."

"Grainger killed four men to get you out of the Solitary Chamber."

"He deserved to be thrown… over." Her voice caught because it was shocking to realize how glad she was that the man was dead. It wasn't ladylike, but it was there, inside her—a complete lack of remorse for the man's demise.

Bion looked back at her, his eyes narrowing to target the telltale quiver shaking her limbs. He let out a long breath and stepped forward, gathering her into an embrace before she realized his intention.

"Guardian Pavola is damned lucky my instincts paid off. I think I might have been moved to violence the next time I saw him if I hadn't found you."

His arms tightened and she heard him inhaling the scent of her hair. She should have been offended. Instead, she leaned forward, nuzzling against his body, the scent of his skin sending a new wave of relief through her. She quivered, her body refusing to remain composed. She needed to be closer to him; it was a yearning that was almost desperate.

"At least I got to kill Grainger." Bion released her slowly, as though he was forcing himself to open his arms.

Stepping back was the correct thing to do—but she loathed it. Her feet felt stuck to the floor and she felt the separation like cold water hitting her.

"I suppose I should thank you for that."

Bion's grin was menacing. "Except that you've never had to express gratitude for someone's death before, Miss Stevenson?"

"You needn't quibble with me," she retorted. "Would you rather I was a woman of rough upbringing? One without a shred of kindness?"

"You'll fare better here without compassion." He withdrew to his favorite pose, crossing his arms across his chest. "These are exactly the sort of men the matrons warned you about."

"As if I couldn't deduce that for myself, thank you very much. I am not a child, Captain Donkova." She expected at least a slight softening of his demeanor, just a glimmer of shame for his ungentlemanly behavior. Instead, Bion chuckled softly as one dark eyebrow rose.

"I am not a captain here." His uncompromising gaze sent heat into her cheeks. "Continue to insist on how much of a woman you are, and I might indeed take notice, my sweet."

"I am not your sweet," she informed him tartly, that yearning making her itch to prove to him that she wasn't what he thought she was.

"I could not disagree with you more."

She was accustomed to his warnings, and orders, and dictates, but what she heard in his tone was a promise, and it unleashed a need that ripped through her like a bolt of lightning. It was shocking in its brightness, and just as uncontrollable. She remembered perfectly how much she enjoyed his kiss. She looked away from him, seeking a moment to clear her senses, but her gaze settled onto the lone bed in the room.

There was a menacing chuckle from behind her, rich with devilish intent. "Don't you know all the really good pirates only have one bed in their cabins? After all, you are trying to impress me with your worldly knowledge." He reached out and quite deliberately patted her bottom. She gasped and turned, ending up nose to nose with the man.

"This isn't a time for jesting, Bion." At last she managed to sound serious instead of sounding as if she was suffering from the vapors.

His eyes darkened and excitement twisted through her belly. It was an instantaneous reaction that stoked the memory of the way he'd looked when he'd kissed her.

"No, it's a far more appropriate time to kiss you."

Bion kept his promise. The words barely had time to register before he'd wrapped his arms around her once more. This time, he cupped her nape, tipping her head so that his mouth might find hers easily. She shifted, not truly pushing against him because he was the only thing in the cabin that she wanted to be near. But she couldn't remain still either. She grasped his vest, crumpling the fabric.

That drew a groan from him—a soft, purely male

sound of enjoyment that pulled her toward him even more. She wanted to kiss him, needed to hold on to him as the world around her shifted out of control. This kiss was deeper, harder, but she returned it with equal passion. They were like mirrors aimed at one another, each reflection being aimed back at the other over and over until it was impossible to think of anything else.

Yes, she understood what the sensations threatening to boil up from inside her were now. It was passion, desire, wantonness. And she wanted to experience all of it. The little girl who had so faithfully listened to the matrons was gone, burned away by the need inside her. Touching him was natural, and his scent more intoxicating than any wine. He pressed her lips apart, the tip of his tongue sweeping inside her mouth. It was intrusive but it also built the excitement. She mimicked him, sending her own tongue sliding along his and felt him shudder.

At last, his iron control slipped in response to her actions. The knowledge soaked into her, making her confidence swell. She slid her hands up his chest until she slid her fingers into his hair, holding him in place for her kiss as well.

Bion suddenly pulled back, holding her biceps to keep her from following him. His expression was hard, his dark eyes lit by something savage. A tremor shook him as he held her away from him. It was a maddening torment. His scent still filled her senses, his taste still lingering on her lips. She needed more, craved him. Everything that she had deemed important paled in comparison to what she wanted from him.

"Damn us both." He uttered each word separately, as if composing a sentence was beyond his grasp.

It was a feeling she shared at that moment. Her mind didn't want to function. Her only desire was to feel and experience. She frowned, shrugging to escape his grip. "Why do you say that? Just because I think you're happiest behaving like a pirate doesn't mean I can't enjoy returning your kisses."

"I want much more than a kiss, Sophia." He slid his hands around her back, pulling her close again. He stroked her, his hand traveling along her spine until he cupped one side of her bottom. The touch was startling and unleashed a wave of excitement that fascinated her. He pressed her body completely against his, making it impossible for her to miss the hard presence of his erection.

That forbidden thing that she suddenly wanted to know everything about—penis, cock, manroot, and a dozen other terms, but it all boiled down to the hard length pressing against her belly.

"A hell of a lot more."

He didn't think she could stomach the topic. It was there in his tone, the sound of warning that grated on her nerves until taking action was foremost in her mind.

"So do I."

Her cheeks colored, but it was arousal driving the blush now. His eyes glittered with challenge and it was exactly the diversion she craved—something that would overshadow everything happening to her. Something that would wipe every thought from her mind except for the feelings flooding her.

Something she yearned to do.

She reached for him, pulling his shoulders down. He stiffened, so she pressed a kiss against his throat. She'd seen a maid do it once, when no one realized Sophia was peeking through the keyhole. He drew in a stiff breath as though she'd surprised him. His hands gripped her bottom tighter, filling her with an odd little jolt of satisfaction.

So, she was not the only one who might be affected so dramatically. The knowledge was like fine scotch, rushing through her system on a course directly to her brain. It was intoxicating and she wasn't interested in any manner of self-control. She kissed his skin again, cupping his nape to hold him in place.

"Where did you learn to do that?"

She laughed softly. Actually it was more sultry, the sound reminding her of a cat's purring. Bion stroked her again, and she arched her back as he petted her. He gripped her hair, angling her chin up so that their gazes fused. Her confidence wavered as she looked into his eyes, because the need raging in them was scorching, uncontrollable. No, not uncontrollable—not if she didn't let it frighten her. Not if she behaved like a woman.

"This is a dangerous game, Sophia, with consequences."

Her throat was trying to close up, but she swallowed, forcing the lump down. She moved her hands over his chest in the same soothing motion he'd used along her back. Pleasure flickered in his eyes before they narrowed.

"Since my future lies with the Illuminist Order, there are no consequences to having a lover. I have as much right to ask you to become mine as you do to suggest such an arrangement to me. And you did mention it first. Perhaps I've been considering your offer."

His lips thinned, a low growl making its way through his clenched teeth. A wave of boldness rose from somewhere deep inside her, some dark corner that she hadn't admitted to knowing about before. But it was there, locked behind all the boundaries she had been raised to fear crossing. Now, they beckoned to her like the gates to paradise—if she were simply confident enough to take the journey.

But Bion set her away from him again. She felt the separation as surely as stepping out the front door in the middle of winter. The chill bit into her.

"You're in shock." His voice was gruff. "And you don't know what you're saying."

She propped her hand on her hip and smiled. "I'll have you know, Bion Donkova, I have a clear understanding of what lovers do. My father didn't much care for the current thinking that innocence is the way to keep young ladies from falling from grace. He made sure I'd know if a boy was taking liberties or not. I know what you have in your trousers and exactly what it's for."

It had to be the most provocative thing she'd ever said, but a sense of satisfaction filled her once the words were loose and there was an answering flicker of appreciation in Bion's eyes.

He reached out, cupping her chin in a delicate hold, then ran the tip of his thumb across her lower lip. She shivered, his touch instantly drawing a reaction from her. It was shocking just how responsive she was to him. The need to explore it was as close to madness as she'd ever felt.

"Sweet little Sophia, I believe I could have done very well without you making it clear how much of a woman you are behind that prim and proper exterior. I do believe you have shattered my illusions about you. It's very much like letting me know that the pie is cooling on the window sill and the cook is out of the kitchen."

He leaned forward, pressing a hard kiss against her mouth. Heat curled through her belly, setting her passage on fire. She gasped, never having anticipated just how carnal her own flesh might be.

Bion smiled and clicked his heels together before offering her a curt bow. "You might know the mechanics of lovemaking, but I assure you, Sophia, you have a great deal to learn about the intimacies." For a moment he looked ravenous until he hid it behind an expression she recognized from countless times he'd placed duty above all. "Something I am not at liberty to remedy in these circumstances."

She laughed at him. "Forgive me, Bion, but there is part of me that simply cannot wonder what more appropriate place there could be than on a pirate ship. Is it not the traditional place for ravishment?"

He grinned, transforming into the rogue she'd spied a few times when the man was in the mood to vex her. She shook her head and sighed. "I think you are not as much of a pirate as you like me to think." Her words clearly shocked him, unmasking the man for the first time in her memory. For just a moment, she witnessed his true nature and found it more honorable than she had expected. But that also shamed her. "Or that I might have been hoping for."

She'd wanted to lose herself in the moment but that was foolish thinking. Reality would be there waiting, right outside the cabin door. She drew in a deep breath and looked around the cabin for the first time with her wits focused on seeing what was of use.

"So, Bion Donkova, what exactly is your plan for getting us off this vessel?"

Bion handed her a pair of purple-tinted glasses. "My entire plan was to join you. Considering just how great a chance I faced of failing in that, I didn't bother to plan past finding you."

Sophia took the glasses and slid them into place over her eyes. "In that case, perhaps we should discover the full extent of our circumstances, so we might strategize a solution to our dilemma."

One of his dark eyebrows lifted. "A fine course of action, Miss Stevenson. It seems someone has instructed you rather well on the merits of helping yourself."

For a brief moment, they were equals. There was something gleaming in his eyes that she had to look at twice before realizing what it was.

Respect.

❧

"You realize the danger this voyage promises?"

Lykos nodded but didn't take his eyes off the pistol he was cleaning.

"And you are still set to sail with us?"

Lykos looked up, annoyed with the captain of the Scarlet Dawn. "What is your point, Captain?"

"The female companion you boarded with."

Lykos stiffened. "Are you by chance referring to Guardian Hunter Decima Talaska? Because if you are, I suggest you remember she has earned a rank far above being addressed by her gender. She is my counterpart, not my personal companion."

"I have no other female members in my crew."

Lykos didn't back down. "Then you should remedy that fact. We are Illuminists. Our judgment is based on performance, not genitalia. A fact Guardian Talaska has proven to the satisfaction of the same board of peers I stood before when I earned my Guardian standing. You might choose to recall there are also female airship captains."

The captain wanted to argue, but shut his mouth and left the small cabin.

"How very noble of you."

Lykos jerked, turning to find Decima in the doorway of the cabin, her dainty foot lodged in the doorjamb to keep the door open.

"To defend my position so passionately."

"Continue to sound so surprised and I shall be happy to behave as you seem to expect I should." There was a warning in his tone that Decima didn't miss. Lykos lifted a hand and beckoned her forward with a single finger. "Come here, Decima, and continue to use that condescending tone that insinuates I lack respect for your achievements simply because I think you should admit you are a woman from time to time."

She frowned, her forehead furrowing. Lykos chuckled and returned to loading his pistol. He heard her leave, the soft step on the hallway floor and the gentle closing of the door.

"Later, my sweet," he promised the empty cabin.

Four

"You will see the seams of the dimensions at some point."

The bridge of the Soiled Dove was more sophisticated than Sophia expected. It lacked none of the cleanliness she had seen aboard an Illuminist vessel. Every gear was gleaming, the brass levers untouched by tarnish, but there was still a feeling of seediness. If evil had a scent, she was sure the odor was lingering in the raised cabin that allowed her to look out over their flight path.

It was a shame that she couldn't enjoy the moment. The heavens stretched out before her, golden sunlight bathing the clouds. The ship cut through them in a smooth, swooping motion driven by the propellers attached to the twin steam stacks at the rear of the vessel. It was the sort of thing a child's imagination might have invented, yet she stood on the deck, watching a member of the crew steer the ship with a large wheel she'd only seen on water-sailing ships.

Of course Bion had been teaching her about such things, but the reality was far more than any schoolroom preparation could hope to impress upon a student.

A bell rang on the port side of the ship. A crew member was jerking the rope handle against the brass body of the bell as he kept his eyes on something he saw through his binoculars.

"Prize at ten o'clock! Bring her around, Mr. Jefferies!" Captain Aetos bellowed as he burst into the bridge. The ship veered sharply as the crewman at the wheel responded. Sophia's stomach lurched as the vessel dipped and tilted like a child's top. Bion slipped a hard arm around her waist just as the bow rose as if they were climbing a wave, and they veered to the left.

"Lower the crystals into the flood basins!"

Crewmen reached for the levers, pushing them down. From the back of the ship there was a hydraulic sound that grew louder until there was an explosion of steam. It erupted through the stacks and sent the propellers violently spinning. The Soiled Dove jerked and catapulted forward.

"All hands make ready with the cannons."

Men ran across the deck, scurrying down the ladders into the center of the ship. Some leaned over the rail, reaching for the cannon doors with large poles. In the distance, another ship was growing larger.

"Disable her outer balloons, Mr. Graves!"

Down on the deck, a man nodded before leaning down and shouting through one of the open trap-doors. The ship vibrated with the explosion of cannon fire, white smoke billowing up and over the rail. Bion was still holding her, and she was clinging to him as the ship in front of them faltered, one of her three balloons punctured. The ship began to turn in a lazy circle, losing altitude as the crew on her deck frantically tried to control her.

"Stand by to board!" Aetos shouted.

Men hurried up from below deck, long rifles gripped tightly in their hands. They braced themselves against the rail as the Soiled Dove closed the distance. A puff of white smoke from the side of the other ship was the only warning she got before Bion shoved her toward the deck. Wood splintered and the Soiled Dove shuddered. Some of the glass windowpanes on the bridge shattered.

"Return fire! But don't sink her just yet!" Aetos yelled. "I'll have her treasure before I send her and the bastards manning her to the earth below!"

The man was lawless. He was leaning out one of the broken windows, grinning as he anticipated his victory. Sophia fought back the urge to retch.

"Swing out the grappling hooks! Get your prize lads! Get your prize!"

There was a roar from the crew. They sounded like a pack of hyenas as they fired off the cannons once more. Then wicked looking iron hooks sailed across the space between the ships with lengths of rope trailing behind them. Many landed on the deck of the other ship. Some of the crew tossed them back overboard but many caught the railings, and the crewmen of the Soiled Dove began to drag the wounded vessel closer and closer. Rifles discharged and the crew snarled as they climbed over the rail.

"Get your prize, me boys!"

"Look away," Bion whispered next to her ear, and for once his tone lacked the commanding arrogance she was so accustomed to. Now, his tone was quiet and kind, offering shelter from the horror happening in front of her.

"She'll keep her eyes forward or earn herself ten lashes and double that number for yourself," the captain shouted.

Sophia sucked in a breath, her temper flaring. What kept her mouth shut was the struggle she witnessed in Bion's dark gaze. She'd never seen him hold back, never watched him bend, and she realized that he was doing it for her. The knowledge humbled her. It also brought her face to face with liking him, something she'd never thought might happen. She jerked her gaze away from his because it felt as if he could read her thoughts. She wasn't even comfortable with them; sharing them was more than she could handle.

But the sight in front of her was truly horrific. She watched the crew of the Soiled Dove charge the crew of the wounded vessel. They tied off the ropes, binding their prey to the side of the ship. The white puff from the barrels of the rifles added an eerie haze to the scene as men fought hand to hand on the deck of the captured vessel. Sunlight flashed off the blades of knives and swords as they clanged against one another, and the screams of the wounded mixed with the discharge of gunfire. Time felt as though it froze, allowing her to see every detail of the mêlée.

Captain Aetos chuckled and slapped her on the bottom. "There will be no pampering aboard this vessel. You're a pirate now," he growled, and jumped down from the bridge to join the carnage.

"Like hell I am," Sophia grumbled, not caring if one of the crew tattled on her.

Bion's hand gently massaged her neck. When she turned to lock gazes with him, she found herself receiving another steady look of approval from the man—and damned if she didn't feel as if she'd earned it.

The survivors were herded into a line. All around them, the crewmen of the Soiled Dove plundered the ship without a care for the bodies littering the deck of the defeated ship. They tore open crates as they came up from below deck. Even the bodies were stripped of their valuables, not a single pair of worn boots left behind.

But it was all carefully placed on the deck of the Soiled Dove. The deck sergeant, Mr. Graves, stood watch as crewmen climbed over the rail and deposited their plunder. Many of them held up their hands to prove they weren't holding anything back while others turned their pockets out, the lining flapping in the wind.

Captain Aetos inspected the survivors, walking down their row with his sword still in hand, its blade stained with blood. "I'm accepting volunteers for my crew," he announced in a cheerful voice that sent Sophia's stomach rolling once more. "Volunteers only."

Three of the survivors stepped up, their expressions grim. The captain waved them over to the rail, then swept the ship one last time. The moment he'd crossed back to the Soiled Dove, his crew hurried to join him. They loosened the ropes and pulled the grappling hooks free. The sacked ship drifted free, the remaining crew looking relieved as the distance increased.

Several members of the Soiled Dove's crew waved farewell to them, which infuriated Sophia. But Bion's hand on her hip tightened, warning her that the horror was not quite finished.

"Fire," Mr. Graves ordered from the main deck. White smoke billowed up from the cannons as another volley was sent into the crippled ship. One of its steam stacks crumpled and fell away from the ship. The survivors all dove for cover, some of them failing to move fast enough. There were agonized screams as the ship groaned and the balloons keeping it afloat were punctured. They released their hydrogen in a ghastly sounding stream as the men left aboard looked around in terror.

In contrast, the crew of the Soiled Dove cheered as they watched the ship falter and drop like a stone. They leaned over the railing to watch as long as possible, and Sophia found her eyes dry of tears. Her horror was too great to do anything but watch silently.

❧

"I do believe you would get more volunteers if you mentioned your policy on grounding ships, Captain," Mr. Graves said.

Captain Aetos cocked his head to one side and grinned. "Maybe, Mr. Graves. Maybe. We won't be learning the answer today."

They chuckled and the sound was sickening. In a way, Sophia was almost grateful to know she still had the decency to be revolted by their savagery.

"Donkova, you'll give a hand on deck." The captain issued his order in a firm tone. "We'll be needing to patch up the Soiled Dove a bit before we hunt again. Miss Stevenson can report to the cook and see who needs a few stitches."

"I am not a trained physician," Sophia protested.

Captain Aetos shrugged. "Neither is the cook, but I'll wager your mother taught you the use of a needle and thread." His eyes narrowed. "No one shirks their share of the work here. You can either make yourself useful in the galley or help us celebrate once the cargo is sorted."

With the window of the bridge shattered, the captain's words floated easily to the men on deck. Several dropped what they were doing, looking up at her with expectation glimmering in their eyes.

"Bloody bastard," Bion said next to her ear. There was a savageness in his tone, but she recognized the difference now. Bion might have the capacity to be every bit as ruthless as Captain Aetos, but Bion had honor. It was in his core and was completely lacking in the captain of the Soiled Dove.

Sophia turned and stepped close to Bion, and she could feel his body heat. A tiny ripple of awareness traveled along her limbs, and this time she smiled in response. "Do not throw him over the rail," she whispered. His forehead furrowed and she tapped him lightly on the chest. "Because I do believe I should like that pleasure for myself."

She had the satisfaction of watching surprise fill his dark eyes as she brushed past him on the way to the galley. The urge to look over her shoulder was intense, but she squelched it, continuing on her way without faltering.

She'd endure well enough. Indeed she would.

⚜

The tiny cabin with its single bed was a welcome sight when Sophia finally got the chance to seek it out. She leaned her head against the door, savoring the solid feel of the wood.

"It won't offer much protection, even if you remember to slide the bolt."

She jumped, startled by Bion's brassy tone. Scanning the cabin, she found the man lying back on the bed in nothing but his shirt and britches. Heat teased her cheeks. She'd never seen him so near to being unclothed.

Listen to you, missy. The word is nude.

"Personally," Bion continued, "I find this more comforting."

He patted something he had been lying on. When she ventured closer, he moved the sheet aside to reveal something that looked like a chemise but it was much larger.

"It's a parachute." Bion lifted it to reveal a leather harness of some sort, then let it go and covered it once more. "Our means of escape—just as soon as I can devise a way to distract the crew long enough for us to use it and we aren't over open water."

"How does it work?"

"We buckle the harness across our chests and jump over the rail. It is designed to open and slow our descent. But it's of little use if we can't make it to the rail unmolested."

He frowned, his eyes narrowing as the word "unmolested" crossed his lips. Sophia was instantly taken back to the moment when Captain Aetos had threatened her with such a fate. It was a chilling thought, but she shook her head and pulled in a deep breath to dispel it.

"I look forward to the experience."

"Ignoring the dangers will not protect you, Sophia."

Bion's warning annoyed her. He was correct, but she did not need to dwell on the possibilities. Hope was what she needed, and she turned on him with determination warming her insides.

"Neither will embracing pity, Mr. Donkova. I am beginning to think you believe me dim-witted and without the ability to understand the details of my own circumstances."

Bion stood up, his arms crossing over his chest. The collar of his shirt was open, allowing her a fine view of the dark hair covering his chest. For once she didn't look away. Maybe she was blushing, but she kept her gaze on the man she was admiring.

"You cannot possibly understand the facts of your circumstances," Bion remarked. "No lady could."

Sophia threw her hands up with a very unlady-like groan. "Oh, for heaven's sake. Just because I know how to conduct myself well has no bearing on what other knowledge I have acquired during my upbringing. You, sir, are far too presumptuous. If all I ever thought about were delicate things and spring flowers, I would have happily ridden out with Jonathon Saddler when he came calling with a nosegay of violets and lavender roses."

Bion's complexion darkened and she scoffed at him turning her back on him. But he grabbed her shoulder and spun her around. A twist of anticipation went through her as she recognized the look in his eyes. It had been there the few times he'd kissed her and it was brighter, hotter than ever before.

"You cannot possibly be jealous."

He chuckled ominously as he stepped toward her. She backed away, instinctively recognizing how powerful he was.

"Now I believe you are the one making assumptions, Sophia." He took one long step, and she felt her back against the wall. Before she could move, he flattened his hand against the worn wood paneling, caging her.

"It's rather insulting to see you reacting—well, in this manner—to the announcement that I had a suitor." Her heart was racing but she just couldn't seem to stop chattering. "I really am not so wretched a creature, you know."

He chuckled again, the sound sending excitement tearing though her. "You may be very sure that I have noticed your charms."

He leaned closer. She propped her hands on his chest, a simple reaction to his encroachment. But his shirt was far too thin, and through it, she could feel the heat of his skin. It was impossible to ignore it for some reason, the desire to slip her hands just a little closer to where the shirt gaped open was nearly overwhelming.

"But I'm suddenly not satisfied with mere observation."

His tone was thick with promise, but she recalled too well the iron strength of will that had seen him turning away from her before. She moved her hand into the opening of his shirt, but she grasped a handful of his chest hair and twisted it.

"Don't tease me, Bion. I've had enough of it."

His lips curled back from his teeth for a moment, betraying the pain she was inflicting. But he didn't budge.

"Aren't you the one who just teased me with the recollection of your suitor?" His eyes darkened dangerously. "Because I find myself agreeing with you." He pressed up against her, trapping her hand. "I am jealous."

Surprise held her in its grip and the kiss he pressed against her mouth ensured that she remained that way. Her wits deserted her, but she didn't make any true attempt to maintain them. His mouth demanded submission, but she kissed him back with every bit of passion she felt. It was like an energy current; once she let it loose, there was no control—only need.

She fought to free her hand, still kissing him. Bion pressed his body against hers, letting her feel every inch of him, and she was eager to do so. The chest she'd so often watched him cross his arms over was something she wanted to feel. Stroke really. Her fingertips were far more sensitive than she'd ever noticed. The shirt wasn't open enough and she fought with the buttons in her quest to free him from the garment.

He pushed away from her, drawing a frustrated sound from her. But she sighed with appeasement when he ripped the shirt up and over his head.

"That sounded like a purr."

Sophia bit her lip, trying to decide what she thought of his tone. He laughed softly, almost wickedly, and beckoned to her with one finger.

"Come here, sweet lady, if you have not lost your nerve, that is."

"You're challenging me on purpose." She stepped toward him but brushed past him to the other side of the cabin. She turned to face him while she toyed with the top button on her shirt. "It's almost as if you need me to prove that I am not too delicate to rise to your provocative statements."

"Or actions," he countered as he undid the top of his waistband.

"Ah yes." The button was free and she moved to the next one. "You have proclaimed yourself a man of action. Yet I wonder if I shouldn't put you in your place and expect you to stand there."

A dark eyebrow rose, but it was the look of raw hunger in his eyes that threatened to hypnotize her. She fumbled with the button, her fingers trembling. A moment later, he had taken over, easily working the button through its hole.

"Never fear, sweet Sophia, I will be happy to assist."

Her top opened and he pushed it back over her shoulders. But instead of sliding it down her arms, he only pushed it far enough to bind her arms behind her back. It left her cleavage on display, with only the edge of her chemise covering the swell of her breasts above the edge of her corset. She was suddenly nervous, confidence a mere whisper in the very back of her thoughts.

"I don't fear you." Her voice was less than convincing.

"And that is exactly where you went wrong, my lovely." He clasped her waist, flattening his hands on her sides, and pressed gently until the metal eyelets of her busk popped open. "I can ignore shrieking maidens quite easily. A confident woman, though, I am powerless against."

The night air was chilly when it made its way through the open side of her corset. Bion pulled the undergarment away, letting it fall to the floor. The waistband of her skirt gave him little trouble and soon it too was puddled around her ankles.

He cupped her face and kissed her again. This time there was something different about the motion of his mouth, something more intimate, more intent. He didn't rush her. He teased her lips, the tip of his tongue brushing along her lower lip, then tasting the upper one. She shivered, once again willingly being swept away into the sensation his touch unleashed. It was as though she'd never experienced what her body was fashioned to feel, never understood what her mouth was for.

Sophia reached for him, eager to touch his bare skin. Her rapid heart rate might have frightened her if it didn't feel so very wonderful. Her breath was keeping pace, pulling his scent into her senses with every agitated breath. She stroked his neck, the warm skin making her tremble. This time the quiver moving along her muscles was welcome, making her almost giddy.

But she wanted more and so did Bion.

He cupped her nape, angling her head back to deepen the kiss. She surrendered. His tongue played across her lower lip for a brief moment before thrusting straight and deep into her mouth. It was the most intimate thing she'd ever experienced. She wasn't sure where to touch him, was only sure that remaining still was impossible. She wanted to be closer to him, and her chemise suddenly felt too warm. His pants irritated her bare thighs, and she reached for the half-open waistband to finish the job.

"We're going too fast." But Bion's tone made it clear that he was fighting to slow down enough to even say that much. Sophia kissed his neck, trailing kisses along the column of his throat as he groaned.

"Minx," he breathed. He pushed her hand aside and finished opening his fly. Part of her wanted to look down at that forbidden part of the male anatomy, but Bion blinded her as he tugged her chemise up and over her head. He tossed it over his shoulder, the thin fabric fluttering like a butterfly until it was out of sight.

"You're ravishing…"

As a compliment, it wasn't so much his words that made her feel attractive, as it was his tone and the way he cupped her breasts, his dark gaze settling on them. Ladies didn't look at their bare forms, but she was fascinated by the way Bion was fixated on her breasts. He handled them gently, stroking and kneading them, brushing her nipples with his thumbs. Both had contracted into tight nubs that he teased with several back and forth motions. Delight spread through her, stunning her with how much she enjoyed being handled. He leaned down and captured one nipple between his lips unleashing a flash of heat so hot she forgot to draw breath.

She twisted for what seemed like an eternity as hunger began to claw at her. Her body refused to stay still, her hips moving toward him in a sultry motion.

She had no concept of where she might have learned it. The tempo pounded through her blood stream. It seemed to target her belly and deeper into her passage, where she felt empty. It was a deep yearning that had her reaching for Bion because she was sure he could satisfy her.

"I should slow down—"

"Don't." Her voice was just as raspy as his. He stroked her sides, his hands pausing for a moment on the curves of her hips. He gripped them slightly harder than before, and it jolted her with pleasure that went all the way into her bones. Between the folds of her sex, her clitoris began to throb. It was so intimate a feeling that all she wanted to do was close her eyes so that she might be immersed in the sensation. "I don't want to think."

"Neither do I."

He grasped the backs of her thighs and lifted her. He pressed her back against the wall and she instinctively wrapped her legs around his hips. Bion held her away from him for a moment. She could feel him shaking with the effort, then he gently eased forward, his cock parting the folds of her sex gently. Fluid eased his way, as his cock sought the opening of her body through the folds. Her body protested the first thrust, pain interrupting her euphoria, but he didn't prolong the torment. Bion thrust smoothly into her, stretching her passage as she gasped and wound her arms around his shoulders. He pressed against her completely, his body holding her against the wall as he waited for her to adjust to the hard presence of his cock.

"It won't hurt like that again," he whispered. His

tone was tender. She opened her eyes in surprise and found him watching her. For a moment they locked gazes, and she was sure she had never really understood what intimacy was because she felt him touching her soul.

But he groaned, his face creasing with strain. His grip tightened before he withdrew. It felt as though he'd been ripped from her, the loss tormenting her with how much she wanted to be filled. Bion didn't let her suffer the need for long. He thrust forward, filling her again and, true to his word, the pain was only a memory. Now there was satisfaction and a growing need to move in unison with him. She met his next thrust, lifting her hips to help him enter her faster. Both their hearts were racing, their breathing more like panting as they strained toward one another. There was no thinking, only responding as her hunger dictated what actions to take.

Something was building inside her. Sensation was gathering beneath the spot that the head of his cock returned to again and again. She wanted whatever it was building up to—needed it—and worked her hips faster in her quest. Bion didn't disappoint her; he kept pace with her, driving into her again and again until she felt something being unleashed inside her. It was a brilliant burst of pleasure, unlike anything she'd ever experienced. It wrung her like a dishcloth, twisting every fiber of her being until she cried out because she just couldn't contain everything she was feeling any longer.

Bion bucked between her thighs, growling as he buried his length deeply inside her. For a moment that felt far longer than it really was, his body was drawn taut, straining toward hers before his seed filled her. The hot spurt set off another ripple of delight that wasn't as sharp but felt deeper.

"Christ that was too quick." Bion sucked in a deep breath before pulling away from the wall. "And I didn't mean to deflower you against the wall as if I couldn't control myself long enough to take you to bed."

He laid her down in the bed, then joined her before the bed ropes finished creaking.

"I believe I rather like knowing you were not completely in control."

Sophia moved over to make room, but Bion hooked her around the waist and pulled her back against his body. She shifted, wiggling because she was suddenly unsure of how she felt. Nothing made sense as she tried to return to not letting him see her feelings.

"You would feel like that."

Bion smoothed her into place along his side. He pressed her head onto his shoulder, doing it a second time when she lifted it to get a look at his expression. He crossed his legs around one of her ankles to keep her in place as he drew in a deep breath and let it out.

"Relax, Sophia. For the moment, the rest of the world may rot."

She choked on a giggle, holding her breath to try and smother the ones that wanted to follow. Giggling was for girls. The stinging walls of her passage made it quite clear that she was a woman now.

"Now that wounds me." He tipped her chin up. "Why can't you laugh in my presence?"

"Because it's, well… girlish to giggle."

He stroked the side of her face, the touch so tender tears burned her eyes. Why was she so emotional so suddenly?

"I do believe we've passed the point of maintaining appearances."

She lowered her chin, uncertainty making her look away before he read how unsure she was.

Bion let out a frustrated sound. "I suppose it's my doing, but I won't apologize for trying to harden you against those who would try to use you."

She sat up, managing to escape his hold and lock gazes with him. "You were correct."

For a long moment he stared at her. He was every inch the stern taskmaster she'd struggled with for the last few months, and yet, he was something else too—the man she'd just clung to in need and hunger, allowed into her body without any hesitation. Somehow, it felt like the climax in their relationship, as though they had been circling one another in a slowly decreasing circle that had finally diminished so much, the only thing they might do was collide.

"Yet we are still landing here."

He reached for her, pulling her back down into his embrace. The facts of their circumstances floated through her mind, but she could not seem to worry very much about any of them. Not while she felt the steady heartbeat of the man holding her. His scent filled her senses, lulling her to sleep where nothing was so bad as it seemed in the darkness of night.

"But you are a man of action," she muttered in

the last few moments before surrendering to slumber completely. "You've proven it so many times…"

❧

Sophia settled into sleep but Bion stayed awake. He would have liked to think that the reason he wasn't resting was because of the lumpy parachute beneath his head. That wasn't exactly true—it was certainly a factor, but that wasn't what his mind was truly occupied with. He was fixated on the woman in his arms—the way her skin felt, the way she lay so trusting in his embrace. Even her scent was alluring, captivating him as though he was some bloodhound that couldn't stop tracking until he found the source of the trail he'd been following.

She believed in him. It wasn't the first time someone had depended on him. Being a captain meant shouldering responsibility for the well-being of others. But this was different. There was no denying it, just as he'd failed to mask the fact that he was in fact jealous of her beau.

Jonathon Saddler. Bion stroked her hair and felt his teeth grinding. It was an irrational reaction, but he was fascinated by it because he had never felt anything like it before. Miss Sophia Stevenson seemed to carry a great number of new experiences with her—at least as far as he was concerned. It was both vexing and surprising. He'd be lying if he tried to tell himself that he wasn't fascinated by her effect upon him. Raw cadets had loose emotions, not seasoned captains such as himself.

But he was still jealous of Jonathon Saddler. It was an unruly emotion he wasn't comfortable with.

Sophia shifted, making a delicate sound as she

rubbed her cheek against his chest. He toyed with the tendrils of hair that had escaped her braids and hairpins, and felt fear rip through his confidence. He couldn't recall the last time he'd admitted to being afraid of anything. Facing the fact that their circumstances were dire sent an unmistakable bolt of fear through him. But there was something else too. Determination.

It grew stronger as he heard her words again.

"But you are a man of action."

"I will do my best to prove my worth to you, sweetest Sophia."

❦

Bion didn't notice the small knothole sliding back into place. Mr. Graves didn't hurry away from the cabin. He left with patient steps and stopped to put his boots back on once he was far enough away to make the sounds blend in with the rest of the crew's movements.

He rapped twice on the captain's cabin door and waited.

"Enter," Aetos barked.

Mr. Graves removed his hat before crossing the threshold because the captain had an unpredictable temper at best. A wise man learned that or didn't last very long among the crew of the Soiled Dove.

Aetos was using a myriad of measuring tools on the Deep Earth Crystals they'd taken from their prey. Length, width, and gender were all being recorded in a logbook.

"How are our guests enjoying their private accommodations?"

"Quite thoroughly," Mr. Graves answered. "He buggered her up against the wall, just as you suspected

he might. The buggering part, that is. I don't recall
you saying just how he'd go about it."

Aetos grinned and shot his deck master a lust-filled
look. "No man is that protective of a female if he isn't
planning on getting his wick wet between her thighs. I
suppose you'll be encouraging me to put into dock soon,
so you can find some lovely to entertain you as well."

Mr. Graves shrugged. "That depends."

"On what?" Aetos set down the crystal he'd been
examining.

"On how long you plan to keep that bloke alive."

Aetos picked up another crystal and brought it closer
to one of the ones lying on the table. They both began
to whine, the sound growing louder as the distance
between them diminished. "Male and female react to
one another in all different sorts of ways, Mr. Graves."
Aetos set the crystal down. "Even in these Deep Earth
Crystals. The reaction is strong enough to boil water
and produce the steam that powers this vessel."

Mr. Graves nodded. "Aye. That's what makes
them worth killing for. It sure beats shoveling coal
into the boilers. Means we can stay in the air for much
longer too."

"Now, with the case of our Navigator and her
trainer, their relationship is the key to controlling
them both." The captain stood up. "She's a lady and
they have sensitive natures. She'd never think that
Bion Donkova is poking her simply because he had
the opportunity to get her skirts up. No, she'll think
it's affection and that, my good Mr. Graves, is the
means to controlling her."

"And what about the bloke? He's a powerful one and

not lacking in smarts. When he gets the idea to cause trouble, he'll do a grand job of it. Mark my words."

"Leave that matter to me," Aetos insisted in a tone every member of his crew knew not to argue with. Men who did ended up dead. "The Soiled Dove is mine and I always make sure what's mine remains mine."

"Right you are about that, Captain."

Aetos watched Graves nod before leaving, then reached into a crate sitting on the floor behind his desk. Straw kept the contents nice and secure during travel. Here was the true prize they'd taken, something so rare it made the Deep Earth Crystals look common. He lifted the lid of a tin box to reveal a velvet-lined interior. Nestled in the middle of the velvet was a Root Ball. Composed of thousands of tiny Deep Earth Crystals, they were often absorbed back into the growing crystal. Root Balls were only found near fresh lava flows.

There were always ways to control men such as Bion Donkova. Aetos closed the lid and grinned. He'd never met a man who didn't have his price. Even Bion would break the tender heart of his mistress in order to get his hands on a Root Ball. Aetos was looking forward to watching it happen.

He chuckled and felt his cock twitch. Virgins didn't interest him, but an experienced woman set on exacting revenge for being betrayed by her first lover? Now that was something he would enjoy.

❧

She heard wood splintering and Sophia sat up.

"My apologies."

Bion didn't turn to look at her, giving her a chance to yank the sheet up to cover her breasts. For all that she understood it was permissible to have a lover as an Illuminist, she still blushed scarlet as the reality of her situation dawned on her.

Bion had the cabin's small dresser on its back. He'd stuffed the parachute into the back of its raised facing on the front. Once he finished, he fit the piece of wood he'd broken free back into place. When he raised it, there was no way to tell that anything was behind the curved face-board of the dresser.

"That should hold, unless someone shakes it."

"Do you mean to suggest someone might inspect this cabin?" Her chemise was draped over the foot of the bed and she quickly shrugged into it.

"I would," Bion assured her quietly, "if I was trying to keep a captive Navigator aboard."

Bion stood up, watching her struggle with her corset for a moment, then came up behind her to press the garment against her sides. With his strength, her rib cage compressed just a little, allowing her to overlap the busk closures in the front. Once it was closed, she felt better but she also realized it was all in the way she thought about it. Being comfortable was really a state of mind, because a few weeks ago, being caught in her chemise and corset by Bion had been unnerving.

She shook her head and looked around for her clothing. "When can we use the parachute?"

Bion was buttoning his vest and offered her a look that wasn't promising. "Darkness and clouds to make sure the moonlight doesn't illuminate us to begin with. After that? Some sort of diversion that keeps the crew from their watch stations and firing off a few shots into our parachute. They don't work very well with holes in them."

Which meant it was almost impossible. She bit her lower lip to keep from voicing her thoughts aloud. There was no point in bemoaning the facts. Bion cupped her chin and used his thumb to gently pull her lower lip away from her teeth.

"I will get you out of here, Sophia. It's my duty."

"Or kill me, right?" She stepped away from him, feeling like the walls were closing in on her. "Isn't that also your duty, Captain?"

Bion caught her and pulled her against his body. She wiggled, not wanting to be comfortable in his embrace. Her emotions were a tangled mess and she needed space to sort them into order.

"I'd sooner wear the title of traitor."

It was an admission she'd never expected to hear from him.

Bion chuckled softly at her surprise. "I do believe I should be offended by your lack of faith in me, Miss Stevenson."

His teasing demeanor frustrated her. "Maybe I wouldn't doubt you had tender sensibilities if you hadn't spent the better part of the last six months being so impossible to please."

"I was ensuring you'd survive. The best path in life is not the easy one."

"I suppose I see your point."

For a long moment their eyes held, his dark ones full of confidence. It was so tempting to just let herself drink in that look, absorb it until she believed him.

She wanted to, but the ship's bell began to clang incessantly. Bion's body stiffened, his expression drawing into a tight mask that betrayed not a bit of his emotion.

"We've got to get off this ship," he snarled.

She couldn't agree more.

❦

"Move your worthless hides!" Mr. Graves shouted at them the moment Bion opened the cabin door. "We've a prize to capture."

Once again, the crew was hurrying below. She heard the cannon doors being opened and froze. If she'd had anything in her stomach, she would have lost it. The images from the last prize ship flooded her mind, sickening her.

"I can't... do... it." She shook her head, her composure crumbling as she saw the ship they were bearing down on.

"Get onto the bridge!" Aetos yelled. "She's making for the dimension seam."

Bion set his arm around her and moved her forward. Somehow, they ended up on the bridge. She didn't want to see the seam, but her eyes had finished their transformation. Still, the seam was clear. She could see the light spilling out from the other side. The other ship was preparing to go through it. The large Deep Earth Crystal array mounted on the front of the other ship like a cowcatcher was being lowered. Once in position, the Navigator would lower the top of it so the male crystals fixed in the top moved close to the female ones in the bottom of the array. A current would form, and it would split the dimension seam open. The array held over four hundred crystals and was worth a king's ransom.

At that moment, it was the difference between life and death for the crew of the ship they were chasing.

"Fire!"

The cannons exploded. Sophia held her breath, watching the ship for signs of distress. The vessel jerked but continued toward the dimension seam. She leaned forward and saw the flashing current beginning to form on the array, but the ship was losing momentum, the large propellers winding to a halt.

"That's it, lads! We've made our mark on them! Fire again, Mr. Graves!"

The cannons responded and this time the ship was knocked off course. She presented her side, and Mr. Graves made full use of the target. They were close enough to hear the screams of the injured. But then came the sound of cannon fire from the wounded vessel as they turned from flight to fighting for their lives. The Soiled Dove shuddered as she was ripped into by the barrage. Bion shoved Sophia down to the floor, curving his body over hers as the remaining glass windows shattered.

"One more volley, Mr. Graves!"

The cannons fired, and this time, the ship was disabled completely. One of the large balloons that held her aloft was punctured and she tipped at an odd angle. The Soiled Dove swooped in like a hawk to claim its kill.

It was only when the boarding hooks were locked around the other ship's rails that Sophia saw the maroon uniform coats the crew wore.

"It's an Illuminist ship," she muttered, too horrified to keep silent. "We have to stop Aetos."

Bion pulled her close, muffling her words against his shoulder. "We'll never accomplish that if we're dead too."

His words were a bare whisper, but the crewman at the wheel looked at them suspiciously. Sophia struggled to swallow her next comment, gently pushing free once she'd mastered the urge to let everyone know what she was thinking.

Once again, Sophia watched the crew of the Soiled Dove scavenge their prey. Her hope was strangled by every hoot of glee coming from the disabled vessel. The crewmen moved their booty across to the deck of the Soiled Dove. She was surprised that they also herded the survivors over the rail of their defeated ship.

The ship's captain and some of his officers were forced to their knees with their hands bound behind them. Two men were set to guarding them with long rifles while the scavenging continued. Their maroon coats were marked with soot, and wet patches betrayed injuries, but they never lowered their chins.

At last, Aetos re-boarded the Soiled Dove and stopped in front of his prisoners. He looked them over before raising his hand and signaling to someone. The crew had settled around them, many climbing the rigging to have a better view of whatever was about to transpire. There was an air of expectancy that set Sophia's nerves on edge. A sense of foreboding tormented her as Aetos inspected the Illuminist crew as though they were livestock being sorted for the slaughterhouse.

"Your captain and Navigator are dead. Which leaves the lot of you with an opportunity to entertain my offer. Who's the youngest?" he demanded at last, still looking at the men waiting on their knees. He paused in front of one man who still had youthful cheeks. "You?"

"I'm old enough."

Aetos clicked his tongue. "That's not what I asked you." The captain moved to another man who lacked creases around his eyes. "How old are you?"

"Twenty-six."

"This one," Aetos ordered.

The man stiffened, lifting his chin as Mr. Graves came forward and two burly crewmen lifted the man to his feet. The deck master held up something and as it unfolded, Sophia recognized another parachute. The man's bonds were cut and his arms threaded through the harness of the parachute. Surprise widened his eyes as it was buckled into place across his chest, thick leather straps securing the parachute to his body.

"To the rail," Aetos ordered loudly.

The crew snickered, some of them laughing as the young man was tugged backward until he was perched on the rail. They made him sit on it like it was a park bench instead of the only thing between him and a fall to the ground below. One of the guards aimed the muzzle of his rifle at the man's chest to keep him separated from his colleagues.

Aetos looked up at Sophia, ordering her down to

the deck with a quick flick of his fingers. There was no point in refusing; the eager looks of the crew made it clear they'd enjoy fetching her.

"Stay right beside me," Bion ordered softly.

Sophia nodded, but she was torn between wanting to let his presence comfort her and needing to worry about the fact that Bion was more expendable than she was in the eyes of Captain Aetos. She pushed her glasses into place and descended to the deck.

"Behold!" Aetos spread his hands wide. "Your Illuminist brethren, on their knees, where they belong." He walked down the line of men, shaking his head. "Having a Navigator makes all the difference, and now, we'll have an array, thanks to this prize."

Her temper ignited as the Illuminist men shifted their attention to her. The disgust was plain in their eyes. "I will not help you, so your nefarious actions will gain you little."

Aetos paused, his lips lifting into a smile that chilled her. "Is that a fact, Miss Stevenson?"

"I assure you it is." Bion was shooting her a furious glare, but she refused to rein in her temper. "I am not like the rest of these cowards who serve you."

There was a grumble from the crew, but Aetos held up his hand for silence. "That's something that I really cannot allow to go unaddressed." He waved to Mr. Graves again and a crewman brought a small table forward. He placed a tin box on the table and a pitcher of water. Aetos tapped the top of the box twice before turning in a wide circle to address his crew.

"No one shirks their duties here, lads! And you know I don't bend the rules for anyone."

There was an answering cheer from the assembled men, many of them laughing, then settling into silence once more. Aetos pegged her with a hard look.

"The normal penalty for disobeying my order is being tossed over the rail."

Bion stiffened, his hand grasping her wrist and pulling her behind him. Aetos didn't miss the motion and the pleased expression that lit his face was horrifying. Sophia gasped and fought against Bion's grip.

"Fine. If I'm the one yer displeased with, then so be it." Her Irish temper came through, but at the moment, she preferred her brogue to sounding frightened.

Aetos clicked his tongue the way he might do with an errant child. "Your eyes are too valuable to waste without at least one attempt to train you."

"I'm an Irish woman. We don't take to training well." She had no idea where the urge to argue with him came from, but she let it burn through her because it was better than letting fear suffocate her.

"Be silent, Sophia," Bion growled. "You'll have to go through me to get to her."

Aetos laughed. Hard and long. He threw his head back and ended up slapping his thighs before he was finished. The crew happily joined their captain. The noise was deafening and nerve-racking, like someone drawing their fingernails across a blackboard. She suddenly understood exactly how early Christians must have felt as they entered the Roman Colosseum to meet the lions.

"Captain Bion Donkova of the Illuminist Order— that is your full title, is it not?" Aetos spoke in a loud voice, making sure the Illuminist crew heard him. They shifted their attention to Bion, disgust simmering in their eyes.

"You can bet it is," Bion snarled. He stepped in front of her, blocking her view of Aetos.

The captain of the Soiled Dove beckoned him forward, pointing to the tin box. "You told me your terms, Captain, open the box. Your payment is inside."

Bion stepped forward and opened the lid. Inside, the tiny points of the Root Ball shone brightly. Sophia gasped and Aetos nodded.

"A Root Ball. Yours to use if you will declare your loyalty to the Helikeian Order and this crew."

"And just how would you have me satisfy your request?"

Sophia moved closer to Bion, a bolt of fear shooting straight through her heart as she recognized the ruthless gleam glittering in Aetos's eyes.

"You'll toss these Illuminists overboard while their comrade watches." Aetos delivered his terms in an icy tone. "One witness left alive to make sure you never try to return to the Illuminists." He nodded at the man perched on the rail with the parachute.

"That's depraved," Sophia snapped.

"Leaving one man alive?" Aetos inquired. "I know it is, but in this case, our young man over here is in luck. I need to know that Captain Donkova is making a solid break with the Illuminists. But don't you worry, my pretty. I haven't forgotten you. Once your lover is my man, I believe he will be more receptive to training you, since he'll have nowhere else to go and he'll be a member of this crew, his obedience bound to me."

Sophia raised a hand to cover her mouth. Helplessness closed around her. She didn't fear Bion hurting her, but the idea of knowing he'd suffer for her disobedience horrified her. Aetos was grinning like a boy in a bakery with a shilling to spend.

"I have your payment, man. Now earn it by showing your devotion to me," Aetos commanded.

Bion looked down at the Root Ball, the morning sun illuminating it and casting a thousand rainbows.

"That's right. There it is. Something you're likely to wait another decade or two for from the Illuminist Order you've devoted so much of your life to. You wouldn't be the first man they took the best years of his life from without paying up. You've killed before; this won't take long. Just toss them over the rail like you did Grainger."

The kneeling Illuminist captain didn't move, but two of his officers swallowed audibly, their complexions paling. The man sitting on the rail with the parachute secured to his back was ruby faced. Shame shown in his eyes as well as hatred.

"Every one of my crew earns his place here in the same way. You'll kill your brethren, with a witness left alive to prove you want to make your place with us. To make sure there is no going back."

The crew snickered again and the sound made something snap inside Sophia. The same urge that had seen her arguing with Aetos rose above everything else. She wasn't going to be Aetos's victim and she wasn't going to let Bion be one either.

She quickly stepped forward, grabbed the pitcher and tossed the water onto the Root Ball. It exploded into a vapor that hit Bion straight in the face. He let out a howl and rocked back on his heels. One well-aimed kick sent the table flying toward the captain of the Soiled Dove. The crew recoiled from the vapor, giving them a clear path to the man perched on the rail. Sophia pushed Bion into the younger man and followed with every bit of strength she could muster.

"Grab on to the harness, Bion! We're going over the railing!"

The younger man was already tumbling over the rail, his arms flailing and grabbing Bion out of sheer instinct.

"Christ in heaven, Sophia!" Bion cursed. He reached for her, keeping one of his arms locked around the man buckled into the parachute. "What in the hell do you think you're doing?"

She didn't hear what he said. They were falling, their bodies cutting through the clouds as the Soiled Dove grew smaller and smaller above. The officer twisted and turned as they fell closer and closer to the ground.

Bion's eyes were closed, but he searched the harness until he found the pull cord.

"Hold tight!" he yelled. When the parachute opened, it was like a huge sail and filled with air instantly, their rapid descent coming to a jarring halt. They were jerked upward and bounced like a toy for several moments before beginning to descend again. This time they glided down gently.

Sophia's cheeks were chilled by the rushing air and her nose turned cold. The wind was numbing her fingers, but she ordered herself to maintain her grip. The ground was coming closer. The parachute was slowing their decent. But the trees still grew large in what seemed like moments. They twirled around in a crazy circle as her heart threatened to explode.

They hit the ground with more force than she'd expected. They bounced and the force broke her grip. She tumbled like an autumn leaf in a windstorm until coming to rest in a heap. Pain assaulted her, flooding her brain as she stared up into the afternoon sky. Her vision was blurry, her mind trying to give in to the urge to simply pass out to avoid the pain, but she dragged in a deep breath and then another to clear her thoughts. There was dirt in her mouth and blood on her lip. One leg burned with agony, and she rolled over to relieve it.

"Sophia!" Bion yelled.

"I'm here!"

He was blind. She vividly recalled the moments after she'd been hit by Root Ball vapor. "I'm coming, Bion."

Her legs were trembling, making it difficult to get to her feet.

"You're a bloody crazy woman," the young officer yelled at her. "You made me leave my captain behind."

"Shut your mouth," Bion snarled. He was already on his feet and fighting to open his eyes. A mere crack was all he managed and tears streamed down his cheeks from the pain the sunlight inflicted. "There was nothing you could do to help them."

"I would have found a way—" The young officer suddenly stiffened and fell over. Something hit the dirt, raising a cloud of dust as Sophia heard a popping noise. Looking up, she stared into the muzzles of two rifles. Mr. Graves and another man were winding their way to the earth with parachutes aiding them.

"Bion, run!" She ran toward him, catching his arm

and pulling him out of the line of fire. He looked up and cussed.

"How many? Christ! I can't make anything out."

"Two," she panted, suddenly hating the corset tied so securely around her straining lungs. "There are trees... ahead."

Bion didn't need any more encouraging. More popping sounds followed them and he pulled her along with his longer stride. They made it to the edge of a forest and had to slow down or run into a tree. She had to tug Bion around the trees. It proved almost impossible because he was still trying to guide her to safety.

"Damn it, Sophia. I can't see."

"I know. You'll have to follow me." She pulled him around a tree and further into the forest.

"It's my duty to protect you," he argued.

She yanked on his arm again to avoid another collision. "Well, now it's my duty," she panted. "Isn't that"—she paused for breath—"the Illuminist way? Gender doesn't set us apart?"

"If we live through this, I'm going to enjoy debating what I think our two genders should be doing." His tone was thick with promise, and it sent a tingle of anticipation along her limbs. The timing was terrible—really couldn't have been worse. She had to fight the urge to giggle. At least he couldn't see her expression. The sound of rushing water became louder and louder.

"Where's the river?" Bion demanded.

Sophia skidded to a stop, pulling on his arm to keep him from going over the edge of the embankment. "It's about ten feet below us." The water was rushing and frothy with white bubbles. It was cutting right through the soil of the forest, trees clinging to the edge.

"It's straight down," she said, uncertain of what to do. A quick look behind her indicated that Mr. Graves was not planning on returning to the Soiled Dove without them. She could hear his footsteps crunching the leaves and sticks on the forest floor.

"We have to jump," Bion decided. He was squinting down at the river and shaking his head as he tried to force his eyes to show him a clear picture. She knew from experience that all he'd see was a blur. But he reached out and clasped her in a solid embrace.

"One. Two. Three!"

Bion launched them off the bank and into the air. They sailed toward the water and hit with teeth-jarring force. The rushing water encased them, the harsh current tumbling them without mercy. Bion released her, and they fought to swim to the surface and draw breath. The water filled her ears, leaving her struggling in a world of rushing sounds.

"Sophia!"

She finally heard Bion and tried to make her way toward him. "I'm here." She swallowed a mouthful of water as she shouted but caught a glimpse of him. It seemed as though time slowed down, but her legs were turning numb, so she knew they had been in the water for some time.

"Sophia!"

She fought the current, her arms burning as she made her way to Bion.

"Close your eyes, Bion." She gripped his hand, her fingers stiff from the cold.

But Bion's strength wasn't spent. He hauled her toward the riverbank by her wrist and they both struggled out of the water.

"Shelter," he barked at her. "We need someplace to hide."

They'd come ashore at a bend in the river. It was a large curved area of smooth rocks. She searched the rocks and turned to Bion.

"It looks as if there is a cave in the bank."

"It will have to do." His teeth began to chatter and she realized he was indeed at the end of his reserves. She remembered how she had collapsed after her encounter with the Root Ball.

"Come on, Bion. I'll take care of you."

"I hate this—" His legs were trembling. She guided him toward a nook where the water had eaten away the bank of the river. There was an indention beneath the forest floor. It was dark, but she dropped down onto her knees and crawled right into it. Bion followed, letting out a groan when the sunlight was left behind.

"Bloody hell. This transformation…"

His legs buckled at last and he rolled over. The cave itself was about five feet deep. She prayed that it wouldn't collapse on them. She reached down and tore a strip from the bottom of her soaked skirt. With a tender touch, she wound it around his eyes to block out the light.

"I'll take care of everything," she promised.

He flinched, fighting to remain conscious. "You shouldn't have to. Leave me… go find help."

She smoothed the wet hair back from his face with

a soft touch. "It seems we are set to disagree once more, Bion Donkova. I will not desert you."

Bion grabbed her hand. "Listen to me. Wait until dark and go. That's an order."

His grip failed. He twisted, struggling to remain awake, but slipped away into unconsciousness. For a moment, she felt a twinge of fear but she shook it off. She was an Illuminist Navigator, able to stand on her own two feet and provide for herself. Duty was something she chose to shoulder, her gender no longer a factor.

Oh yes, she would see to what needed doing. Bion was not the only one who might be counted upon when action was needed.

❧

Aetos peered over the rail.

"Should we land?" one of his men asked.

Aetos shook his head. "We'd be sitting ducks in this area. There're too many Illuminist ships."

He looked up and stared at the crystal array sitting on the deck. Disappointment bit into him and the satisfaction gleaming in the eyes of the Illuminist prisoners ignited his temper.

"Toss them over."

"All of them?"

"You heard me, man."

There was a scuffle as the condemned men fought for their lives. Aetos watched it without a shred of compassion for the life and death struggle. Three of his own men went over the rail before the last Illuminist was off his ship.

"Plot a course for the airship port. We need Trackers."

Aetos didn't wait for his men to answer his orders. He walked toward his cabin and the chart books there. It took him several hours to decide where to begin his search. At least luck was on his side, because they were over the borders of Russia. It was a no-man's-land as Europe moved closer to war with the crumbling Ottoman Empire. There were few Illuminist Solitary Chambers in the area. He cursed as he considered how much gold it was going to cost him to hire Trackers. There were men who dealt in information and had a wide network of spies in the area, but they were also men who knew how to sell information to the highest bidder.

Men such as Jordon Camden. Aetos studied the report he had on Camden, frowning when he found evidence that Camden often sold his information several times over.

But there wasn't another option. Jordon Camden was the best and Aetos needed the best. He shut the book and prepared to disembark. He was going to enjoy getting his hands back on Bion and Sophia because the moment he had them, he was going to sell Bion Donkova and make sure Sophia got a good view of her lover being led away in chains.

❧

Sophia crawled to the edge of the cave and watched the river rushing past. She began to close up the opening to their hiding place with rocks from inside the cave. The light diminished as she built a crude sort of wall, until they were hidden from view.

When she returned to Bion, he was shivering. There was plenty of driftwood along the riverbank, but she didn't dare risk a fire that might give away their location. So she pressed herself against him to keep warm. As soon as the chill of the river had been chased away, she nodded off into slumber.

❧

"How long are we going to tromp around out here?"

Mr. Graves turned to peg his crewmate with a deadly look. "Until we find them. Even as big as that bloke was, he'll not have gotten too far before the shock of that vapor blast laid him low. That Navigator can't be carrying him, not as delicate she is. They are here, I tell you."

"The river might have done them in."

Mr. Graves shook his head. "Maybe, but I'm not quitting."

They continued along the edge of the river and the sunlight faded. The forest creatures eyed them as they walked past and both men gripped their rifles to give them comfort. Graves far preferred the shining eyes of the wolves to facing Aetos without the prize he'd been sent after.

Part of him was also enjoying the freedom of being away from the captain. He toyed with the idea of losing his comrade in the dark, but he stayed too close. It was only a fleeting idea anyway, one he shouldn't give too much attention to. He had nowhere else to go. The Illuminist Hunters would track him down for sure if he tried to settle into a life on the ground.

❧

Aetos was in a foul temper. The official waiting for him at the base of the escalator that led up to the docking station was wearing a frown that Aetos had no intention of suffering. He liked being the master of everything he surveyed, which was why he only put into an air station when he couldn't avoid it.

"You should have donned civilian clothing to hide your identity, Captain Aetos," the official reprimanded him. "A Hunter might spot you and follow you back to this docking station. That's trouble I don't need."

His fingers itched to lock around the man's throat, but while on the ground, he had to restrain himself. "So noted. I need to hire the best Trackers possible. I have a pair of Navigators to run to ground."

The official raised an eyebrow. "Did you say pair?"

Aetos grinned. "I did."

Aetos moved past the official. The biggest prizes often required the most risk. He thrived on such challenges, which was why he was captain and the man staring at his back only a dock attendant.

Five

SOMETIME NEAR DAWN, BION MUTTERED AND JERKED for what had to be the hundredth time. Light was making its way through the cracks in Sophia's stone wall. She worried her lower lip as she felt Bion's body burning with fever. When she'd been hit by the vapor of the Root Ball, Bion had taken her to a medical facility where there had been soothing compresses for her burning eyes and medication to ease her pain. The water rushing by only a few feet away might help him, but she hesitated, fearful of revealing their hiding place.

"Bion?" She gently shook him, but he remained locked in fretful slumber. He thrashed again, causing dirt to fall from the ceiling of their cave, and Sophia rolled over. She would have to take action.

The rocks she'd piled up moved away easily. She looked around before crawling out of the cave. The morning was bright and clear. Overhead birds called to each other as they searched for food.

"What are you doing sleeping in the riverbed?" She jumped and turned to face a man in baggy pants, white shirt, and vest. He had a bushy beard that covered his chin and his eyes sparkled merrily. "Even we gypsies do not sleep in the riverbed." He said something over his shoulder in another language. "Even if many countries would rather we adopted their ways and gave up our caravans."

Behind the man was a circle of gypsy wagons. Inside the cave, she hadn't heard the sounds from the camp just above. They were Roma people. Their wagons were small houses on wheels, and many were decorated in bright colors. They had tiny windows and even stovepipes rising from the roofs. A miniature door was set into the back of each one for the inhabitants to enter through. The camp was a cheerful scene, but Sophia looked all around her twice as she searched for any members of the Soiled Dove's crew.

"Come and share a morning meal with us. I am Abraham, leader of these people. What is ours is yours."

It was very tempting. She suddenly felt like moving was beyond her tolerance. From her fingertips to her toes she felt like she had been stretched and yanked beyond endurance. But she still turned and looked over her shoulder, scanning the other side of the forest for Mr. Graves. Bion was completely dependent on her. She suddenly understood his unwavering attitude and her cheeks heated with shame for the arguments she'd flung at him.

Well, at least some of them. But she felt her lack of experience with the Illuminist Order keenly. She had no idea how to go about searching for a Solitary Chamber. That lack of knowledge could see them back in the hands of Aetos.

"Are you a convict?" the Roma leader asked.

She turned back to face Abraham and shook her head, biting her lip as she tried to decide what to tell him. She simply didn't have much experience with lying and nothing came to mind.

But she was going to have to adapt quickly.

The older man stroked his beard and his expression became pensive.

"We were shanghaied," Sophia offered. "And you see, I'm not sure if it's safe to come out."

His eyes widened. "The very reason I tell my brethren to avoid the waterfront. Greed has driven men mad enough to enslave his own kind. Where is your companion?"

Part of her resisted trusting him, but she had no other choice. In fact, the gypsies just might be the perfect solution to their dilemma. The Roma people were known for their love of the open road and their own kind. They rarely became involved with civilization, except to trade their wares.

"He's here…"

Action. She had to take action and that would mean trusting someone. Abraham motioned to his people and soon Bion was being lifted up and out of the river cave.

Sophia sighed with relief. She just hoped their luck held.

❧

Aetos disliked waiting.

But he didn't have a choice because Jordon Camden only took the appointments he wanted. There were few people who had actually seen the man's face, and that was due to his very selective nature. Aetos studied the map on the table in front of him. The rented room was simple but clean enough. Since he was accustomed to his cabin on the Soiled Dove, it was really quite spacious, but he wasn't in the mood to enjoy the luxury.

Someone knocked on the door.

"Come in."

"Mr. Graves, Captain," the crewman at the door informed him before disappearing in a flash. The reason behind his hasty exit was reveled when Mr. Graves entered the room with only the crewman he'd parachuted off the Soiled Dove with.

"I don't care for disappointment, Mr. Graves." Captain Aetos was in a dark humor. He glared at his deck master and the all-too-apparent lack of his prizes in tow.

"It's likely they are dead," Mr. Graves informed him. "They jumped into the river."

Aetos snorted. "They aren't dead unless you saw their bodies." He flattened his hands on the top of the table and leaned forward. "Did you see their corpses?"

"No."

Aetos cursed and slammed his fist on the desk. "They aren't dead," he snapped. He looked at the map open on his desk. "No one escapes my crew. No one. We'll track them down and bring them back, or we'll make sure they don't tell any tales of the Soiled Dove. You will take to the road again and find them."

Mr. Graves didn't nod or offer any comment. Captain Aetos wasn't the sort of man who enjoyed crewmen who shared their opinions without being asked. The captain studied the map, then straightened.

The crewman outside the door knocked again. He didn't wait for Aetos to give him permission to open the door but still turned the doorknob and pushed the door in.

"Message for you, Captain."

His man handed over a folded parchment that was sealed with a large splotch of red wax. There was a crest pressed into it, but Aetos broke it without studying it too closely. The script was nearly perfect, the strokes of the pen even. Aetos read through the details of the message twice before nodding with approval.

"I'm going to see a man who will assist me in getting results."

And he was going to enjoy setting eyes on the elusive Jordon Camden.

Mr. Graves ended up alone and in the rather unexpected predicament of having permission to leave again. The crewmen in the hallway stared at him as he passed and the smile on his face grew larger.

Aye, he'd take to the road again and enjoy being accountable to no one.

❧

"Your man needs rest."

The Roma had a simple way of talking. Barbara, Abraham's wife, stopped in front of Sophia and instructed her in a tone of voice that made it clear she was used to being listened to.

"My man has given you both a wagon."

"Thank you."

Barbara looked her up and down. Sophia fought the urge to straighten her top. There was little point in attempting to correct her appearance. Her skirt and top had more dirt on them than a coal miner's boots. The few hairpins she had left failed to keep her braids secured. The strip she'd torn off the bottom of her skirt left a ragged hole and there were rips all along her sleeves.

"You need to bathe," Barbara decided. "We do not need the greedy men who tried to own you here. You will dress like a daughter until your man is able to rise from his bed. You must not be different. Go to the washing area."

Other women gestured to her, guiding her to the far end of camp. There were lines strung up for laundry and two women were busy working over scrub boards. The women waved her further away from the camp until she passed what looked like blankets drying in the morning sun. Maybe they were freshly washed, but they also formed curtains that surrounded a large tub.

Sophia let out a little sigh, shaking with anticipation. Just the sight of the tub made her skin feel ten times filthier. It was an old tin tub with a high back. Two fires burned nearby with caldrons of hot water steaming over them. They were up by the riverbank, making it easy to fill the tub. Sophia even fended off blushing when the women took every last bit of clothing she had. Her nose wrinkled when she smelled her chemise. The women laughed and tossed her underclothing toward one of the laundry tubs.

"Pretty golden hair."

One of the women searched out the remaining

pins in her hair and began to brush out the tangles. The Roma were mostly dark-haired, and they seemed fascinated by her blond locks. Sophia didn't care, so long as she was clean. They filled the tub halfway before adding hot water. After a stir, she climbed in and sighed as the water hit her skin. Someone poured water over her head and then worked soap through her hair. When they finished with her, she rose from the water and ordered herself not to blush.

"Your man must protect you better," Barbara insisted as she joined them.

"He came after me. Something I didn't think anyone could accomplish, yet he did. He is the best protector."

The older woman smiled in response. She held out clean clothing. "You dress like a daughter now."

The gypsy women all wore long skirts that were colorful and decorated with reflective spangles. They gave her a chemise sort of blouse, and Barbara clicked her tongue in reprimand when Sophia reached for her corset. A woman quickly submerged it in a laundry tub.

Barbara gave her a vest to wear instead and a scarf to cover her hair. Once back in her shoes, Sophia felt relieved, but it was short-lived. With a determined stride, she went back to where Bion was, worrying her lower lip as she tried to think of what to do next.

The honest truth was, she had no idea. But she was going to have to think of one, because she'd be damned if she would falter when it was her turn to let him depend on her.

She was going to protect him and get them back to the Illuminists.

And that was that.

꙰

Bion fought his way to consciousness. His body resisted. Fatigue smothered him, and he struggled to break the bonds of slumber. Finally, he jerked and sat up, smacking his head on something above him.

He fell back again as pain tore through his head. When it subsided, he was treated to a second wave of pain that didn't wash away. It was persistent and lingering. Something was tied over his eyes and he pulled it off. His first view of his surroundings was blurry, but his eyesight finally focused, even if it was a bit fuzzy.

The bed he was in was only about six feet by four feet. For a moment, he was confused, the wooden walls and ceiling making him wonder if he was in a crate. But there was a comfortable bed beneath his back and a warm blanket tucked over his legs. The only wall that wasn't solid had thick curtains drawn across it. He swept them open and stared at the inside of a gypsy wagon. He recognized the colorful decoration of the Roma culture instantly.

There was a small potbellied stove that accounted for the warm interior. Cooking utensils hung on the wall near the stove and there was a long seating area on the opposite side of the wagon. Every inch was utilized and decorated. Even the ceiling was carved with intricate depictions of animals and trees, some of it even gilded.

He sat up, making sure to avoid hitting his head, and crawled out of the bunk. His head touched the ceiling as he walked down the aisle. The door opened easily, but he flinched when the sunlight sent agony through his eyes. How could he have forgotten?

For a moment, he leaned on the closed door, face to face with the reality of something he'd devoted himself to earning for years. The pain became a treasured confirmation of his eyes' transformation. It seemed surreal, but the persistent discomfort was a hard fact.

And he owed it to Sophia.

For a moment, he indulged himself and grinned. His trainee was a bundle of surprises. Their tumble to Earth replayed itself and he shook his head. As much as he needed to scold her for taking such a mad risk, part of him enjoyed it immensely. She had courage and the spirit of a warrior.

His grin faded and his grip tightened on the door handle. He had no idea where they were, which made it a very inconvenient time to have his encounter with a Root Ball.

When he opened the door the second time, he was prepared for the shock of the light. They were parked under some trees, other wagons forming a circle. Women were tending pots over fires while children ran about. All of their clothing was bright, much of it decorated with spangles that flashed in the sunlight.

Bion's boots were placed at the bottom of the steps that led down from the wagon. Balanced across the top of one was a pair of purple-tinted glasses. He picked them up, feeling a rush of satisfaction that quickly died. He could not be content while Sophia was still so exposed to danger.

"You're supposed to put them on, not hold them, Bion. You need them."

He flinched, his hand tightening around the glasses as Sophia appeared from the side of the wagon.

"What I need is to teach you not to take such chances with your life."

She propped her hands on her hips. The gesture made the spangles on her Roma gypsy scarf dance. She had it draped over her head like the other women and was dressed in a colorful tiered skirt as well. If not for her blond hair, it would be easy to take her for a Roma woman.

"I got us off that ship and managed to get you what you wanted too," she insisted.

Bion flipped the glasses open and slid them into place over his eyes. Sophia watched him through her own purple lenses as he stooped to put his boots on. She could tell he wanted to continue the conversation, but it would wait until he decided he was ready to face their situation. He really was a man of action.

She rather liked him without his boots on.

Without anything on, you mean.

"You need me at my best, Sophia."

"We needed a diversion. You mentioned the necessity yourself." She paused for a moment, trying to keep herself from sounding too pleased. She was ecstatic, but it felt like a weakness in the face of his stern disapproval. He was such a complex man, almost like the Roman god Janus, who had two faces. He loomed over her once his boots were on, and it irritated her.

"I am doing rather well at taking care of you," she muttered.

Surprise registered on his face before frustration made his nostrils flare. "You are my trainee."

"It seems we are both trainees now." She smiled slowly. "And I am a more senior student."

His eyes narrowed to slits, promising her an argument. Instead of being annoying, she found herself relieved to have him restored to his normal, overbearing self.

Someone laughed nearby. Bion spun around, throwing out a protective arm to keep Sophia behind him.

"That's Abraham. He's our host and the leader of these people," Sophia explained.

Abraham had a full beard that covered his collar and was speckled with gray. "I see you are awake at last. Good. I was worried you might starve to death."

"Bion, behave. Abraham is our host. We were sleeping in a riverbank cave before he found me," Sophia warned in a low tone.

"So you thought revealing our position was a wise move?" Bion demanded.

"Better than waiting for Mr. Graves to discover us." She shot a hard glare back into his dark eyes. "And Abraham promised to take us as far as a city. I couldn't do it without help. You were unconscious."

"A fact you are responsible for." His voice had lowered, making her lean closer to make out his words.

She slowly smiled, recognizing the wounded pride of a warrior in his tone. "Well now, Mr. Donkova. Do not lavish me with so much praise; my head will surely explode."

He groaned softly and relaxed, allowing her to move away from him, but he reached down and swatted her on her rump as she went. She jumped, her face turning scarlet.

"Are you mad?" she sputtered.

Abraham smiled brightly. "No. He is making it plain you are his." The Roma leader locked gazes with Bion for a long moment. "And that he is your protector. Your man knows the Roma way."

Abraham spread his arms wide. "You are welcome in our caravan. The wagon is yours until you leave us." He offered them a half bow before leaving.

"Wait," Bion called, but Abraham was already extending his hand to another person.

"What did you expect?" she groused. "You greeted him like a mastiff intent on establishing his territorial boundaries."

Bion turned on her, his lips set into a mocking grin that she recognized instantly. She stepped back but he'd already cupped her cheeks and claimed her mouth. She should have tried to escape. Should have pushed him away. Instead she gripped the edges of his vest, her lips following his lead. He showed her no mercy, not a shred of concern for her modesty. The kiss was hard and passionate. Without a care for how many watched, he continued the kiss until she was breathless and fighting to maintain her composure. Only then did he release her.

"Now I've behaved like a mastiff." There was a pleased smirk on his lips, and he reached up and mimicked the motion of tipping his hat to her, then turned and went after Abraham.

"Damn you," she flung after him.

And damn her for liking it so very much.

❧

Jordon Camden was not a man who gave away his feelings. His expression was controlled, along with his body. No fiddling fingers to betray eagerness or a tapping foot to help Aetos know when the man was getting excited.

"I was told you were the man to see about Trackers," Captain Aetos repeated himself as his cup of Turkish coffee went cold.

Camden didn't let his own suffer that fate. He sipped at it slowly, allowing the aroma to fill his senses before taking another taste.

"Are you going to answer me or not?" Aetos growled.

Camden shot the captain a deadly look. Aetos wasn't blind to how dangerous the man might be if provoked. Beneath his silk vest and fine shirt was solid muscle.

"The art of tracking is one of patience." Camden continued to enjoy his coffee. "In this case, the prey is loose and highly valuable. This is not the same civilized Europe you are from. Here, the regions are controlled by noblemen still operating under the rules of serfdom."

"Are you saying you cannot find them?"

The coffee was set aside. "If you are willing to pay the price, anything can be yours."

"I thought you were a compatriot."

"I am also a businessman," Camden countered quietly. "As are you. So kindly spare me the lecture on loyalty. Neither of us are Helikeians for the glory of the cause. You are here because you have lost a fledgling Navigator." He clicked his tongue in reprimand. "Very careless of you."

"She dove over the side," Aetos defended himself.

Camden drew in a long, deep breath. "An obvious reaction to her circumstances. Females require special handling. An accomplished man can make any member of the gentle sex his pet, but only if he can master his own impulses."

Aetos snickered. "You seem to have a talent for it."

The two females attending them were both nude from the waist up. One was a trim girl with small breasts crowned with rosebud nipples. The other was a curvy woman with dark skin and fire in her eyes. Around each of their necks was a collar of plain leather. A bell dangled from the front of each, ringing delicately every time one of them moved.

"Do you like my pets?" Camden waved them forward. Each wore a single garment, a wrap of sorts that tied at their left hip. When they moved, the fringe trim shifted to give him a peek at their mons. "Each is unique."

"I heard that about you." Aetos worked to speak up. He was finding it hard to concentrate with so much female flesh on display—and so willingly too. "You're like some pasha. The rumors say you have a harem and that you use it voraciously."

"What I am is a connoisseur, a collector of art. Females are only one of my collections." He finished off his coffee and the darker-skinned female took his cup away, her bell tinkling. "You see, I find the challenge of transforming vinegar into sweet wine irresistible."

"Wine comes from grapes. There's no secret there."

Camden smiled wickedly. "Ah, but I enjoy the challenge of testing my stamina. Any fool born with a cock can fuck. I demand more of myself. I have an experienced Tracker. He can begin tonight. My fee is nonnegotiable. I assure you my network of informants is unsurpassed, much like my collection of pets."

Aetos had to swallow to clear his throat. "Deal."

"In addition, you will provide me with one unique item to add to my collections. Disappoint me with my object of art and I will have my doorman turn you away next time you ask for my help."

"I heard you were picky about how you were paid. I don't have time to find you a gift. I'll double your fee."

"I am a connoisseur and gold is not the only thing worth collecting. You'll bring me something unique or find another man to track your Navigators." Camden let out a sigh and leaned back.

Aetos fought the urge to argue. He also had to temper the urge to look up at the heavens, where he would far prefer to be, far away from having to bend to the demands of anyone. He shrugged. "If those are the terms, I'll meet them."

Jordon grinned. "You might just enjoy looking for my gift. Seeking out the unusual is its own reward. You really should consider approaching life as an admirer."

Aetos shifted his gaze to the other female. "I can do that. I'd be very happy to let you know if your pet's skill is the best I've encountered."

Camden chuckled once again, the tone dark and sinister. "You show promise."

"I enjoy a good challenge, Captain."

For a moment, Aetos studied the man, surprised to discover someone very much like himself.

⌘

Lykos held out a gloved hand for Decima. For once, she took it. There was a smile on her face any high society matron would approve of as she allowed herself to be escorted. Lykos touched the brim of his beaver silk top hat several times as they strolled past other couples. Anyone watching them would think they were taking the air before continuing on their journey.

At last, another couple stopped to greet them, the gentleman extending what looked like a calling card. Lykos slipped it into his vest pocket. In a few moments, the couple moved on. Lykos guided her around the park a few more times before moving back to the escalator that led away from the afternoon promenade. The park was near the rail station. Trains connected Europe, and it was the best place to seek out the newest information. Their Illuminist pins drew the right attention. Other Hunters recognized them by the gold insignia.

Still, it was a slow, frustrating process. But there had been no word of Bion or Sophia at the air station. Coming to the park was a desperate action, but there were Hunters who did not wear their pins in plain sight. They were firmly established in their roles among the non-Illuminist society and would not risk being discovered by going to the Solitary Chamber.

"Delightful afternoon, Miss Talaska."

"Only if we have something to show for our efforts." Decima withdrew her hand before Lykos could place a kiss on the back of it. She lowered her eyelashes to avoid making eye contact with him when he frowned at her.

He sighed and withdrew the card. It was actually a small envelope. The letter inside it was written on eggshell parchment so that it might be pressed flat and masquerade as a calling card. He scanned the card, trying to fit together the bits of information gathered from their network of Hunters across Europe. No one ever disappeared completely. There was always *some* clue, and it was up to him to discover where to look for his comrades.

Decima came close again. Her presence was distracting, dividing his focus. For all that he teased and toyed with her at times, he did not have time for distractions. They so often proved fatal in the field.

She pointed at one line of ink. He looked closer, rereading the bit of information: *"Pirate attack on the vessel Crown Jewel. No survivors. One man found on ground with parachute attached dead from gunshot wound."*

"Only one man in a parachute?"

"He might have panicked and deserted," Lykos remarked.

"Which would not account for the gunshot wound," Decima countered.

"No, it would not." He folded the letter and tucked it back into his vest. "It seems we are not long for fair France. That body was found in Germany."

"Along the passageway returning from the Arctic volcano fields."

"Exactly," Lykos agreed.

The body was their clue. The trade routes between the Arctic Deep Earth harvest fields weren't known by the Society around them. But the Illuminist airships used them all the time. It was the most likely place a Navigator would be needed.

Decima didn't wait for Lykos to take action. She raised her hand for a carriage to stop for them. He watched her, enjoying the way she confidently took on the world. Unlike the other ladies strolling in their afternoon frocks, Decima wouldn't wait for her escort to get what she needed. She was an accomplished Hunter and her gender made her unique. Even among the Illuminists, a female Guardian was rare.

That was the only reason he thought about her so much.

❧

Sophia leaned against a tree, darkness wrapped around her as the members of the caravan enjoyed a communal fire. Someone was playing a lively tune on a violin. The older members of the group sat close to the fire, babies on their knees. The younger people stayed back from the light, many of them disappearing into the darkness two by two.

You wouldn't mind a little of that yourself.

Her inner voice was intent on prompting her into action. It needled her, reminding her of the long hours she'd shared that cave with Bion, worrying that he might not recover. Or how she had felt when Captain Aetos had made it clear that Bion would be the one to suffer if she didn't perform.

Go to him.

Enough!

She hugged herself and leaned her cheek against the tree. The bark was a poor substitute for what she wanted touching her—what she longed for. She huffed, taking the opportunity to express her frustration.

"You should not hide in the dark." Abraham's wife, Barbara, walked up, the firelight reflecting off the two gold hoop earrings she wore. Her earlobes were stretched from their weight, indicating that she'd had them for many years. "That man is brooding; he is more stubborn than you," she said. "Go to him before he strangles on his pride."

Sophia shook her head. "It is not simply pride."

Barbara cackled with amusement. "Daughter, it is his wounded pride keeping him watching you from across the way. Men do not like it when we women prove our strength to them. Go to him. I see the longing in your eyes. Youth is too quickly gone to waste such a night."

Was he waiting on her? She scanned the darkness beyond the firelight. Her Navigator's eyes could see the layers, the places where light had different shades, and she spotted Bion directly across from her. Watching her.

Her body erupted with a flood of sensations, as if the darkness granted her permission—or at the least would mask her wickedness.

Ye cannot be wicked alone.

Oh, she certainly could. Her mind was already full of the things she might like to do, but her mouth went dry as she recalled the whispers she'd heard during her time at the Solitary Chamber. Illuminist females were raised differently than ladies were. It wasn't about manners but about sensuality. Nestled inside the huge library were books on passion with illustrations no matron had laid eyes upon.

But Bion had. Of course, it was his world. Her confidence wavered with that thought. The man had taken her, but she honestly had to ask herself if he would have chosen her if there were other women

available. After all, Illuminist men were not expected
to suffer celibacy simply because they were not
married. Weddings only took place when a couple
loved one another. Satisfying lust didn't mandate a trip
to the altar. Once wed though, adultery wasn't tolerated. It was considered a violation of an oath, and if a
member wasn't going to keep one oath, there could be
no trusting them to maintain their oath of allegiance
to the Order.

The violin player changed tempos and the mood
changed. Several other musicians joined in. The
wrinkled faces around the fire split with smiles as
they moved back to make room. Someone let out a
loud whoop and a moment later a man in a dark vest
was dancing around the fire. He slapped his hands
together, then stretched his arms out wide, dancing in
a small circle. It was a slow dance but every motion
seemed packed with power. She would have sworn
that she felt it radiating across the space between them.

More whoops followed and then several men were
dancing. The violins played faster until they reached
a zenith and went silent. Then drums began to beat.
The violins joined again but the men left the circle.
Barbara let out another throaty ripple of amusement.

"Then go dance…" She pushed Sophia away
from the tree and swished her hands at her when she
hesitated. "Go and tempt him. Entice him to abandon
his pride."

Tempt him?

Now that was a wicked thought. It sent heat curling
through her belly like a whip uncoiling. She watched
the area around the fire as women filled it, their hair

unbound and flowing behind them. They swirled their skirts up, offering tempting peeks at their thighs, then weaving and dipping and turning again. Their upper bodies bent and their hips swayed as they danced. This was not the kind of dancing she'd learned in parlors.

Sophia felt the first snap of the whip inside herself. The sting traveled along her limbs, raising gooseflesh. She walked toward the fire, her hips swaying in a sultry motion. She seemed to know the motions instinctively, her heartbeat helping her keep pace with the tempo.

The women welcomed her, and once in the center of the firelight, she could no longer see Bion. But she felt him, which was better—ten times more intense than watching him. She danced for him, for his keen dark eyes. She wanted him to see her, to watch her hips moving and her body flowing. Sparks from the fire drifted up into the night sky, making her feel as if she was part of the blaze. It was primitive and likely undermining to her discipline, like all the matrons said. Even the Royal Navy warned against pagan dances, but she let her thoughts slip away until all she heard was the wild rhythm of the music. Time stretched, feeling as if a minute lasted for an hour, until the men whooped and jumped into the firelight to join the women.

Her breath caught in anticipation. She turned, her eyelashes fluttering. She lifted her chin and looked up to see if Bion had joined her.

"You doubted I would join you?" His voice was gruff with frustration.

She nodded. Maybe it was dangerous to let him see

how little confidence she had in her ability to draw him to her.

"Don't."

He didn't dance. Bion circled her, settling a hand onto the curve of her hip and turning her around and around. Her belly tightened like she was spinning on a ballroom floor. But the chill of the night air teased her with just how much more exciting her night might be because she was so far from the reaches of society. There were no limits to what liberties he might take.

Or she might demand from him.

The music changed tempo again, slowing down as the couples moved closer to one another. Bion brushed her cheek with the back of his hand. The touch was so simple, yet it set free a riot of sensations. His glasses were hooked into his vest pocket and she smiled when she realized they were truly comrades now. He watched her, reading her emotions as clearly as he always had. Finally, she was thankful for how perceptive he was because he captured her wrist and turned toward the caravan wagon Abraham had given them.

They left the firelight behind and Bion pinched out the candle that had been left burning inside the wagon. The aisle was narrow, but he pulled her around him and lifted her up onto the bunk. Without her Navigator vision, it would have been dark. But there were a hundred sources of light that cast a magical glow, like the single candle she often took to her bedroom at the end of the day. It would grant her a limited amount of light but the semidarkness was where she felt at liberty to dispense with clothing and hairpins and all the trappings of society.

"I am drawn to you." He shrugged out of his clothing, letting it drop behind him. The wagon swayed as he crawled up onto the bunk with her. Poised on all fours, he was more magnificent than she had noticed before. The pinpoints of light traced the muscles and contours of his form. He tossed her skirt up and stroked her bare legs.

"So much so, the idea of not touching you is a torment…"

He stroked her, running his hands along the outside of her legs from calf to knee and then further up to her thighs. She quivered, falling back onto the bed as her clitoris began to throb. He ran his hands back down to her calves and sat for a long moment on his haunches. His cock stood up straight and swollen, promising her the pleasure she'd enjoyed before.

But he didn't move to cover her. Instead, he moved his hands over the top of her shins until they rested on the inside of her legs.

"We didn't get the chance to savor the moment last time." He slowly slid his hands to her knees. "Something I plan to rectify tonight." And on to her thighs. "By touching every part of you." And at last to her mons.

He barely made contact with that forbidden place and she jumped, the softest pressure sending a bolt of sensation through her passage. It was so intense, she gasped and found her breathing labored. He laughed softly, the sound full of intent. He lowered his hands and pressed her thighs apart once she'd settled.

"Every part of you, Sophia," he warned again in a tone she knew signaled his intent to bend her to his will.

"You're trying to frighten me."

He loomed over her, crawling up her so his face was even with hers. "I prefer to call it trying your nerve. The question is, are you woman enough to meet me on the field?" His breath teased her lips, and he pressed a kiss against her mouth. She lifted her head to kiss him back, needing some outlet for all the excitement brewing inside her. It was like sitting through a thunderstorm and waiting for the next crack of lightning.

"You know I am. I will stand steady while you do your worst." Her voice was full of husky confidence. His chest rumbled with amusement, but she didn't snap her thighs closed when he slid down the bed to hover over her open slit.

She'd seen this in a book, and the memory served as an aphrodisiac. Her clitoris throbbed with anticipation, the growing excitement almost too much to contain. She gripped the blanket beneath her, digging her fingernails into it as Bion's breath teased the moist skin of her slit.

"I hope you will be moved to action…" He separated her folds and stroked the center of her slit with the tip of a finger. "Just as I hope you made it to the erotic section of the library."

She jerked, the single touch nearly sending her into climax. He pressed her back down with a hand over her belly as he chuckled.

"I believe that means you did, Sophia." He returned to fingering her, this time drawing his finger back and forth and never withdrawing. Sweat beaded on her forehead as her nipples began to pucker.

"Right now, you are poised on the edge of reason and all because of what you think I might do to you…" He clicked his tongue and looked up at her. "And I promise to do every wicked thing you will allow me to."

"Oh… yes." The response came from deep inside her, from that place where she was starving for his touch.

"Yes what?"

She was so needy, her body yearning so much for release that his question frustrated her. She bared her teeth and snarled at him. It was a primitive sound and seemed to fit the moment. Outside the music was still swirling. Lying on her back was suddenly intolerable. She didn't feel submissive, didn't think she could control all the impulses filling her body.

"Yes, I want to take you."

She sat up so fast, he knocked his head on the top of the wagon as he got out of her way. Sophia didn't care. She pushed him onto his back and climbed over him.

"Then get in the saddle," he insisted as he pulled the fabric of her skirt out of the way. "And make sure you keep a good grip on me or I'll toss you."

"You'll not find me that easy to unseat." It only took a moment for her to gain what she wanted. He guided her onto his length, easily penetrating her as she lowered herself. Satisfaction filled her as her body stretched around his flesh. She'd never noticed how empty she felt, not until now when she was finally full.

But she needed friction. The urge was demanding and unruly. She lifted her bottom and Bion guided her back down a second later. When he pressed her down, he bucked beneath her to drive his length deeper into her body. Pleasure speared through her, returning with every thrust. All of her energy was focused on their bodies moving in unison, lifting and plunging, rising and falling in time with the violins.

Her climax caught her off guard, snapping like a corset lace. Delight went rushing through her. Bion bucked frantically, burying himself to the hilt, then flipping her over onto her back. The wagon rocked as he began to piston her. She gripped his hips, locking her legs around him as he growled, stiffening when his seed erupted inside her.

He caught himself on his elbows to keep from crushing her. Her lungs were burning for oxygen, the frantic pace of her heart demanding that she pant. He nuzzled her neck, kissing the tender skin before gently biting her. It was shocking but exciting too. The feeling of his teeth against her skin touched off some sort of trust that she'd never realized she might feel for another human, the sort of trust that meant being completely comfortable with placing her life into his keeping.

Of course, he'd already been responsible for her when she was helpless after the Root Ball had vaporized in her eyes. Now she stretched her neck out, offering the column of her throat to him. He groaned low and deep, grazing her with his teeth, then beginning to move once more.

"This time, we'll slow down."

He proved true to his words. The music had become mellow and slow and Bion kept his pace even. It rekindled the passion in her, building it slowly this time. By the time it became a raging need, her skin was coated with perspiration and every muscle ached from straining toward her lover.

Bion rolled off of her once he was spent, pulling her into his embrace as he had before. He smoothed the hair back from her face, toying with one lock that curled in front of her ear.

She should have fallen asleep. Instead, she found herself savoring the moment, lingering in it as she tried to memorize the way his embrace felt. She couldn't recall ever being so secure, so certain she was safe. It was a whimsical idea, considering their circumstances, but she couldn't seem to change her thinking—not even a tiny bit.

"Why did you doubt I would join you?" The night was quiet now; the music had died away outside.

His question accomplished what she had been unwilling to do. It forced her to acknowledge reality with all its sharp edges.

"You aren't sleeping, Sophia, and you aren't often a coward. Answer my question."

"How could I not doubt? There must be many Illuminist women happy to be your lover." It was the closest she would come to admitting her fear that he'd only taken her because she was near. In his society, that was accepted behavior. It was not an injustice if there were no promises between them. *And there weren't.* She really needed to remember that before her tender feelings were bruised.

He toyed with her hair. "You have the right to take other lovers too, Sophia."

His voice was a mere whisper, but she was certain

she heard the tone of an admission. She lifted her head so that she might look into his eyes.

"I only want you."

She was pinning her heart to her sleeve. All he had to do was shatter it now that she was offering it so openly.

"And I cannot seem to ignore you, Miss Stevenson."

He rolled her onto her back, sealing her response beneath a kiss. He spent a long time just kissing her before rolling back over and holding her against his side once more. The camp was silent and fatigue finally took over. Later, she'd remember that he hadn't really declared any tender feelings for her. For the moment, while the night surrounded them and the gypsy wagon offered them a hiding place, she would simply be happy.

It had been a very long time since she'd been happy.

Lykos felt his hold on his temper straining. He was back in an Illuminist Chamber but the information his brethren were giving him wasn't very helpful. "What do you mean there are only a few telegraph lines?"

The Illuminist member facing him shrugged. "Winter is hard in those areas. The lines snap under the weight of the ice. It's pointless to try and repair them until summer. Besides, the Russian government is not very appreciative of our Order. There's talk of abandoning all the Solitary Chambers inside the country, now that Russia is getting ready to go to war over the Ottoman Question."

"Damn those fools. Still fighting over land as their

fathers did," Lykos lamented. "They waste their lives on petty squabbles."

"Cursing them will not change the fact that Russia is intent on scooping up as much of the crumbling Ottoman Empire as she can," Decima remarked. "If Bion and Sophia are on Russian soil, it might be impossible to aid them."

"Difficult, sure, but there isn't anything I consider impossible," Lykos informed her. "We'll have to ride horses from here."

They were on the edge of Russia. The country was so vast that crossing it on horses wasn't a pleasant idea. But Bion and Sophia were likely traveling by the same means, so it was still possible to catch them.

"There is something else, sir," the Illuminist member interrupted. "We intercepted a message last evening."

Lykos took the page from the man as Decima joined him to read it at the same time.

From Jordon Camden stop.
Reward offered for information stop.
Two Navigators in Russian territory stop.

"Two?" Decima questioned.

"So it would seem," Lykos answered. "Who is Jordon Camden?"

"He's a recluse with amazing influence. He has a network of spies that he employs for anyone willing to meet his price. He has Helikeian ties but is more devoted to his own interests."

"Do we have anyone inside his network?" Decima inquired.

"A few, which is why we have that information. But we do not know who hired him or if he has already found his prey." The Illuminist member continued, "We do know that it is likely he will sell the information to more than one party.

"This is turning into a fox hunt," Lykos groused.

"One we'd better plan on winning or the dogs just might tear the prey apart."

Decima's tone was dark and fit the moment all too well.

❧

Jordon Camden pushed his slumbering concubine away from him, then stood up. He rolled his shoulders and stretched as the early morning breeze blew across his bare skin. His current home had a lovely secret that allowed him to enjoy his collection of females in true Ottoman fashion. The front of the house looked normal enough, but the back was built into an open terrace that faced the Caspian Sea. Lengths of sheer silk hung from the arched openings to the patio, the colored-glass lanterns from the night before having burned out. A soft tinkle of a bell warned him that one of his pets was nearby. A red-haired Scottish girl offered him a robe. He stopped and let her clothe him.

"You may join me tonight."

Joy lit her blue eyes. She pressed her hands together and bowed. He chuckled on his way to where his pigeons were gathering for their morning meal. He did enjoy seeing obedience in her eyes, but he admitted to missing the defiance she had spat at him for the last year.

Knowing that she was now a truly submissive conquest was all the more reason to ensure that someone had a reason to gift him with another pretty amusement. He detested boredom.

He walked past the gardens and the fountain until he came to where the birds were eagerly enjoying the kitchen scraps put out for them. He watched them, looking for new arrivals. He caught one and pulled the small pouch off its talon. No one opened the messages except for him. He was master of his empire and information—the selling of which was what kept his empire thriving.

Once he'd inspected all the birds, he left with their messages clasped carefully in his hand. The flowers were blooming, but he didn't let the sweet morning air tempt him into lingering outside. There was money to be made.

Navigators were so very rare after all. A healthy female of breeding age was even rarer. He entered his office and looked through a few of his ledgers. He stopped when he found the information on Janette Aston Lawley. What drew his attention was the notation of Dr. Nerval. The man had been a client from time to time and had a reputation for paying well for information on the location of rare individuals such as Navigators.

He'd never promised Captain Aetos exclusivity.

❧

Bion was gone when she woke.

Sophia stretched and paused when she saw her glasses placed carefully beside her. "It does seem that the good captain is feeling better," she muttered to herself. "Or at least he's intent on proving he is."

She opened the door of the wagon and made her way down the steps. She turned around to the back side of camp for a moment of privacy before facing the day. But Bion was waiting for her, his expression one she recalled very well. The man was not pleased.

"Do not disappear on me, Sophia."

She stopped close enough to him that their conversation wouldn't drift. "You are the one who was missing when I woke this time."

Not even a hint of remorse flickered in his eyes. "I was discovering where we are and you are my trainee."

His tone was condescending, but she was too distracted by the idea of returning to London to quibble with him. "So where are we?"

"It isn't good news."

"Well, it can't be any worse than what's already happened."

His lips twitched for a moment, revealing the man she recalled from last night.

Your lover, you mean.

Fine, her lover. During the day it was hard to see him. Bion had his expression controlled just as tightly as he might have while standing on the bridge of one of his beloved airships.

"You aren't going to abandon your hopeful attitude, are you?" For just a moment, his tone was playful. "I believe we have crossed over into Russia, which is a problem because Russia is moving closer to war in a quest to claim land from the weakening Ottoman Empire."

"Are there no Solitary Chambers here?"

"Very few, and Abraham is intent on making it farther north now that spring is giving way to summer."

The gypsies recognized no borders. All around her, they were getting ready to move on. They were tinkers and traders and sometimes musicians for festivals. During the spring and summer, they would follow the merchants on their ways to open-air markets and circuses.

"I am grateful for his help," she stated firmly. "I'm not sure what I might've done if he hadn't come along."

"We don't blend in, so we can't stay with them." He nodded, seeming to reassure himself that his logic was sound. "As much for our protection as theirs. Be ready to leave the caravan when I tell you it's time."

His on-guard stance swept away the last of her happiness. It had been so simple to relax during the night, but she realized that she'd really just been naïve.

As an Illuminist, she needed to watch out for herself, not depend on Bion. To travel north with the caravan would be foolish.

"You're right," she admitted, the admission squeezing her heart a little.

The caravan got underway, giving her the privacy to deal with her emotions without Bion noticing. Being lovers did not mean she didn't have to make her own way. Even as that idea brought her heart-ache, it filled her with a sense of pride. Her future would be something she earned. The matrons of society's upper crust were very fond of preaching about how young ladies enjoyed security, but the same walls were also a method to keep women from achieving the same positions as men. She smiled because she knew that those matrons would never have the opportunity to shred her reputation. Their opinion meant nothing in the Illuminist world and Sophia was going to be a Navigator.

She'd bloody well earned the right.

❦

He was being an ass and he knew it. Bion let the label sink in as Sophia settled into the seat beside him. She was struggling with her emotions, her eyes full of uncertainty. But only the strong survived.

Tender feelings could translate into death so easily when fate turned her nose up. Captain Aetos would have gladly used Sophia's kindness against her. Training her entailed stripping away anything that might hamper her survival. It was his duty.

So why did he feel like such an ass?

❦

The caravan stopped outside a small village the next night. They parked their wagons in a circle and began to cook an evening meal. Sophia went with the other women to pull fresh water from the river. But Bion reached out from behind a tree to stop her from returning to the camp with them.

"We need to leave."

"Now?"

He lifted the yoke off her shoulders and left the buckets where they landed.

"Yes, now. Anyone watching us will think we've

retired and not miss us until morning. With any luck, there will be a Solitary Chamber in the next village."

"What if Captain Aetos is there instead?"

Bion motioned for her to begin walking away from the Roma camp. "He might as easily be coming up the road behind us."

It felt odd to be leaving the caravan, and yet, she hadn't known their hosts for very long.

"Stop looking back, Sophia. I assure you, there is at least one man among them willing to sell us out for the right price."

"Well, that is a very harsh way to put it."

"And you don't care for how it wounds your pride? As a Navigator, you need to always control your impulses and carefully weigh the consequences of your actions." Bion peered at her over the rim of his glasses. "It was foolhardy of you to impair my abilities while in such precarious circumstances."

She propped her hands on her hips, his words stinging. "Do you mean to tell me you are going to quibble over the timing when you have been waiting for years for a Root Ball?" Bion's face tightened. He was fighting to contain his emotions and that stung her too. In fact, it felt as if he'd delivered a harsh slap to her cheek. "You should be thanking me," she declared.

"Impossible." Bion's tone cut through her attempt to maintain her dignity. "Once again you have failed to grasp my level of dedication to duty. I would never place my needs above the mission goal. You allowed the desire to please me to interfere with sound judgment."

"You might wear an Illuminist pin, but you still think that because I am a woman, I need a protector. Well, I dealt with things quite well while you needed protecting."

She almost broke through his stern exterior. Something flickered in his eyes that hinted at his true feelings, but he made a slashing motion with one hand before she decided just what it was.

"You do need a protector, Miss Stevenson, and I plan to perform my duties without fail." He stared forward, denying her the chance to see his expression. The gravel crunched under her feet as they made their way up the road.

"Oh yes, you are a man of action. You've proven that time and again."

Only today the action was breaking her heart. At least the sun was going down, offering her darkness to hide the tears flooding her eyes. She blinked them away, satisfied at least with the fact that none slid down her cheeks. There were few people on the road now and those who were hurried to make it to their homes before the night made it too difficult to find their way.

They were no different, and yet, the darkness was no longer something to shut the windows against. Now it was the time of day when she could at last take off her glasses and be at ease.

It was also the time of day when Bion might be her lover—if only until sunrise.

"It should be on the east end of the village."

"Have you been here before?" she queried as Bion tugged her along behind him with a firm grip on her wrist.

"I grew up in Russia and have a good recollection of most of the major Solitary Chambers."

In spite of the darkness, the man was still in his stubborn, commanding form. She twisted her hand up and over his wrist, breaking his grip. He stopped and glared at her.

"I am not a child to be pulled around." She continued past him, offering him a contented smile as he glowered at her. "I understand that Russia is a very large country. How could you recall a single village?"

"Because there are not many Solitary Chambers here. The czar is not fond of secrets," Bion answered. "Still, he has gained little for the number of our Chambers he's burned."

"Burned?" She hesitated and Bion captured her wrist once more.

"Did you think I was hurrying you because I long to be rid of your company? Quite the opposite in fact. The promise of a private bedroom draws me like a lighthouse."

For just a moment, his tone held a teasing note. She fought off the urge to giggle, horrified as a soft sound made it past her lips. Only simpletons giggled.

Bion answered her with a soft chuckle. "I do believe that was a challenge, my sweet." He stopped and surveyed the road where it split in front of them. His fingers gently massaged her wrist, sending little ripples of delight up her arm. He shot her a look that was hard to decipher in the darkness. "I've yet to enjoy your charms in a bed that wasn't owned by a ruthless pirate or a gypsy." He tugged her close, his warmth wrapping around her like a cloak. She wanted to snuggle against him. The impulse was so strong, it hurt to resist it. Bion leaned over to place a kiss against her throat. "Let's find our brethren and a bed free of impending peril."

"Yes." She was breathless and unsure of which of his suggestions she was agreeing with. Her thoughts had clouded so quickly, frustrating her with how fast he reduced her to naught but a creature ruled by her passions.

He made a growling sound that cut through the fog holding her wits hostage. His pleased tone was impossible to miss. She broke his grip once more.

"You are entirely too sure of yourself, Captain Donkova."

She walked past him, intent on using action to clear her thinking. A firm slap landed on her backside, earning him a hiss as she jumped with surprise.

"No gentleman spanks a lady," she protested.

Bion Donkova grinned at her, the starlight illuminating his teeth. "Yet as you have so often noted, I am a pirate."

"What happened to your sense of duty?"

He shrugged and pointed. A few paces away were a pair of doorways with the seal of the Illuminist Order painted on them. Her shoulders suddenly felt lighter and every muscle in her body began to ache. Bion hooked an arm around her waist, his teasing demeanor vanishing. She looked away, fearful that he'd transform into the stern taskmaster again, the man who knew so much more than she did, the one she couldn't quite seem to best.

"Easy, Sophia." He held her close for a moment, placing a soft kiss against her temple as she shuddered. Control was slipping through her fingers like sand, the days of uncertainty taking their toll now that safety was so close at hand.

"You've done as much to bring us here as I did," he admitted. His voice was gruff and she lifted her face so their eyes locked. He cupped the side of her face. "And I do appreciate the gift you managed to bestow on me, even if I could not say thank you until I knew you were safe."

She shivered but not from the cold. It was emotion and the certain knowledge that she stood on even footing with him. For sure, she didn't expect him to tolerate it for long, but she realized she didn't want him to. Part of her enjoyed being possessed. At least by him.

"Let's see if anyone is home," he muttered, sounding as reluctant to end the moment as she was.

The street might have looked deserted, but a wise man learned at a young age to be unnoticeable—at least in a country such as Russia, where men were still bound to the land as serfs. Sergey was no different. He might have been named for an important man, but he himself was very common and a serf. He made his way as best he could, for tonight there was a man willing to pay for information. Sergey watched the couple, feeling a stirring of pity for them. The fact that they were lovers was clear. It was there in the way the man touched her and in the trusting way the woman leaned against him.

Sergey stiffened. Pity would see his children crying in the winter when he had nothing to feed them. One man's misfortune was another's gain. There were men who paid well for information, and it was easier to produce than working all day in the coal mines.

A pair of Navigators arriving at the Solitary Chamber dressed as Roma gypsies was certainly something unusual. The Illuminists didn't travel in wagons like a common man such as himself. One good thing about there still being serfdom in Russia was that it made it easy to spot outsiders. Sergey waited long enough for the couple to disappear behind the doors of the Secret Order, then hurried off to wake up his friend who ran the telegraph office. Information was worth money, but only if it was fresh.

Six

THE SOLITARY CHAMBER WAS SMALL. USED TO THE blocks and blocks of hallways that the London one had, Sophia found herself rather disappointed—except for the sense of relief that came with seeing the seal of the Order on the large double doors. Bion had pounded on the door.

"I just hope someone is home. These outposts are often deserted during the winters, and it's still early enough that no one may have returned yet. Winter lasts longer this far north." Bion knocked again as the last of the villagers made their ways home for the night. It left the small town deserted, the homes all shuttered now that the sun had set. A prickle of suspicion touched her as she looked up and down the streets. There was absolutely no one in sight. Since it wasn't too cold, it was odd. It was like no one wanted to be seen.

"Why are the streets deserted?"

Bion wasn't keeping his back to the streets for long. He continued to watch every possible approach as he knocked again. "This is Russia. Most of the people are serfs and the landowners like them obedient. Drawing attention to one's self isn't wise when you are owned. Anyone suspected of plotting rebellion will be shipped off to Siberia. Solid evidence isn't a requirement, so it makes it wise to disappear as often as possible."

"That is barbaric."

Bion shrugged. "Many corners of the world are. But there is also adventure if you are willing to abandon the notion that Britain is the only place with anything worth experiencing. Life can be bigger than the confines of the society you were raised in."

"I've noticed that." And honestly, she felt she was better for it.

The door suddenly cracked. "The church is at the other end of town, gypsies." Without their pins, the doorman wouldn't open the door for them.

"We are Illuminists. Navigators."

Bion stuck his foot inside the doorway, wincing when the man tried to close it. "We were shanghaied by Helikeians and need assistance."

Sophia wasn't sure if the doorman believed Bion or not, or if it was just pure response to the authority in Bion's tone that made the man pull the door open. Bion didn't bother to discuss the matter further. He crossed the threshold with a determined stride, taking her with him.

"I need to see your Chief Guardian immediately." Bion was already moving down the hallway looking for the office. "Where is he?"

"Another two doors down, but you shouldn't go in there just now..."

Bion didn't listen. His grip remained firm around

Sophia's wrist as he headed straight for the door to the Guardian's office. He applied a quick rap with his knuckles before opening it.

"I told you. I ain't no Helikeian. I was shanghaied. It's the truth," a man argued. He was facing the Chief Guardian and didn't turn around.

"Who are you?" the man behind the desk demanded. He was an older man with spectacles perched on the end of his nose. His face was lined with wrinkles and his waistcoat was ten years out of date with worn patches at the tops of the pockets.

"I am Captain Bion Donkova. This is Miss Stevenson, Navigator trainee. We require immediate assistance."

"Captain Donkova, I am conducting a very sensitive investigation into the pirate attack upon one of our vessels."

"If it was the Crown Jewel, I can provide you the details of the matter."

The Chief Guardian stiffened and the man facing him turned. Sophia gasped, recoiling as she recognized Mr. Graves.

"Oh, they know right enough, since they were on the pirate ship that done the deed." Mr. Graves had abandoned his shipboard attire in favor of something that looked almost respectable and he pointed a finger straight at them. "They are pirates. It was these two who put an end to your son."

"This man is a member of the pirate crew." Bion didn't have any difficulty standing up to him. He stalked across the office toward Graves. "You really believe you can accuse us?"

Mr. Graves didn't back down. "You've got gall,

I'll admit that, for thinking you could get away with pushing the Guardian's son over the rail. Poor bloke was only twenty-six."

"We were escaping when that happened," Sophia interrupted.

"See? See there?" Mr. Graves shook his head. "She admits it."

"Of course she does," Bion snapped. "And it was your finger that pulled the trigger of the rifle that shot him. As Illuminist members, we'll be happy to make a full report of what happened aboard the Soiled Dove and your part in it."

"Enough," the Chief Guardian shouted. "For all I know, you are all in league with the Helikeians."

Sophia jerked around to argue with the man but the words never crossed her lips. Tears glistened in his eyes, but he drew himself up stiffly as grief clearly tormented him. "I will send for a Marshal."

Bion slowly grinned. It was a menacing expression and one he aimed at Mr. Graves. "I look forward to it."

Mr. Graves lost some of his color but he began blustering to cover it. "So do I. Why I've got plenty to tell and don't you think I won't."

"In that case, we shall make sure all three of you are here for the occasion," the Chief Guardian decided. He pressed the earpiece covering his right ear and the door to his office opened. Several muscular men entered, their stiff composure making it clear they expected to act as jailers.

Bion moved back toward Sophia, reaching out for her wrist. She offered him her hand instead. He cut her a surprised look before the Guardians led them down the hallways to a section of rooms. Unlike the London Solitary Chamber, this one had no gates to make it harder to escape from. Only a pair of Guardians stood guard.

Bion's fingers tightened on her hand. He looked back at Mr. Graves as he was escorted into a room across the hallway and then back at the two Guardians on duty.

"That man is a Helikeian pirate. I insist that he be better secured."

The Guardian escorting them pointed through an open door. "He will be."

There was an ominous promise in his tone that perplexed Sophia until she followed Bion through the doorway. The chamber wasn't really a room; it was more like a prison cell. Beyond the wood-paneled hallway was a room constructed of stone blocks. She felt the chill immediately, making it clear that the stone was thick enough to not warm during the early summer days.

A rattle of chain interrupted her study of the walls and her inattention proved costly. One of the Guardians had snapped an iron manacle around her wrist before she realized his intention.

Bion wasn't so easy to subdue. He flung away the Guardian who was foolish enough to try and shackle him. The man hit the floor but was back on his feet a second later. Bion was ready for him and his comrades.

"Well now," the Guardian cooed like he was trying to calm a spooked horse, "here I thought you were worried that we didn't know how to secure things."

"Sneaking up on me isn't a wise idea," Bion answered, his tone lacking any hint of apology.

The Guardian wiped a handkerchief across his lower lip and scowled at the bright red stain left behind. "I've a mind to let the boys drag you down the hall. You're big but you're outnumbered sure enough."

"I am also a captain," Bion declared firmly. He sounded as if he were on the bridge of an Illuminist ship, attired in a freshly pressed uniform, instead of in a stone prison with chains set into the mortar.

"That hasn't been proven yet," the Guardian argued.

Bion stepped up so that he was looking down at the man. "Nor has it been disproven."

The Guardian weighed Bion's threat and it was clearly a warning. Sophia could practically taste it. Tension filled the room as the moments felt like they were stretching. She set her teeth into her lower lip, horrified by the concept of being separated. She jerked away from the chain binding her, the iron links clattering. The sound bounced off the stone walls with an eerie effect.

"You've got a point there." The Guardian waved his comrades back. "If you're telling the truth, you won't have a problem with me slipping this on you."

He held up the manacle, opening the twin sides of it for Bion to place his wrist into.

"An incorrect assumption." Bion moved away from the man, placing himself in front of Sophia. "Miss Stevenson is my trainee. I cannot perform my duty chained, nor would I ever leave her."

The Guardians waiting just beyond the door frame leaned forward. Bion grinned at them. He whispered something in Russian that made two of them swallow audibly.

The Guardian holding the manacle eyed Bion and the position he'd taken up between Sophia and her jailer. He finally nodded.

"That will be simple enough to prove, but if you open the door, my men will not be leaving until you're chained up like the lady." The Guardian stepped into the hall. The door shut with a firm sound before Bion chuckled.

"Have you taken leave of your senses?" Sophia demanded.

He was laughing so hard, he sat down on the bed the room was furnished with.

"Not that I'd blame you," she offered softly.

He stopped laughing and lifted one dark eyebrow. "I haven't lost my mind, just the burden that has been weighing me down since I was informed you were missing."

She jerked her arm up so that the chain rattled. "I do not call this being free from burden."

He reached down and grasped the chain that was attached to her shackle. He tugged her closer, using both hands to pull the chain.

"I had thought chaining you to my bed in London was a fine idea, and I must confess—" She was forced to move toward him and ended up between his spread knees. He stood up, hooking an arm around her waist. "The fact that we are not in London doesn't matter. We are back in a Solitary Lodge, hence my satisfaction."

"You're talking nonsense—"

Bion smothered her argument beneath a kiss. She hadn't realized how desperate she was for his kiss. In fact, she was starving for it. Bion was just as ravenous, cupping her nape to ensure his mouth might plunder hers. He claimed her mouth, pressing her lips apart as though he owned her.

She wanted to contest that claim, needed to show him that she was his equal. She had no desire to understand her emotions, only to act upon them. With a soft snarl, she trailed kisses along his jaw and onto his neck. His skin was hot beneath her mouth and smelled undeniably male. The scent was intoxicating. It swept logical thought aside as she tore at the buttons on his vest to open it. Once done, she pushed his shirt aside to kiss more of his bare skin.

Bion caught her, pushing her back. She hissed at him, earning a chuckle.

"That sound makes it seem I'm in danger of being seduced by you, sweet Sophia."

He pulled his clothing off, the sound of tearing cloth proving how eager he was to be at her disposal.

"Since you enjoy being a pirate so much, maybe I want to be your Grace O'Malley." She opened her dress but couldn't take it off because of the shackle. Bion reached for the scarf she'd covered her hair with and sent it fluttering to the floor. He combed his fingers though her hair, grinning with wicked anticipation, then grasping it firmly. He controlled his strength, stopping just shy of causing her pain. There was a gleam of enjoyment in his eyes that touched off a strange reaction inside her. It was a form of enjoyment that she never would have guessed she'd experience from rough handling. It was sharp and intense, fanning the flames of need flickering in her belly. His strength impressed her and part of her liked knowing that he was stronger.

But that didn't mean she wasn't in the mood to prove her own worth to him. She reached forward, boldly stroking the front of his pants. His cock was hard behind the worn wool, and she stroked it several times while his lips curled up to show her his teeth.

"I find myself intrigued by the idea of you abandoning your ladylike demeanor."

She grasped the waistband of his pants and opened them swiftly. One of his dark eyebrows lifted. "And I never truly considered just what sort of skills you might have learned in your father's tailor shop."

She pushed the sagging britches over his lean hips and they slithered down his legs. "It was quite the family secret." She pushed him back and he sat back down on the bed. On some men, it might have been a submissive position, but not Bion. He spread his knees, his cock rising hard and promising from his groin as he watched her with roguish delight.

"No lady should understand the mechanics of a gentleman's wardrobe?" he asked mockingly.

"Of course not," she answered.

He reached forward and teased the swells of her breasts where they rose above her corset, then slid his hands down her sides. She had only a moment to lament the loss of his touch against her bare skin before he pressed the sides of her corset inward and the busk fasteners popped opened. Her breasts were free and Bion eagerly cupped them now that nothing covered them.

"Knowing the mechanics of clothing can be very useful."

He slid one arm around her waist to draw her close. The other hand cupped one breast and held it steady for his lips. She gasped, never realizing just how hot a kiss might feel. Against the soft, pink skin of her nipple, it was scorching. Bion sucked the entire point into his mouth, drawing on it, then teasing it with his tongue. Her clit throbbed with need as she suddenly became a prisoner to it. It was that intense. She was certain she would have denied him nothing so long as he satisfied her desire.

The other side of her desperation sent her reaching for his cock. Once her hand was wrapped around it, he stiffened, releasing her nipple with a little popping sound, then arching his head back. The single lamp in the room was turned to the lowest setting to accommodate their eyes, but she could clearly see the corded muscles along his neck and jaw—the sort of reaction he normally inflicted upon her, the gnawing need that overshadowed everything else so clearly evident in his body.

And she very much wanted to make him twist with it. Memory stirred and she knelt between his spread thighs. She heard him draw in a breath but didn't look up. She stared at his cock and felt her cheeks warm. It seemed rather odd to realize that she didn't really know what this part of his body looked like. The skin was smooth and hot, the head of it crowned with a ridge of flesh that circled it and directly on top was a slit. She stroked it, marveling at the texture of the skin.

"Sweet Christ," he whispered.

She lost the battle to control the urge to look up at his face. He was watching her, hunger flickering in his eyes. She maintained eye contact as she worked her hand up and down his length. His eyes narrowed. For a moment the man she so often battled with appeared, the part of his nature that wanted to be her protector, her mentor, and was always devoted to duty. She stroked his cock again and again, searching her memory for the information she'd glimpsed only once in the London Solitary Chamber library.

From a book of erotic arts.

There had been many volumes from all over the globe. Asian, Indian, and more, and all of it had made her blush. What she wanted to know was, would it reduce Bion to the same state he'd put her in, inside the gypsy wagon?

She opened her mouth and licked the slit on the top of his staff.

"So you did find that section of the library. I wondered…"

His voice was strained, his control compromised. The sound fed her confidence. It was amazing how empowered she felt. There wasn't a hint of the revulsion the matrons had so often hinted went hand in hand with marital duties. Instead, she opened her mouth and took the entire head of his cock inside without even a shudder. He made a sound that was deep and husky. She took more of his length into her mouth, lowering her head and then pulling it back up until his cock was free.

Bion's hands were fisted on the edge of the bed, his fingers crumpling the bedding. She closed her eyes and took his cock back between her lips. She was as lost in the moment as he was, her attention on the sounds he made as she licked and sucked. The portion of his length that didn't fit inside her mouth, she stroked with her fingers before grasping it with both hands and pressing all the way down to the base as she lowered her head. He jerked, snarling as if fighting against something. His cock was becoming harder, the slit producing a salty drop of fluid before he captured her hair and pulled her head away.

"Let go, Bion."

He leaned over and kissed her hard and fast, then he stood up and pulled her along with him. "I'm a pirate, remember? I take what I want, and right now, that is you, my sweet."

His voice was hard and unyielding. Just like his body. She wanted to melt against him, the need inside of her making her weak. Bion didn't give her the chance. He turned her away from him, the chain rattling as he caught one of her ankles with his foot and spread her legs apart.

"Chained and bound for my pleasure… a pirate's feast to be sure."

"I'm your lover—"

A soft swat landed on her bottom, popping loudly in the stone-walled room. Bion pressed her body over, until she laid her hands against the bed to support herself.

"What you are is *mine*."

Yes. It was more than a word; it was an emotion that swept through her. She felt suspended inside it, like being in the center of a wave. Everything was crashing around her, the unseen place in the middle an unexpected haven. Even if it was going to crush her, she still longed to stay in its grip.

"And I plan to take what is mine."

He grasped her hips, his grip sending a spike of hard need through her belly. It was carnal, even if her knowledge of the word was limited. She knew it in that moment, would have sworn that she tasted it as the head of his cock burrowed between the folds guarding her entrance. He held her tightly, keeping her as his possession while pushing his cock deep into her body.

She'd never felt so connected to another human being—never needed to strain toward one as she did at that moment. The sensation was clawing at her, making it impossible to not fight against the grip that held her in position.

"Mine, Sophia," Bion snarled at her. "To take as I please."

Arrogance coated his words as he worked his length in and out of her all the while holding her still for his ravishment. She gripped the bedding, her fingers curling into talons as she used it to give her something to push off of. At last she defied him, moving backward into his next thrust. Satisfaction rippled through her as she let out a contented sigh of achievement.

"You really are a pirate wench," Bion scolded her. "Never content to do as I tell you."

He was breathing hard and she was straining toward him. The bed cracked and the chain rattled, but she didn't care if every single occupant of the ancient building heard them. All that mattered was meeting his next thrust.

"I'm not your wench," she insisted. "I'm... Grace O'Malley... your counterpart."

Bion growled and pulled free. He scooped her up and tossed her onto the bed. She bounced in a tangle of limbs, her shackled arm falling heavily to the surface of the mattress.

"I'm going to make you scream."

His voice was savage but when he joined her, she found herself once again delighted by the harsh edge of the moment. He'd seduced her gently before, but tonight she was too consumed by need to be sweetly satisfied. She wanted his weight and wrapped her thighs around his hips when he pressed her down beneath him.

"And I am going to hear you cry out, Bion Donkova."

He thrust hard and deep into her body, the bed rocking beneath them. Sophia lifted her hips, straining to take every last bit of his length. Pleasure knifed into her, sharp and hard. When he withdrew, her muscles gained only a moment of relaxation before she was rising up to meet the next plunge and then the next. She cried out, unable to contain the pleasure inside her. Each thrust pushed her closer and closer to the edge of insanity. She clawed at him, somehow not feeling close enough to him.

She did scream, the sound torn from her as the pleasure crested and tumbled down over her. It turned her over and over, tumbling her in what felt like an endless moment of rapture. She couldn't move, couldn't relax her viselike grip on her lover. Bion snarled and bucked. He groaned with his release, the sound harsh and savage. Deep inside her passage, his seed set off a second eruption of delight. This time it was duller but no less breathtaking. She lost her grip on reality, floating along in a bubble of contentment that was so warm, she had no idea when Bion rolled off her. He lay next to her, breathing heavily as she tried to calm her racing heart. Every inch of her felt too hot.

Bion moved at last, rolling onto his feet and pushing the bedding aside. She rolled toward him, kicking at the coverlet until she had the cool feeling of the sheet against her skin. Her lover joined her, laying along her back and trapping her feet between his ankles. He nuzzled at her neck, placing soft kisses there before settling her head beneath his chin.

"The matter will be sorted out within the week."

Mr. Graves nodded to the Guardian as the man left the room. Since he'd been living on an airship, the place looked like a palace. He lifted his arms, stretching them out wide and turning around simply because he could, but the chain locked around his wrist kept him from completing a full circle. He glared at the manacle, bringing it closer to his face to inspect it. He was so close and yet still an eternity away from freedom.

What a piece of bad luck.

He scanned the room, searching for things to use to escape the shackle. He was no stranger to fate turning her ugly side on him. No, sir, he was not. He sat down and pulled the lamp closer so that he had a good view of the lock. Fate had dealt him more than one losing hand over the years, but he'd always managed to stay alive. Escaping the Soiled Dove had been something he'd thought beyond his doing and yet he'd done it. Now, there was just one more shackle to overcome.

He'd find a way.

⌘

"Did you hope I had found that section of the library?" She must truly have lost her wits to ask such a thing, but the question tumbled out of her mouth while her brain was still hazy with satisfaction.

Bion choked and tried to cover it with a poor attempt at a cough.

"Are you actually shocked, Captain?" she scolded softly. "How very un-pirate-like."

"Pleasantly shocked, which is very much in keeping with the roguish code of the lawless." He cupped one of her bare breasts. "Yet I confess, I enjoy the differences between us."

"You would prefer me always beneath your authority."

He blew out a hard breath. "Must you always balk against it? My position is something I've earned."

"And now you are a Navigator completely," she whispered. "You must be happy about that."

He shifted and stroked her cheek gently before answering. "As opposed to your own feelings about your transformation?"

"You needn't sound as though I was acting ungrateful." But her cheeks still heated with a guilty blush. "I'd never even heard of such a thing before that day."

His fingers detected the heat, tapping gently against the spot that was turning scarlet. She shook her head, trying to wiggle away from him, but he locked her in place. Her emotions were unfurling inside her, completely disobedient to any sort of self-control.

"Let me up, Bion."

"No."

His tone lacked the arrogance she was accustomed to hearing when he was issuing commands. It made it no less of an order. She heard the expectation of obedience clearly.

"I mean it. Let me up so I can dress."

He rolled her onto her back instead and kissed her. It wasn't as hard of a kiss as he'd given her when they had been consumed by passion, but she tried to turn her head away. He followed her, covering her lips with his until need bubbled up again. Desire was slower this time, their coupling less frantic, and when pleasure broke over her, she surrendered to the need to simply sleep without deciding how she felt.

Because she very much feared she was losing her heart to a pirate.

❧

Sergey held his hand out, waiting for his payment. The man in front of him carefully counted out the amount agreed upon, double-checking before giving it over. Sergey didn't linger, didn't wait for the man to begin tapping out a message on the telegraph machine. It was better to leave before anyone noticed he was there. He wasn't the only man who sold information and he didn't need anyone knowing he had money. People liked to find reasons to ask for gold when they knew you had some.

The man who had paid for the information smiled when the door to his tiny shop closed. Sergey was a simple man, one who had no idea how important the information he'd discovered was. He turned and opened a large book, looking through it at the messages that had come in during the last few days. Yes, Sergey had brought him something very useful, and he didn't really care who acted upon the information first because he was going to sell it to everyone interested. The battle between the Illuminists and Helikeians was not his; it was simply a situation to profit from.

⌖

"The master is busy."

The moans coming from beyond the arched doorway left no doubt as to what Jordon Camden was busy doing. A wispy, gauze drape was pulled across the opening, but when the pigeon keeper stepped in front of it, he could see right through to the interior of the harem. He had good reason to be there, but his palms were clammy as he took a moment to steady his nerve.

The master didn't like to be interrupted, and his mood was always poor when he was taken away from his sport.

The pigeon keeper cursed his bad luck. He peered through the curtain, hoping to catch the master after he had obtained a peak. Jordon Camden was on his back, a redheaded beauty riding him hard. Her face was twisted with need, her breasts bouncing as she rode. She let out a high-pitched sound as she climaxed, but the master only shouted with victory.

"He likes to best them in the battle of wills," the guard explained. "Likes to make them work to unman him."

The pigeon keeper felt his hands shake as the master stood up and displayed his rampant cock.

Bad luck, but there was nothing for it. He had to take the message to him immediately or Jordon Camden would be even more displeased. He brushed the curtain aside and walked into the harem, keeping his eyes off his master's pets.

"What do you think you are doing?"

The pigeon keeper simply held out the message. Jordon snatched it from his grasp and read it quickly.

"I must depart, my lovelies."

There were cries of disappointment.

"Amuse yourselves with the pigeon keeper for as long as the man lasts."

There was laughter and the pigeon keeper looked up, startled by his master's words. Jordon Camden was pleased and patted him on the shoulder, then left him to the menagerie of females. If they were surprised by their master's words, they didn't show it. None of them hesitated to do exactly as they had been bidden.

His luck had changed for the better. Much better.

Jordon Camden ignored his cock. It was simply a matter of discipline. The message in his hand was worth money, a great deal of it. He sat down in his office and considered the information before writing out another message to Dr. Nerval and Captain Aetos. His informant in Russia had done a good job. His pigeon master was enjoying his pets as Jordan walked out to where the birds roosted. He selected the birds he needed and placed the messages in their pouches. No one was allowed to know everything about his network, not even the pigeon master. Jordon set the birds free, watching them flap away with a satisfied grin on his lips.

❧

"It simply wouldn't be proper."

Decima tilted her head to one side and the telegraph operator gazed longingly at her exposed neck. For a moment, she allowed him to think she was offering herself to him before she looked back at him and fluttered her eyelashes.

"Of course, you have your duty…" She let her voice lower until the man was leaning forward to catch her words. "I would never ask, except that my mother is so very upset. She's thinking the worst, you see."

The operator cleared his throat and looked around the deserted office. He hastily scribbled down a message and folded the paper before sliding it across the desk to her.

"I couldn't very well sleep if I thought your mother was upset in such a fashion."

Decima fluttered her eyelashes again, then left the office with a sweep of her skirts. She made her way down the sidewalk and around the corner to where Lykos was leaning against the building. His posture was deceptive, as was his rough clothing. She walked past him without stopping, and on to the Solitary Chamber three blocks away.

"You had that poor bloke ready to polish your boots."

Decima looked up from the message the telegraph operator had given her. "It seems only fair that he should have enjoyed it. I am certainly pleased with my end of the transaction." She held out the message. "I do believe we have found our two Navigators."

"Two?"

Decima nodded. "It would seem there is much more to this tale."

Lykos read the message twice. "So it would appear, but I rather suspect we are not the only ones looking for our comrades."

Lykos abandoned his teasing demeanor. He was a fierce Guardian and it was moments such as this that Decima was reminded of it. There was a hardness in his blue eyes that warned of just how deadly he might be in defense of the Order and those few men he called friends.

She was not sure if that dedication would be enough. The circumstances were grim. Russia was a backward country, and the czar made his own laws. More and more Solitary Chambers were being abandoned because the czar was cracking down on the Order, and members didn't want to remain inside a country that was still clinging to serfdom. It wasn't the first time the Illuminist Order had left an area due to mankind's greed. Decima doubted it would be the last. The only thing she feared was the all-too-grim fact that she trusted that Bion would perform his duty—even if it was to end Sophia's life to keep her from falling into Helikeian hands.

"We have little time," she said, but Lykos was already heading down the hallway.

❧

Sophia stirred and frowned. Her head ached and she was almost positive it would be easier to notice how many places *didn't* hurt as opposed to how many that did. She stretched her foot and let out a little sound of discomfort.

"I could not agree more."

Her eyes flew open and she jumped. Bion grunted when her head smacked his chin. But he caught her before she went rolling over the edge of the bed.

"There's no need to worry that your father is going to burst in on us." He made sure she was steady before sitting up and stretching.

Sophia was fascinated. She was certain she should have looked away, but the opportunity to study him was just too rare.

Admire him, you mean.

Well, yes. All of the things she'd always been told should endear a man to her didn't seem to matter when compared to the simple reality of what Bion was. Songs spoke of fair features and merry eyes, but she found herself absorbed by the way his upper torso moved. He'd always struck her as a powerful man in uniform, but there was something very intimate about the way seeing him in nothing but his skin made her feel.

Breathless.

She rolled over and stood up. The room was cast in shades of gray. There were two windows set up at head level. Outside, the sky was covered in dark clouds.

"With that storm brewing, there will be no Marshal arriving."

Sophia tried to smooth out her clothing. The skirt was crumpled from having slept in it. The chain rattled as she moved.

"We need to get you out of that chain."

"I thought you enjoyed having me bound."

He was up and getting into his discarded trousers. "I did. I find immense satisfaction in knowing exactly where you are while I am sleeping. The night was far more restful."

She propped her hands on her hips and pouted. "That isn't very nice. I do believe I would be far more sympathetic if our roles were reversed. You make it sound as though I am an errant child."

"I believe I have taken ample notice of your womanly attributes." He reached for his shirt and shrugged into it as she considered his words. "But your stubbornness tends to keep me awake."

"What do you mean by that?" she asked. A little warning bell was trying to get her to drop the subject, but her pride just wouldn't let it go.

Bion offered her a piercing look. There was no relenting in it and she recognized it very well.

"Becoming an Illuminist means I don't have to follow all the silly rules of always staying in the parlor until some grand gallant takes me out for a stroll. Don't tell me to stand up and face your training challenges and then insist that I sit about waiting for an escort the rest of the time."

"Being a Navigator sets you in a rare category, which means you should not place yourself at risk."

She raised her chin. "Is that so?"

"It is," he insisted in a tone that grated on her nerves.

"You might want to be careful, Bion Donkova. You're a Navigator now, so the rules you are imposing will bind you too."

His eyes narrowed. "Hardly. I am not helpless."

She gasped. "Neither am I. Why, I've protected you as much as you have me."

He didn't agree with her. She could have screamed out of frustration but shook her head instead.

"Don't shake your head, Sophia. We owe a great deal of our success to luck. Maybe now you will understand why I insist on certain things. I'd appreciate it greatly if you didn't place me in the position of knowing it's my duty to take your life because you fail to take proper precautions."

The chamber went silent.

"Don't look stricken. Would you really want to end up a member of the Soiled Dove's crew?" Bion looked like he wanted to curse but his gaze remained unwavering. The man didn't know how to allow his feelings to interfere with his actions.

She was a fool to even toy with such an idea.

She shook her head and turned away. He followed her, the sight of her back impossible to bear. But the door opened before he could touch her.

"I would say good morning but from the sounds coming from inside here, you are not having such a good morning." The Guardian shrugged. "But I must admit that I am happy to hear you, for it seems our other guest departed during the night."

"Mr. Graves is gone?" Sophia asked.

"I warned you he was a Helikeian," Bion snapped.

The Guardian removed a key from his vest pocket

and fit it into the manacle locked around Sophia's wrist. There was a metal scraping sound as it released.

"It does look that way." He replaced the key and gestured toward the doorway. "We do not have enough personnel here to set a night watch. He's made good on his escape plans."

The market was busy. Mr. Graves listened to the sounds as the merchants opened their stalls for the day. People were already inspecting the fresh produce and haggling over the prices. Maids walked by with baskets on their arms and freshly pressed aprons. Some of them had young boys following them to help carry away what would no doubt end up as some rich man's supper.

There was plenty of noise, horses, chickens, and children. He picked out the easy openings to steal something to eat, but for some reason, didn't act on any of them. For the first time in a very long time, he didn't have anyone to impress or please—only himself—and he smiled as he realized the next steps he took would be entirely up to him.

No more worrying that he'd be tossed over the rail if he didn't please someone. Even his rumbling stomach didn't dampen his mood. He moved through the market, enjoying the scent of fresh baking bread.

"You there." Graves looked up and found a plump merchant pointing at him. The man's arm was wrapped in fabric and bound to his chest in a sling. "You look hungry, sailor," the merchant continued. "I need a pair of able arms to unload the wagon. Do it quickly and you eat your fill."

He needed food to live, but somehow, the offer sounded much better than that—better than anything Aetos had offered him. Graves touched the brim of his cap before climbing up onto the wagon. He'd almost finished when the sound of approaching hooves grew loud. People scurried out of the way as two columns of mounted men rode through the market without a care for anyone. Their uniforms were buttoned to their necks and each man wore a polished helmet. The horses they rode were fit for battle.

"Someone is going to have a bad day," the merchant remarked. "Prince Afanasi always gets what he wants and he has the men to make sure he is never disappointed."

❧

The Head Guardian wasn't very apologetic. In the kitchen of the Solitary Chamber, he sat down to eat around a long table where two women were serving up the first meal of the day. There was no eating hall, no other tables. There were also less than twenty people in the room.

"Is this your entire membership?" Sophia asked as she passed a plate of morning biscuits to Bion.

The Head Guardian nodded as he swallowed what was in his mouth. "Maybe you understand the need for the shackle a little better?" He poured fresh milk into a cup from a pitcher. "There are few freemen here and many of our membership have left for countries that have outlawed serfdom."

"It seems like more than a few," Bion remarked.

The kitchen seemed quiet, as though the entire

building understood how empty it was. Sophia shivered, feeling like she was sitting at the bedside of an old man as he drew closer to his final moments. Everyone at the table had a look in their eyes that reminded her of a family gathering to await the death of their patriarch. There was no energy, no bright faces looking forward to the day, as she'd seen in London. Here, they were just holding on.

"I'm surprised you are still here," she muttered.

The two women at the hearth turned from where they were tending the pots on the hearth to look at her. Hope was flickering in their eyes until their head Guardian squelched it.

"We will not abandon our posting," he said in a firm voice. "We are Russian Illuminists. Proud of our dedication to the Order."

"You mean you will not ask to be relocated," Bion countered. "Or admit that this location is not performing the true function of a Solitary Chamber."

The Head Guardian turned red. He flattened his hands on the surface of the table, opening his mouth to draw in a deep breath. "Now, see here—"

"I see very well." Bion sliced through the man's outburst with a razor-sharp tone. "I see you being too proud to take a position at another Solitary Chamber where you might not be the Head Guardian. The Order is about the preservation of knowledge and the furtherment of education."

"Which is in good order here."

Bion shook his head. "I doubt it, and I am going to make sure the matter is investigated. By maintaining your position, you have placed all the members under your authority in jeopardy. The books in your library could easily be stolen since you do not have the Guardians to protect them."

"No one here is in any danger and no one outside the walls even knows of our vast collection of books," the Head Guardian argued, but Sophia was busy watching the women behind him. They nodded in agreement with Bion, relief shimmering in their eyes.

"I disagree." Bion stood up. "Had I known how few members you had last evening, I never would have allowed my charge to sleep here."

He reached out for Sophia, surprising her by offering her his hand instead of grasping her wrist. She placed her hand in his without thinking, too stunned by the fact that he was granting her a choice. Her chair skidded back but just then someone pounded on the front door.

"Open up in the name of the prince!"

"Don't," Bion commanded.

The Head Guardian was already waving his men toward the door. "This is Russia. When the noble landowner demands something, we give it to him."

Bion pulled Sophia from the kitchen, searching for an exit. There was the sound of boots running down the stone hallways, but she didn't have time to decide if it was theirs or the men demanding to be admitted to the Solitary Chamber. The building was solid stone and the only door they found was locked with a thick chain.

"Stop there!"

Bion turned in a flash, shielding her with his body. Something snapped inside her, some emotion that made it impossible to let him protect her.

"I am your counterpart, Bion Donkova," she snarled, drawing a perplexed look from him. "And you're going to learn to respect that if I have to lock you in chains."

"You will come with me." The man wasn't really asking. He was staring down the barrel of a gun as his comrades leveled their own weapons at them. Her stomach knotted, but a strange sense of calm settled over her as well.

She'd endured this before and she'd rise above it again. They both would.

⚜

Lykos sniffed the wind and frowned. The sun had set long ago, but the horizon was glowing orange. However, it was still too early for dawn. According to his map, the Solitary Chamber where Bion and Sophia were was close. Which was welcome news. Lykos was sure he could happily face a solid month of not having to sit on a horse.

"Something's burning," Decima said. She lifted a pair of binoculars and looked through them. "Up ahead."

They rode on toward the village, the scent of smoke growing stronger. A large building was smoldering, its roof caved in. The heat of the fire had shattered the windows but the stone walls still stood, portions of them glowing red-hot from the fire that had fed greedily upon the contents of the building.

Lykos dismounted and climbed the stone stairs. Lying across them were the double doors that had once been mounted in the huge front entrance. The seal of the Illuminist Order was still visible.

"We're late," he said, his voice thick with emotion. "Too late."

"Not necessarily," Decima offered with a touch of hope that seemed misplaced amidst the wreckage. Lykos cut her a hard look that she returned. "We aren't too late if there aren't bodies inside."

Lykos nodded as he moved to look inside the building. There was still enough heat coming from the smoldering remains to burn his face. He had to back down the steps, furious at the delay in discovering whether or not Bion and Sophia were dead.

If they were, the delay wouldn't matter.

The need to know gnawed at his insides. Even a hint of possibility that they might still be rescued promised him a restless night. The sky was clear now, offering him no hope of a rain shower to expedite the matter. Which left him nothing to do but wait, though waiting was better than knowing for certain that his comrades were dead—even if he found that poor comfort.

Chains rattled for what must have been the hundredth time, the sound echoing through the lavish dining room. Sophia didn't bother to look at Bion; she knew that he was restless and didn't need to see his white knuckled fists to confirm how frustrated he was to be in chains.

You don't need to see it because you feel the same way.

That was a solid truth. Fate had an odd sense of humor at times because the frustration she had felt last night paled in comparison to what she felt now. Both her hands were clamped in shackles like Bion's. On either side of them were guards, both men holding guns on them.

They stood in a hallway, just inside a doorway that was open to a dining room, kept back like servants waiting on the master's whim. The room was lavishly furnished. A dining table with ornately carved legs was draped with a lace tablecloth. Its surface was set with fine bone china and silver flatware, which gleamed in the light. There were no candles in the room; the lamps used Deep Earth Crystals to produce light. Prince Afanasi seemed to enjoy Illuminist technology as much as he did pomp. The butler serving the table wore white gloves and a formal three-piece suit. His shoes shone and he made only the barest sounds as he waited on his master.

The Russian noble sat in a throne-like chair at the head of the table. His military uniform was covered in gold braids and there were numerous medals secured to it. Two servants stood beside him, their attention on his hands. All he had to do was lift a finger and they hurried to serve him. The man did not even pick up his own flatware. Instead, he lifted his hand and his butler placed it in his hand from a tray. The man never used soiled utensils.

Another servant passed by Bion and Sophia, her hands full with another dish to present to the master of the house. She curtsied the moment she stepped out of the hallway and twice more before offering the tart she held to Afanasi. Meanwhile, she and Bion stood waiting, their bellies empty while the scent of the meal being served made them even more aware of their hunger.

"We're nothing but chattel to him." She'd have been wiser to hold her tongue but couldn't seem to keep silent.

"Exactly," Bion spat softly. "Perhaps facing the reality of our circumstances will soften your judgment of my dedication to duty." There was a note in his voice that surprised her. Somewhere past the frustration and stubborn devotion to honor was an undercurrent of injury.

"I wasn't judging you, Bion."

He pressed his lips into a firm line and peered at her over the rims of his purple-tinted glasses. The man was a fully dedicated to his duty, and she realized she would have him no other way.

"Then why did you turn your back on me?"

It was there again, the note of injury. Heat teased her cheeks but she maintained eye contact with him.

"Because I realized if I truly wanted to be your counterpart, I would have to shoulder the same duty you do. I did not like the feeling of knowing I might have to harm you or that I have belittled the burden you carried in the past by not realizing that I am considered a commodity beyond the walls of the Solitary Chamber." His eyes were beginning to show the amber streaks now, the transformation continuing its course. "Or that I sentenced you to the same without asking you if you wanted it."

"Sophia—"

"Who is talking and disturbing my dinner?" Afanasi pounded his fist on the table. One of his servants whispered in his ear and he snapped his head about to look at the opening that led to where they were being forced to wait upon his leisure.

The two men guarding them made a slashing motion with their hands, but Afanasi slapped the table again. "Well, bring them in, since they cannot maintain their place while I finish my meal."

"You've done it now," one of the guards threatened in a low tone as he prompted them forward with his pistol.

"Better to be done with waiting," she insisted as she stepped into the dining room.

"I agree," Bion said.

She looked toward him, suddenly fearing that it might be the last conversation they had. It wasn't her own fate she feared but his. She felt as she had on the deck of the Soiled Dove, but now it was much stronger. It was no longer the simple desire to not see someone else harmed; this was a very personal emotion attached to Bion himself.

You're in love with him.

She didn't have time to argue with herself. The guards pushed her forward when she hesitated too long.

"The prince has called for you."

The Russian nobleman was drumming his fingers on the table. Sophia stared at his fingers, astounded by his arrogance. She was sure she'd never seen anyone so spoiled—except for perhaps Captain Aetos. A chill traveled over her skin as she realized how similar the two men were, as well as the circumstances they had thrust upon her and Bion.

"Closer," the prince insisted. "I need to see their eyes."

The guard made to push her forward but Sophia stood fast. "I do not need your assistance."

Afanasi frowned. "You were not given leave to speak in my presence and where is your curtsy?" He

looked at Bion, his face turning red as Bion refused
to bow.

One of the guards hit Bion on the head, but the
man had made a grave error. Bion lifted his leg and
sent an Asian back kick at the man. The guard went
rolling as the pistol fired into the air. A chunk of
plaster fell from the ceiling, making a dull thud as it
landed on the polished wooden floor.

"Insufferable!" The prince hit the table several
times like a child stomping his feet during a tantrum.
"I am a prince!"

"Which is the same as an earl in my country,"
Sophia informed him.

"And an earl may not put anyone in chains," Bion
finished with a snarl. "I am no serf."

For a moment, Afanasi looked like he might choke,
but he finally recovered himself and drew breath.
"Here, on my land, you are what I say you are."

Another chill shook her as she noticed just how
subservient those waiting on the man were. They
were all bowing, bent over and looking at the floor.
She could feel the tension in the air as every last one
of them tried to be invisible.

That fact told her everything she needed to know
about Prince Afanasi. The man was a bully and an
abusive lord. He ruled by fear and she would be
foolish to not understand she was at his mercy.

"Did you enjoy watching your Solitary Chamber
burn?" He smiled wickedly. "The czar distrusts
those who keep secrets. I am sure to be rewarded for
removing the blight from my land."

"Your czar is making ready to go to war over the

Ottoman question," Bion spoke up. "He'll have to promise the men who fight for him something and that something will be freedom. The days of serfdom are drawing to a close."

Rather than growing angry, the prince smiled once more. "The future is very far away and very much out of your reach." He stood up, the servant behind him hurrying to pull the chair out of his master's way.

There was a flurry of footfalls as more guards entered the dining room. Bion looked around, taking in their number as Sophia did. Horror clogged her throat as she recognized a very familiar look in Bion's eyes. She wasn't sure the man knew how to bend. It was noble and honorable, but often, those traits were recalled by others long after a man ended up dead for upholding his duty.

That thought ripped a jagged path across her heart. She clamped her stinging retort behind her teeth.

"Now," the prince continued, his tone restored to its full arrogance, "in spite of my czar's dislike of your Order's secrets, I myself find several things about you Illuminists very much to my advantage."

The guards moved, rushing Bion and clamping him in their hold. Bion resisted, struggling against them. Sophia gasped when the guards behind her grabbed her. There were simply too many of them to struggle against for long and it simply wouldn't gain them anything.

"You will be still," Afanasi ordered Bion. "Or she will suffer the consequences."

Sophia hissed, her temper flaring. Bion froze, only the rage burning in his eyes betraying his true feelings.

Now she'd seen the man bend and it brought her no happiness. Instead, she hurt even more to know she was his Achilles heel.

Afanasi grinned very much the way Grainger had. He stopped in front of her, cupping her chin and peering into her eyes. She shuddered, revolted by his touch. She strained against his hold on her, unable to master the urge. It was pure reaction.

The man moved on to Bion. His eyes gleamed and his lips curled back. Afanasi began to reach for his chin but stopped and only looked into Bion's eyes.

"I understand Navigators are worth quite a bit." The prince returned to his throne and took his time settling into it. Only when he waved his hand did his guards release them. Sophia rolled her shoulders, trying to erase the memory of their touch.

Bion merely cocked his head to one side. There was a loud pop from his neck as he sent a venomous glare toward Afanasi. "Return us to the Order and you'll be rewarded."

"I rather think you will fetch a far higher price on the black market." Afanasi lifted his hand and his servant placed his goblet in it. "I've already spread the word of your presence here. Tomorrow night, I am having a gala ball, and after I have shown you both off, you will be auctioned to the highest bidder. Take them away."

It felt like someone had kicked her in the chest. Drawing breath was impossible as she was dragged away. Bion snarled and she looked over her shoulder and saw that he was being dragged toward a different doorway. The separation was too much to bear. She struggled, finding strength she didn't know she had and using it to fling the guard holding her arm away. Her chains rattled as the man tumbled to the floor, but his comrades rushed at her to fill the spot he'd occupied. Bion struggled as well, but he was pulled through the doorway and beyond her sight.

It was very possibly the last time she would ever see him.

Seven

SOPHIA WANTED TO CRY. HER EYES STUNG WITH TEARS and even having her shackles removed didn't grant her any relief.

Stop acting like a child. If you're Bion's counterpart, devise a plan of action.

A plan would require information. She lifted her head and blinked away her unshed tears. She needed to discover where she was. The guards had taken her to the upper floor of the grand house. The lavish ornamentation wasn't confined to the dining room. The hallways were all afforded with gleaming wood flooring and the ceilings decorated with wood molding. The chamber she stood in had two parts. The outer room had couches and plush chairs for receiving visitors. There were glass-paned windows without a speck of dust on them and silk valances edged with tassel trim. Books lined one wall and even a phonograph sat on a side table. She couldn't resist trailing her finger along the edge of its large sound funnel.

Had it only been months ago that she and her

sisters had danced around after supper to the tunes played on the phonograph her father had bought them for Christmas?

"Would you like some music?" one of the maids asked. The women were so silent; Sophia hadn't noticed that there were four of them standing in various places just to wait on her.

Sophia shook her head. The woman frowned and wrung her apron. The worry in her eyes was disturbing. To have someone fearing her displeasure did not suit Sophia.

"Perhaps I might bathe."

The woman nodded, relief easing the tension on her face. She snapped her fingers at two younger maids who were standing near a closed doorway with their hands folded and their eyes downcast. They opened the doors, reveling a large bathtub. There was an old pump positioned near the tub to fill it with water.

One girl began to kindle a fire in the hearth that the tub was placed in front of. The other went to a large wardrobe and opened it. She pulled out a length of toweling and spread it on a warming rack. There was a jingle of keys as the maid who seemed to be in charge went to one of the drawers in the wardrobe and unlocked it. One of the younger girls was already behind her, waiting with a silver tray. The older woman placed a bar of soap on it and a silver brush.

There was a sizzle as a kettle was pushed over the fire. Orange flames crackled to life as one of the younger girls worked the pump to fill the tub with water.

They would certainly adore the Illuminist bathing facilities, but she doubted they would ever be allowed off the prince's land. Sophia pitied them and suddenly realized just how much she had allowed herself to overlook while missing her family.

A year was a long time until her novitiate was complete and she could contact her family. But the year would end and she would have her adventures too. The transformation of her eyes was a most wonderful thing and it was time she appreciated it.

It's time you figured out how to escape.

Or at least how to rejoin Bion. While the maids filled the tub and heated water, Sophia walked to the bedroom. A huge four-poster bed sat on a raised dais. Bed curtains were draped at each pole to be drawn once the occupant retired. She walked to the windows, which were open, but it was a sheer drop to the ground. Beyond the house, there was a huge green. White gazebos sat under trees and the entire estate was surrounded by a wall. It looked similar to the construction of the building that had been the Solitary Chamber. At the end of the main drive, there were two wide iron gates that were closed. Men sat nearby, clearly on duty to prevent uninvited guests from entering.

Or anyone tired of being Afanasi's property from leaving. Well, she was going to be leaving… *somehow*.

"Miss? Your bath is ready."

Sophia turned and realized the woman waiting on her might be her best resource. They knew the house and she needed to be free of the house before she could ever make it past the gates. But first she needed to find a way to get to Bion.

Somehow…

✎

"Brooding will not help."

Bion grinned at the man laying out formal evening attire.

"Neither will trying to sweet-talk me into dressing up for your master's little event."

The man straightened his lapels for what must have been the tenth time. He looked rather exhausted, which was a vast improvement over the confidence he'd had when he first arrived with his staff.

Bion shook his head. The men waiting on him had no concept of freedom. It would be impossible for them to understand why he was not happy with his current circumstances. It was a sad reminder of why he was proud to be an Illuminist, the core reason why he was so dedicated to the Order. Now, with his new sight coming in, he had more reason than ever to remain steadfast in his thinking.

There would be no auction.

He liked the sound of that idea but not the feeling of uncertainty that followed it. The room he stood in was guarded and on the third floor of the house. Some of Afanasi's men were patrolling the grounds beneath the windows and Bion still wore his shackles.

Difficult, but not impossible. At least that was what he was going to believe. Sophia deserved a better effort. She deserved a hell of a lot more than being sold. He would find a way.

"If you would please try on this coat, we shall see that it is fit to you for this evening's gala." The servant held out the coat, unknowingly offering Bion an opportunity.

"Someone will have to relieve me of these shackles first."

The servant paled, lowering the coat as he worked his mouth without any words coming out.

Bion pushed away from the wall he'd been leaning on and shrugged. The lazy gesture seemed to put the servant at ease. "I haven't worn decent clothing in too long." Bion held out his wrists, the chains dangling from the manacles locked around them. "But my hands won't fit with these chains on them."

The servant sniffed. "Yes, that is clear. Of course."

The man went to the double doors of the suite and opened them. The guards were still there and after a few muffled comments, one of them entered with a ring of keys.

Action, at last.

❦

Decima was in a hurry. Her steps echoed in the hallway as she rushed toward him. He picked out the way her hand was crushing the piece of paper she'd retrieved from the telegraph office and her teeth were worrying her lower lip. From Guardian Hunter Talaska, the emotional reactions were a red flag. His muscles drew tighter because he'd already been unhappy about having to rely on her. But there were times when Decima's gender produced more results than his. Just because the opposite was often also true, didn't ease his frustration.

"They are set to be put on auction tomorrow morning."

Lykos flinched.

"A Prince Afanasi has them and intends to hold an

auction," she explained. "What worries me the most is just who might be invited to the event, since our Order wasn't."

"At least we'll get a look at the scum on this side of the planet," Lykos remarked. "Because we will be attending."

He wasn't sure just how he was going to make that happen, but it wasn't the first time he'd beaten the odds.

~❧~

"The prince has been most generous."

Sophia looked up from the book she was reading as the head maid returned. The woman still hadn't introduced herself; that fact struck Sophia as sad because it was as if the woman didn't think herself important enough to be called by her name.

The prince was a spoiled brat. Like someone from the Middle Ages who had been raised to believe that they ruled by divine right. Being born into a noble family line didn't mean God had decided you were infallible.

You sound more like an Illuminist than a tailor's daughter.

She smiled, pleased with herself as a line of maids filed into the chamber until six of them passed by. They practically marched and never looked at her or anything else. They kept their attention on the person in front of them as they delivered a small collection of boxes before turning about and leaving.

"Yes indeed," the older maid continued. "The prince sent to the tailor for you and there is everything a lady should need for a ball."

"What is your name?"

The woman drew herself up, considering her for a moment. "Yaneta, but you are leaving soon, so it really doesn't matter."

It would have been easy to become offended, but Sophia noticed the pity in Yaneta's eyes. The maid clearly didn't care for what the prince had in mind for Sophia but was powerless to intervene. A chill traveled through her, attempting to steal away her confidence. Sophia brutally ordered herself to maintain her composure. Bion's stern orders came to mind, making her smile again as Yaneta began to open the packages and exclaim over their contents.

Like someone trying to distract a child—or dupe an innocent.

"A fine chemise. It will feel so nice against your skin, and there are three silk taffeta petticoats to hold out your skirt."

All the better to ensure she sold at a high price. She might refuse—her pride would certainly like her to—but Sophia chewed on her lip as she considered her options.

An Illuminist Navigator always weighted the situation carefully. Bion certainly did.

And she was his counterpart.

"You will make a very pretty picture in this silk brocade; all the men will rush to fill up your dance card," Yaneta cooed. "Many of the bidders will be attending; surely one of them will become smitten with you. That will not be so bad an arrangement."

Sophia could not have disagreed more. But Yaneta's prattling did bring to mind Bion and the fact that he was her lover.

"My heart could not bear it," Sophia said, "for it belongs to Captain Donkova."

"You shall have to forget him," Yaneta cautioned sternly. "You will fall in love again, with the man who takes you away in the morning. You are young; a young heart can heal quickly."

The expectation on the maid's face made Sophia pity the woman once again. She finally understood what Bion had been trying to teach her about fates that were worse than death. The firm belief in Yaneta's eyes that people could belong to others was sickening. It made Sophia's stomach churn and her temper flare. But it also made her frantic to escape ending up like the woman, and for that, she needed Bion at her side. Together, they would succeed and she would never leave him behind.

"I suppose if I am to be parted from him, I shall refuse to feel guilty about taking him for my lover. But I shall have to hope I am not with child, for it would never know its father."

Sophia looked down at the ruffle of one of the silk petticoats, but she was also watching Yaneta through her eyelashes. The maid didn't look startled by her words. Instead, a gleam entered her eyes and a tiny smirk lifted the corners of her lips before she turned and opened another package.

So the woman was duly reporting Sophia's every word back to the prince. Good. There was one thing Sophia might depend on and that was that the prince was a greedy man. Afanasi saw only her worth on the black market, so she would do her best to dangle the possibility of a third Navigator beneath his nose.

It was a slim chance, but it was just possible that the prince might decide to double his odds by letting Bion spend another night with her.

Slim. Very slim. Yet it was better than nothing.

❧

Russia might have been stuck in the past in some ways, but Prince Afanasi certainly knew a thing or two about hosting a gala ball. Yaneta and her staff set Sophia's hair perfectly, crowning it with fresh flowers and ribbons. The silk brocade dress had an organ-pleated skirt that the silk petticoats held out flawlessly. The bodice had a deep point and a small waist that fit well once she was tightly laced into the corset. There were small pleats going from her shoulders to midchest and just the right amount of cleavage was on display.

"Your gentleman will be enthralled by you," Yaneta cooed.

A maid set out a pair of sugar-heel shoes with a single strap over the top of her foot to keep the shoe in place while she danced. Sophia lifted the hem of her skirt and petticoats so she might fit her foot into one. It fit well, and the maid knelt down to fasten the strap.

The last thing Yaneta handed her was a set of long evening gloves. Once, Sophia wouldn't have dreamed of stepping foot outside her home without a pair on her hands, but that seemed a long time ago.

She recalled enjoying the feeling of Bion's skin against her own and a soft blush heated her cheeks. There was no shame in it now; instead, she enjoyed it as she turned and looked at her reflection. The dress was a summer-sky blue and it matched her eyes perfectly. In fact, it accentuated the amber streaks in her eyes. She picked up her glasses and set them in place, the light purple lenses something she enjoyed seeing on her face. Her lips curled up into a smile.

"The prince will be waiting."

Yaneta held out a cream dance card. A silk ribbon dangled from one corner. Sophia slipped it onto her wrist and heard the double doors open. The two maids who stood on either side of them stared at the floor. It was a blunt reminder of how the prince viewed the world and everything in it—including herself. It might crush her confidence if she allowed it to, but she lifted her chin and strode through the open doors. Satisfaction filled her as she descended the grand staircase. Below, the house was lit by Illuminist lamps, the Deep Earth Crystals filling the room with a soft, golden light that didn't offer any smoke to stain the ornately decorated ceiling.

The air smelled of flowers. There were greens and blossoms draped along the banisters of the staircase. Her petticoats rustled as she moved, drawing the attention of several men standing guard at the main doorway. They bowed to her and one extended his hand toward the back of the house. Sophia took a moment to look out the open front doors. Night had fallen and there were lanterns placed along the long driveway to welcome the arriving guests.

The guard moved, blocking her view with his body. Once again he extended his arm toward the ballroom.

She heard the music and could smell the scents of fine food, but it did not beckon to her as the night did—freedom.

But if she wanted it, she would have to outwit her captors. She'd done it once, which meant she could do it again. Would do it again.

At the base of the staircase, she turned and heard the delicate sound of crystal clinking. Conversation floated through the house as the musicians played. The doors to the ballroom were open and the prince was there to receive his guests—not standing as she might have expected, but once more the man was seated in his throne chair. It was set on a raised platform so that he was at eye level with those greeting him.

"Who gave her a dance card?" Afanasi complained. "She must be with her companion—sets sell so much better."

He looked her up and down with the same critical eye that one might use on a mare. He lifted a hand and indicated that she should turn around. Instead of annoying her, his commands amused her, so she turned and stopped in front of him as he offered her a satisfied smirk. She curled her lips back so he might see her teeth.

"Impertinent peasant," he sneered.

"If that is meant to imply that I am not anything like yourself, I accept the compliment."

Someone offered her a soft applause from behind. She turned to discover Bion closing the distance between them without a single tap coming from his polished boots. He was turned out in grand fashion, his vest a dark amber silk that also complemented his newly transformed eyes. He wore a dark overcoat that fit him superbly and a silk cravat was knotted at his neck. He looked over the rim of his purple-tinted glasses at her, a hint of amusement flickering in his eyes before he masked it.

"Try and escape and you will be shot by my men," the prince informed them. The butler standing behind him didn't even blink to indicate that he was startled by his master's words. "I assure you, there are ample men on duty. The people on my land know who their betters are and how to mind their places."

The hard tone of certainty in his voice irritated her beyond every lesson her mother had taught her on politeness being absolutely necessary no matter the circumstances. Somehow, she knew her mother would understand. She turned and offered Bion a curtsy.

"My dear Captain, might you possibly offer me escort? I find I am in desperate need of fresh air. It seems unbearably stuffy here, the company beyond stifling."

Bion bent at the waist and offered her his hand with all the polish of a gentleman. The prince grunted, managing to sound like an overgrown child.

"That was delightfully skillful, my dear," Bion remarked as they swept into the ballroom and the guests turned to look at them. "I doubt your mother taught such a skill, so I am left wondering just where you learned to insult with such grace."

"Fishing for compliments, sir?" She realized she was gripping his hand too tightly but couldn't seem to defeat the impulse to hold on to him. Had it really only been less than a day since she had watched him being torn away from her in chains?

Oh yes, her heart was upon her sleeve. Actually, she was sure she had already given it away to Bion.

"Do you think I crave kind words of praise any less than you do?" He spoke softly, but she heard something in his tone that sounded very much like the same emotion she felt. It may not be true, but it was better than focusing on the blunt details of her current situation. For the moment, she was dressed in her finest and on the arm of the most dashing man present. Being happy was within her grasp; all she had to do was choose to be so.

"I will be most happy to lavish you with praise tonight if you will indulge me by being my escort."

❦

"We may return for the auction tomorrow, but that is the best I was able to do. The guards weren't letting anyone not on their guest list through, no matter how good the bribe offered." Decima climbed into the carriage Lykos had been ordered to remain inside of with a huff. Her frustration matched his own and in a way made it possible for him to dispense with some of the tension that had been hounding him.

"You have employed far more charm than I ever might have and still we are defeated."

Decima shot him a chilling glance from her place on the opposite side of the carriage. The excessive volume of her skirts and petticoat made it necessary for her gown to be draped over his legs. Lykos stretched out his leg, brushing hers slightly.

"This is not the time for toying with me, Guardian."

Lykos used his cane to knock on the wall behind his

head. The driver instantly set the horses into motion. The carriage jerked and rocked.

"I disagree, Guardian Talaska. Toying with you will distract me from the rather primitive experience of riding in a horse-drawn carriage. At least we shall be able to end this visit to the backwaters by tomorrow."

"I don't like leaving here." Decima moved her leg away and looked out the window. She was studying the grounds, searching for a weakness.

"If you discover a way out, we should return in more suitable attire to wait there." Lykos became serious. "Because if there is a way out, my money says Bion will find it."

"No faith in you for Sophia?" Decima asked but didn't give him time to answer. "She might be just what Bion Donkova needs to assist him in an escape."

Lykos considered the view for a moment. "Because she might employ charm where Bion tends to forget that the lowest maid might be persuaded to grant mercy to the imprisoned if given a little attention? True."

Which was what made Decima a very effective Hunter Guardian. Lykos fought the urge to look at her. She was gowned in rich silk that complemented her emerald green eyes. The fabric puddled around her, making her appear as if she was rising from a garden pool like some fae maiden. She was delicate in appearance but what made her almost irresist-ible was the strength in her eyes. One never saw it until they were too close to escape. She was like a snow leopard—smaller than their counterparts but no less deadly.

"What time is the auction?"

"Sunset. Apparently, the prince likes to stretch his gala celebrations until nearly sunrise. So he won't be ready to conduct business until late in the day." She tapped her gloved fingers against her fan. "And yet the telegraph said it was dawn. I cannot help but be suspicious."

"So it seems we will have to remain watchful or risk having our Navigators sold out from beneath our noses."

                                       ~

"I do believe you are challenging me, Miss Stevenson."

She wasn't unaccustomed to Bion taking issue with her, but there was an amused twist to his lips that surprised her.

His eyes narrowed for just a moment when the musicians struck up a waltz and his grin became mocking. "Ah, the opportunity to prove myself."

"How so?"

Bion didn't answer her. He captured her hand and tugged her toward the dance floor. Years of lessons on etiquette kicked in and she glided along beside him without a single misstep. But her mind was full of doubts as he swept her into the flow of dancers. Her skirts whirled up as he turned her around and around. She looked over his shoulder and then across to the opposite side and back, as her dance teacher had taught her.

But for the first time she was tempted to look into her partner's eyes. As she passed the doorway, she caught a glimpse of a guard and there was no more hesitation. She locked gazes with Bion, uncaring of the gossip that might result. Let them see her fascination with him. What mattered most was allowing herself to savor the moment. It might well be her last one in his embrace.

But she wouldn't dwell on that now. No.

Instead, she enjoyed the feeling of his body next to hers, the hard power that seemed to flow from him. He might be dressed in finest silk and wool, but where her hand rested on his shoulder she felt the iron strength of his flesh. His eyes narrowed, the hand resting on the small of her back pulling her closer, as if he couldn't resist the urge either. Hunger flared in his eyes and she felt a blush teasing her cheeks. His attention dropped to her lips, the tender surface tingling with anticipation.

But the waltz ended, and the couples around them broke apart as they softly applauded. Bion blew out a breath before stepping back from her. Frustration nipped at her and she was certain she saw the same thing in his eyes. There wasn't much time for her to think about it because the musicians began a lively polka and Bion's lips twitched again into an amused grin. He caught her up in the rhythm, and they were sweeping across the polished dance floor once more.

"You doubted my expertise on the dance floor?"

The polka left her breathless; the corset was so tightly laced beneath her brocade bodice it restricted her efforts to draw in deep breaths. Bion didn't really need an answer; the man was quite clearly pleased with his efforts.

"True, I did doubt your ability to partner me."

He lifted her hand and raised it to his lips. For a

moment they were once again impossibly close, and this time, her lack of breath had nothing to do with the corset. The cause was the look in his eyes. It would be so simple to believe he was smitten with her.

"I'm accomplished in moonlight kisses along garden pathways as well. However, I doubt Afanasi's guards will be kind enough to allow me the opportunity to prove myself."

He kissed the back of her gloved hand and retreated to a respectable distance. It was only a single step, yet it felt like a vast canyon separated them. Drawing him back to her was the only thought in her mind.

"Now, that skill is something you have proven to me, Captain Donkova."

He frowned and slowly shook his head. "No, Sophia, I haven't, to my regret. There has been no sweet courting between us and that is my failing. Perhaps you will be generous enough to allow me to make the most of the evening, since it appears we shall be denied the garden."

He settled her hand on his forearm and began to walk her slowly around the room. A few gentlemen tried to step into their path and reach for her dance card but a scowl from Bion sent them away. She let herself become immersed in the moment, ignoring the guards stationed at every doorway. She refused to acknowledge anything except for the feeling of walking on the arm of the man escorting her.

❧

"I only want the woman," Captain Aetos urged. "And I need to be gone before their Illuminist brethren return. Accept my offer and auction the man tomorrow. It was my Root Ball that created him."

"The woman is more valuable than the man," Prince Afanasi countered. "She has confessed to being lovers with her trainer, which means there might be another Navigator growing inside her."

"I need a Navigator now; babies don't interest me," Aetos snapped.

"But they do interest me." A third man stepped from where he had been standing in the shadows. He ignored Aetos and offered the prince a formal bow. "The offspring of two Navigators is born with its parents' abilities. Once weaned, it could be raised to be loyal to the Helikeian cause."

Dr. Nerval peered through his spectacles at the couple at the other end of the ballroom. For the first time since he'd been forced to flee from Britain over the loss of his newly discovered Pure Spirit Janette Aston, he was excited. "By rights, it was my actions that helped create this Navigator. You should accept my offer for the female and let her spend the night with her lover again."

"You have no rights on my land that I do not give you," the prince insisted. "They will be auctioned tomorrow at midday. Now leave me to my guests and do not let my merchandise see you. I do not want my guests disturbed by their panic."

Aetos and Dr. Nerval didn't care for his orders, but Prince Afanasi smiled as his men stepped forward to ensure his will was done. That was as it should be. The prince's captain of the guard returned and bowed, obviously wanting to ask a question.

"Yes?"

The guard straightened. "We told the Illuminist members the auction was at sunset as you instructed."

Prince Afanasi stood up and descended from the platform his chair was positioned on. He stopped and allowed his valet to straighten his vest and help him into an overcoat. Only when his manservant had bowed did Afanasi answer.

"This auction is about more than gold. The Illuminists might be able to best the other bidders in that but not in connections. They hold to their Oaths of Allegiance too strictly for what I want."

"Then why tell them to return at all?"

The prince shook his finger at his captain. "Because, in business, it is always wise to keep your options open. Besides, I might decide to allow those Illuminists to pay me to tell them who has their Navigators after I have sold them to someone else. Jordon Camden is not the only one who understands the value of information."

Bion and Sophia caught his attention through the arched doorway of the ballroom. Many of his guests were turning to bow to him as he joined them, but Afanasi paused just outside the doorway. Sophia was smiling sweetly into the face of her escort, leaning toward him as he covered her hand where it rested on his forearm. The attraction between them was genuine and unmistakable.

Which of course meant he should capitalize on it. Dr. Nerval had a very good suggestion.

"Captain, I have a new instruction for you concerning my merchandise."

❧

Time escaped her.

Sophia didn't care, not a bit. But the world would not be ignored forever. Bion stiffened, alerting her to the end of their evening. She looked up to see six guards marching toward them. The few remaining guests looked on with curiosity but no one took exception.

"It seems our chaperones have taken notice of our familiarity." Bion spoke quietly.

Bion placed a kiss on the back of her hand as sedately as any suitor might have, but flickering in his eyes was pure hellfire. She laughed softly because it was better than allowing a sob to break free.

Later.

She sunk into a low curtsy as the guards surrounded her. It felt like a firing squad came to take her to her execution. Their impending separation was tearing a hole in her heart, but she lifted her chin. She was no coward. No, only a woman in love and she would cherish it.

Yaneta and her two maids waited just outside the ballroom. Sophia glanced at the large clock ticking slowly away in the hallway and found that it was just past midnight. Rather early for a gala ball to end, but there was a steady line of carriages pulling up in front of the main entrance. As she climbed the stairs, she watched footmen return wraps and overcoats to those making ready to depart.

It seemed the prince would not be hosting his guests in the numerous rooms in his large house. *Of course not, he's planning a flesh sale and couldn't possibly want witnesses to that.*

"Hurry now," Yaneta encouraged Sophia once she'd climbed to the top of the stairs. The maid seemed flustered and waved her forward. Yes, yes, better to be locked up before she made a run for it.

Sophia hesitated, looking behind her for Bion. It felt like a noose was tightening around her neck, the sensation destroying the delightful mood she'd enjoyed throughout the night. The double doors to the bedroom she'd dressed in were open, more burly guards standing ready in the hallway should she decide to resist. She walked past them and heard the doors close. The moment it did, the maids closed in on her.

Someone had started the phonograph and there were candles lit on the side tables. Sophia turned in a circle, taking in the details of the rooms and her nape tingled with suspicion. It looked like a scene set for seduction.

"Take the dress off her." Yaneta clapped her hands and pulled the flowers from Sophia's hair herself.

"What is the hurry?" she asked, but none of the women answered. They were all tense, as if they expected something was going to happen. Sophia turned away from their hands.

There was a knock on the door and Yaneta gasped. "We took too long," she lamented.

Sophia stared at the woman. The doors opened and Sophia hugged her partially opened bodice closed. The three women scurried toward the door, slipping out as the guards shoved Bion through it.

"I'll lock you back in shackles if you even turn the doorknob," one guard warned. The door slammed shut the moment the warning was issued. The sound echoed through the chambers, followed by the soft sound of Bion chuckling.

"What can you possibly be amused by?" she asked softly.

Bion walked toward her. "The fact that I am content to not meet that puppy's challenge because it would cost me your company."

His tone was dry and serious, but the compliment made her blush. "I see. Are you quite certain your reputation as a man of action shall survive?"

He stopped in front of her as her belly tightened with anticipation. He pulled his glove off, one fingertip at a time before tossing it onto a nearby table. With a gentle touch, he stroked her cheek. Sensation rippled down her body, raising gooseflesh.

"I believe I have been grossly mistaken on just what manner of action is more important." His second glove joined its mate. "And God forgive me, I know Afanasi is a calculating bastard, but I don't really care because his plans favor my own desires."

"Plans?" Her brain was having difficulty functioning. All she wanted to do was drown in the flood of sensation he inspired.

Bion shrugged and pulled his cravat off with a satisfied grunt. "I believe he wants to increase your value by being able to claim you might be carrying."

Her cheeks burned scarlet, but she smiled with satisfaction. "I told Yaneta we were lovers. I can't believe it actually worked." She rubbed her hands together, trying to think. "Now we can escape."

"Escaping this room isn't the challenge we need to overcome. It's getting off the grounds," Bion offered.

"Our best chance will be in the morning, when the kitchen takes deliveries of fresh supplies and the hounds have been called in."

"Hounds?"

Bion nodded. "My jailers were happy to share the details of how Prince Afanasi prizes his dogs. They are trained to hunt as pups and will run anything down at night. A rather helpful habit for keeping serfs on his land."

"That's ghastly."

Bion walked to the window and moved the curtain a small amount. He looked down, his expression focused. For once, she was happy to see it because it awakened hope inside her. He dropped the curtain. "So we are here for the night." He looked past her at the turned-down bed. "And here I thought for certain I would never thank that bastard prince for anything."

He shrugged out of his overcoat and her mouth went dry. It really was a foolish response, for they had been together before. But every inch of her skin was begging for release from her clothing, her senses heightened as he moved back toward her.

"Um… what are you doing?"

Bion's eyes narrowed at her question. He opened the first stud on his shirt and then another and another until his shirt was open.

"Disrobing." His voice was dark and edged with promise.

"You're toying with me," she decided.

Instead of the mocking smirk she expected, he cupped her chin and raised her face until their gazes locked. What she witnessed in his eyes mesmerized her. It was hotter and deeper than anything she'd ever seen before.

"The circumstances have provided me with the rather unexpected opportunity to prove the afore-mentioned Jonathon Saddler is not the only man who might seduce you gently."

"Jonathon never seduced me."

"And neither have I." He leaned down, sealing her lips beneath his. The kiss was surprisingly tender and soft. He didn't rush to press her mouth open but teased her with unhurried motions until she yielded of her own volition.

"But I should have," Bion offered softly against her ear. He inhaled the scent of her hair while stroking his hands down her back. She felt him tugging on the laces on the back of her bodice. They made the faintest sounds as they were pulled free and then he stepped back so he could pull the open garment down her arms.

"I've been very remiss in remembering you are a respectable woman, one who should have been enticed into bed with gentle words."

He turned her around, wrapping her in his arms. For a moment, he simply held her, stroking her neck with warm fingers. She shivered, feeling the wave of sensation cresting over her. She was eager for more. He settled his hand over her heart, feeling its accelerated rate.

"Words I am rather unaccomplished at saying." He pressed his hands against her sides to release the busk on the front of her corset. The metal closure snapped, allowing her to draw in a deep breath.

"I don't much care what you say, your actions please me quite well," she sighed as she drew in another breath and fought the urge to massage her breasts. "I've never been fond of tight lacing."

Bion dropped her corset. Sophia settled for rubbing her sides, where her waist had been constricted. Bion brushed her hands aside and took over the duty. She was sure that someone, somewhere would tell her no gentleman should perform such a task, but Bion was a pirate, so it was perfectly fine.

Better than fine. She let out a sigh and then something that was closer to a moan. His touch awakened the need inside her once more.

"And let us not forget these..." He cupped her breasts, the thin silk of her chemise offering little protection—not that she wanted any. No, she craved his skin against hers. Blunt, primitive, base, she really didn't care what upper society might label it. She pressed back against him, reaching for his thighs because standing still was impossible.

"Let us not forget that I consider myself your counterpart," she said. Sophia turned and reached for him. Her hand was small against his nape but that didn't stop her from pulling his head down so she might kiss him. She rose onto her toes, needing to prove that she might initiate as well as receive. This time the kiss was harder, and he responded in kind, his lips parting hers, then his tongue stroking the length of her own.

Pleasure tore through her. It was like a bolt of lightning and it left behind enough heat to make her frantic to be free of her clothing. The petticoats were stifling, and she reached for the hooks on the waistband.

Bion happily pulled one up and over her head once it was free. It crinkled when he tossed it aside, and he grabbed a second one.

"Are you in there?" he asked as he fought with the third petticoat.

"Yes," she answered, and a very soft giggle escaped from her lips. She slapped a hand over her mouth, horrified by the sound, but Bion merely raised an eyebrow at her.

"There is the proof that I've neglected your tender sensitivities. There is nothing wrong with laughter."

Her chemise was floating free now, the few lamps in the room illuminating her curves.

"You're a pirate."

Bion tilted his head to one side and moved toward her. She hadn't realized she'd stepped back, but couldn't stop herself from doing it once more. Her belly tightened with anticipation as he slowly approached her.

"Not all the time."

He offered her his hand. In some ways, the invitation was more arousing than the slow chase he'd been giving her. She blushed and fluttered her eyelashes, but she was already moving to meet him. He clasped her hand and pulled her against him. His kiss was hard and demanding, but she met him measure for measure.

Now that her petticoats were removed, the hard bulge of his cock was impossible to miss. She rubbed against it, impatient to have him inside her once again. He lifted his head, earning a soft hiss from her as frustration broke through her enjoyment of the moment. But he scooped her up, easing her impatience.

"We are not going to let that fine bed go to waste," he muttered as he carried her through the open doorway and into the bedchamber.

"I should hope not. You'd certainly lose standing among your pirate peers if you did."

The bed was turned down and the mattress soft. There was a soft scent of wildflowers as she crawled across its surface and faced her lover. He was freeing himself from his trousers, but his attention was on her. Sophia rose onto her knees and fingered the hem of her chemise.

"I swear you have only to ask me to beg you for your favor and I will."

They weren't flowery words, but from Bion Donkova, they were everything she needed. "I see." Sophia tugged the silk up to reveal her thighs. His dark eyes were focused on the rising hem. She leaned forward and he shifted, moving his attention to the gaping neckline.

"Tease," he accused softly. The bed shifted as he placed a knee on it. His erect cock was clearly in sight now, neatly turning the table on her.

"Somehow, I doubt Jonathon would have let me see any of his parts." She drew the chemise up and over her head. The night air was brisk but she was too hot to be bothered by it.

"I doubt you would have looked to see if any were in sight if you'd been his bride."

She shook her head. "No, I would have been put to bed, to await him." She lay down and reached for the covers.

Bion tore them back, beyond her reach. "Pirates take everything."

She lifted her arms and he came to her. Conversation became irrelevant as they communicated through touch. She needed to feel him—all of him—against her. As playful as their foreplay had been, she couldn't fend off the frantic need to hold him one last time. It drove her, consuming her as he pressed her back against the bed.

"I am going to enjoy taking you, Sophia."

His voice was low and menacing, but she purred with enjoyment. He spread her thighs, and she lifted her hips to welcome his first thrust. They moved together, giving and receiving, each trying to touch the other. There was pleasure in every motion and it built until there was no holding back the explosion. Her hands became claws as rapture twisted through her. Her nails dug into his skin while he bucked and drove his length hard and fast into her core. His body grew taut, his seed erupting deep inside her and for one moment, they were as close as two humans might ever be.

But it was a fleeting moment. Tears stung her eyes when he gathered her close.

You can cry later.

It was good advice but her heart wasn't listening. She struggled against the advance of time and the harsh reality Prince Afanasi had promised her. But a memory stirred, and she laughed softly with it. Bion shifted and raised her face so he might lock gazes with her.

"Somehow, I doubt that the prince has heard of the policy of killing new Navigators before they fall into the hands of the Helikeians."

"I believe he thinks me too smitten to do you

harm." Bion pressed her head back onto his chest. "He's correct."

Maybe some would not have considered his words a declaration, but Sophia knew better. For the moment it was enough. In fact, she was sure she would hear his words in her dreams for the rest of her life.

He tipped her head up. The light from the outer room cast him in shadow, but it suited the moment.

"Perhaps you'll consent to join me in an escape attempt."

"How?" She tried to sit up but Bion held her in place. "I know it would be simple enough to use the bedding to climb out of the window, but I suppose you could have done that from the third floor…"

He chuckled softly, shaking his head. She clearly had been thinking ahead. "I was locked in shackles and chained to the wall. Without your clever little announcement to Afanasi's staff, escape would have been beyond my doing. You're a better Illuminist than you realize, Sophia, and more of a counterpart than I gave you credit for."

He rose up, turning her over so that he looked down into her face; her back was on the surface of the bed.

"And as much as I should be focused on your attributes as my colleague, I confess I am far more interested in kissing you until there isn't a thought left in either of our minds."

"I wouldn't dream of arguing with you."

He pressed his thumb against her lower lip as his eyes narrowed. "Yes, you would, Grace O'Malley."

He kissed her before she might reply, and true to

his nature, the man employed action until there wasn't a thought left in her head—or his, which pleased her greatly.

∽✧∾

Dr. Nerval fingered the grooves in the top of his walking cane. The Deep Earth Crystal was carved and set like any ordinary glass cane topper, but he knew what it was. Those he was interested in knew what it was too.

"I wouldn't have thought you were a man more interested in listening than doing, Doctor."

Jordon Camden stepped out of a darkened doorway and offered Nerval a half bow.

"What interests me is the production of another Navigator. I am not paying for the possibility that that female is carrying if she spends the night alone."

"As thick as the doors are, they might well be arguing."

The doctor cleared his throat. "I very much doubt it. They could barely keep their hands off one another in the ballroom."

"I concede the point."

"Only because you came to make certain of the facts too," the doctor accused. "You have really no use for either of them. Why are you here?"

Jordon smiled at the doctor. "I always have an interest in profit, and there is profit to be made here. I promise you I will be bidding against you. But feel free to underestimate me."

It would do him no good. Dr. Nerval made his way down the hallway to the rooms he'd been provided.

No good at all. He would have the Navigator his actions had created. Failure was not an option. He was a Helikeian and only the best were allowed to survive.

~~~

Decima Talaska sat at the window of the room she'd rented for the night. It wasn't modern or even in good repair, but it had a fine view of a tavern across the street. She sat in darkness, so she might watch the residents of the village without their knowledge. It was frustrating not to be able to walk among them, but a stranger would have been noticed.

Still, there were details to take in—the type of clothing the women wore, the way the men toasted one another, and a hundred other things. It was a skill she'd had since she was a child, noticing details. It was the core of her success as a Hunter Guardian. She saw the little things that so many others overlooked. They might form a trail or, in this case, offer her the opportunity to blend in.

"Planning to try and replace the morning delivery boys?"

She jumped and bit back a curse. Lykos was already too sure of himself for her to let him know he'd startled her.

"Since the prince is planning an auction and seems to enjoy lavish displays, I suspect his kitchens will be taking in supplies at dawn."

"We are no match for the number of guards the man has."

"Which leaves us trickery," she informed him.

"A skill you are accomplished at, I admit." Lykos spoke in a tone rich with praise.

He leaned against the window frame and looked out at the revelers below. Decima eyed him warily, far too aware of his presence. It was simply a response triggered from the approaching battle. That was all. And she would not think about it anymore.

Eight

A RIPPING SOUND WOKE HER. SOPHIA OPENED HER EYES, but the room was still dark. The candles had been pinched out, but with her altered sight, she could see the residue of light in the room. The ripping came again.

"Is it time?" she asked, her mind clearing instantly. She should have been tired, but the anxiety of the past day made her far past ready for freedom. "Have the hounds gone in?"

"They will soon. Get dressed." Bion tore another strip off a bed curtain and added it to the rope he was making. "Wear something, well—"

"Besides the petticoat?" she offered as she found her chemise and shrugged into it.

He nodded, his focus on the rope. Sophia opened the wardrobe and searched through it.

"Your eyes have finished their transformation." Bion spoke softly from behind her, a touch of envy in his tone.

"Yes." She looked over her shoulder at him. "It's really quite amazing, I'll never kick the bedpost in the middle of the night. You'll see soon."

For a moment his hands were still, his attention locked on her. "Thank you." He knotted the rope again but stopped and looked back at her. "I never said that, but I should have."

"Even if it's landed you on an auction block?"

His teeth flashed at her as he pulled another knot tight. "Even if it ends with us breaking our necks as we climb out of the window, because I'll be double damned if I'll waste the chance you've provided to try and escape."

There was hope in his tone and his actions. She watched him continue working, then turned back to find something to wear. She'd go out the window in her chemise if she had to.

She wasn't going to waste her opportunity either.

Decima was frustrated. But at least she was faring better than Lykos. Her partner was currently fighting to maintain his composure as they chased down one false lead after another. No one was sure who provided the morning milk to the prince's estate. The duty seemed to be passed around like a chore because the prince would decide how much he was willing to pay and there was no room for bargaining.

"It seems we're at a crossroads."

Lykos angled his head and glared at her. "How so?"

"We can reserve our funds for the auction or use some of them to provision a wagon and deliver it to the prince's holdings," Decima said. "But if we buy the provisions—"

"We'll not have enough gold left to defeat the other clients," Lykos finished.

He scowled, but Decima expected her own expression was just as dark. They would have to make a decision and Bion and Sophia's fate would hang in the balance.

❧

Captain Aetos rose early. The maid he'd enjoyed during the night rubbed her eyes, then gathered up her clothing. He stretched and reached for his pants. The sun was just beginning to brighten the horizon. He frowned as he looked back at the rumpled bed. A few more hours of rest would be most welcome, but he wanted to get back in the air by sunset.

He'd have to commence with tying up the loose ends of his business dealings. Beyond the gates of the main house were the village and a bustling marketplace. Traders came through the village from the Far East as well as Europe. There might even be merchandise from Africa this time of year. The nobility of Russia liked spending their money on treasures, but they rarely left their land for fear of being suspected of treason.

Surely there would be something appropriate to settle his account with Jordon Camden, even if he didn't care for just how the man had kept his end of the deal. For a moment Aetos indulged his anger. Jordon Camden had done exactly what he'd said he'd do and not one thing more. He'd tracked Bion and Sophia and given him the information and then sold it to a dozen other interested parties. It was a betrayal, at least to Aetos's way of thinking. There was one thing Jordon Camden could count on and that was that

Aetos didn't suffer being played for a fool. But he'd still get the man his gift because vengeance was far better when it was unexpected. Aetos finished dressing and checked his pistol before hiding it in the interior pocket of his vest.

No one need know that Aetos was going to enjoy knifing the man in the back just as soon as an opportunity presented itself. Until then, he'd be finding the gift Jordon had demanded.

❧

There was a sharp whistle in the distance. Bion leaned out of the window as the dogs began to bark. They were moving away from the main house; the next whistle came from further away. Bion nodded, his body tensing.

"Don't look down."

"I'll look where I please, since these might be my last moments among the living," Sophia groused.

Praying might serve you better than being snippy. She sucked in a deep breath. It was only one floor.

Plenty high enough to kill you, girl.

"I suppose I can't take exception to your tone." Bion scanned the yard once again before tossing their rope down the side of the building.

"Because it saves you the trouble of trying to decide how to talk me into following you?"

He gave the rope a yank and the bed remained solidly in place. The look he gave her was rich with challenge. "I expect Grace O'Malley to have no problem following."

He shot her a grin and a wink before he went

through the window, the rope pulling tight as it supported his weight. The edges of the horizon were pink. Soon there would be too much light for them to make it down the expanse of the wall without being seen. Sophia poked her head out and swallowed to force a lump down her throat.

If she were going to die, she'd go out like a pirate queen.

The rope Bion had fashioned was easy to hook her hands into. She swung her leg over the windowsill, but the side of the house was slick. She lodged the tip of her boot into a groove between bricks and ordered herself to leave the house behind.

Bion was right; she shouldn't look down. But her pride refused to allow her to heed his advice. She was suddenly grateful for every sore, aching muscle her Asian fighting class had given her because she needed the strength she had built up. Her arm shook but she took one step and then another down the side of the house. The distance was no more than that of crossing a bedchamber but it seemed to take forever. Her heart was racing and sweat popped out on her forehead. She had to slide her feet along the smooth surface of the stone wall because the riding skirt she'd found to wear kept trying to get under her boot heels. Her fingers began to ache and it seemed as though the sun was rising impossibly fast.

"Almost there," Bion whispered from below.

She was panting but moved her feet a few more steps. At last Bion reached up and caught her. She wasn't even willing to quibble about the fact that he grabbed her hips in a far too intimate fashion for out of doors.

They were outside!

She drew in a breath and savored the feeling of the earth beneath her feet. "We did it."

"Not yet we haven't." Bion's voice was edged with urgency. "It won't take them more than an hour to see that rope."

He clasped her hand and tugged her around the back of the house. He slipped along the wall and she mimicked him. The chickens were waking up, the rooster beginning to crow. Behind the main house the stables stood in the predawn light. The master of the hounds was shepherding his charges inside, the animals eager to be fed.

Someone struck a bell in the distance, the sharp sound carrying through the morning stillness.

"That will be the watch changing at the gate."

A few moments later, there was the steady sound of marching feet as the men who had manned the gate returned to the barrack buildings. The back doors of the kitchen opened, two youths appearing with their hands full. One carried an iron pot with steam rising from its top while the other balanced a huge pitcher. Behind them a younger boy hauled a basket of freshly baked bread. They trudged toward the long, low building the guards had disappeared into.

"That will keep them occupied for half an hour." Bion pulled a small pocket watch from his vest pocket and noted the time.

Sophia scanned the area around them, desperate to find somewhere to hide. Dawn was still breaking, but it felt like high noon on an August day.

"Here," Bion announced at last. He pulled her a few more feet toward the kitchen doors, then reached down to lift a small trapdoor.

She hurried inside, crouching down to fit through the entrance. The air was musty and stale, but she could make out the shelves that lined the walls. The air was chilly, which would keep the food stores fresh and she hugged her arms to keep warm.

"Now we wait." Bion's voice was hard. There was no going back for him and she realized she felt the same. He kept the door to the root cellar open just an inch or two. They watched the boys return to the kitchen, their feet kicking up dust as they stomped the dirt loose on the steps.

The light was increasing and all they could do was wait. She was straining to hear the sound of an approaching wagon. Every second seemed to last for hours.

She jumped when it came. She was so desperate for escape that Sophia doubted what her ears were telling her. She pressed her face closer to the opening and peered out into the dusky morning light.

"Your sight is better than mine. What is it?"

She blinked, forcing herself to believe what she saw. "A wagon. Oh yes, Bion… and it has a cover over the back of it."

She was so happy she shook, but Bion didn't share her joy.

"Let's hope they unload quickly. If not, it won't take them long to find us here."

She looked behind her. The shelves were only half full. No, it wouldn't take long at all.

Mr. Graves whistled, then stopped, realizing what he was doing. It had been a mighty long time since he'd felt merry enough to whistle a tune while he worked. His new employer was perched behind the counter of his stall as Graves continued to set up the boxes of spices the man had for sale. There were cloves and cinnamon and their scents reminded Graves of his mother's kitchen.

He whistled again, remembering the song his mother had so often sung to him. He felt younger than he had in a long time; freedom seemed to be a magical tonic. There were men who would call him foolish for giving up his rank among the crew of the Soiled Dove, but he was more than content with his choice. He'd happily remain a lowly merchant's man.

"Exotic birds Camden can get. The man lives in the Ottoman Empire."

Graves froze, his blood chilling at the sound of the familiar voice. He looked past the boxes he'd just stacked and felt his eyes widen. Captain Aetos walked among the stalls, members of his crew trailing behind him.

It was fate coming to get him, all his misdeeds refusing to be left behind. He didn't deserve happiness. His hand gripped the small box he held so tightly that the wood cracked. The sound drew his attention and when he looked back up, Aetos had moved on.

Graves set the box down, his arms shaking as sweat dotted his brow. How in the hell had he gotten so lucky? He couldn't find a reason, which left him with the sure knowledge that a reckoning was coming.

He certainly deserved it.

❧

"We'll have to make a run for it."

Even if Bion's voice had held hope, Sophia doubted she would have placed any faith in it. There were just too many opportunities for failure.

But she mustn't dwell on that. No, it would be better to feel the strength in Bion's grip as he prepared to leave the root cellar behind. There was plenty of light now, maybe not full daylight but enough for anyone to spot them. She drew in a deep breath and tried to muster her courage.

"Let's go."

He cut her a sidelong glance and she stared straight back at him. "I'll be right behind you," she promised.

He nodded and lifted the cellar door. They climbed out and hurried across the distance toward the wagon. Inside the kitchen, the sound of people moving about drifted out the open door. Outside, someone was arguing with the owner of the wagon over the price as the rest of the kitchen staff scurried inside to escape it.

Bion climbed up into the back of the delivery wagon with one long step, pulling her along with him. The cover that had protected the goods from dust was pushed toward the back of the bed. Sophia knocked her shin as she followed Bion but she didn't slow down. Pain shot up her leg as she crawled down the bed of the wagon and beneath the thick cover Bion held up for her. It smelled of road dirt and spoiled milk, but she decided it was the best scent in the world.

They were huddled in the corner and she realized

Bion's jaw was clenched. Of course it was; he wasn't one who hid from trouble. But there was nothing for it. The driver muttered something in Russian that Sophia didn't need translated. Profanity had a tone that was universal.

The driver climbed up onto the seat and set the horses in motion. The wagon swayed as it turned in a circle and began the trek back to the gates. It was so simple, yet every second felt like an hour. All of her senses were heightened as they neared the gate and it opened.

She shivered with happiness and Bion squeezed her hand in response. Hope filled her as the wagon continued on its way, no shout for it to stop coming. It seemed too good to be true.

Which was what frightened her most.

Captain Aetos didn't like being on the ground too long. His temper was being tested as he walked through the stalls of the marketplace. He had more important things to do than buy gifts for a spoiled businessman. But offending Jordon Camden meant losing an important contact.

The morning was well underway as he continued to pass stalls because their merchandise seemed too common. Everything was beginning to blur as he became more frustrated with the need to procure something before the auction time arrived.

He checked his watch and growled. It would have to wait. Aetos turned to retrace his steps to where his horse was tied on the outskirts of the market.

❧

"The prince only gave me half of what it was worth."

Bion held up a hand to warn her to be silent as the wagon stopped.

"Not even enough to pay for the feed for the horses," the driver grumbled as he walked away.

Conversation drifted around them and Bion lifted one corner of the cover. They were parked on the outskirts of the morning market, horses and wagons lined up along a fence that was being used as a hitching post.

"The prince will send his men after us, you can bet on it," Bion warned her.

"Then we'd better hurry."

Sophia climbed out of the wagon, not caring for the feeling that was churning in her belly—as if everyone around them was watching them.

"We'll have to try and hire some horses. A cart will be too slow, and stealing anything would give the prince the legal right to imprison us if we were caught," Bion said as he led her past the delivery wagon.

"With what money?"

He shrugged. "We'll promise them payment when we arrive."

"How about I collect payment for you, Captain Donkova?"

Bion whirled around in a savage motion, pushing her behind him as they came face to face with Captain Aetos. He pointed a small pistol at them.

"It seems only fair since it was my Root Ball that transformed you into something of value," Aetos continued.

Every muscle she had drew tense. Bion snarled softly and stretched his arms out wide.

"Do stay right there," Aetos warned.

"It's going to take more than that peashooter to stop me," Bion assured him.

Aetos never faltered. "But I don't need to stop you, Captain Donkova. Just burden you enough so that you can't outrun my men."

Aetos shifted the gun and understanding dawned on Sophia. Her memory flashed with a vivid picture of Hawaii and Grainger shooting her to keep Janette in line.

Not again! She would not let it happen. They'd reached the stalls, and she brutally shoved a table over. Its contents went flying into Aetos as she reached out and grabbed Bion by the waist of his trousers.

"Run!"

Aetos let out a snarl as he tumbled backward. Sophia didn't wait to see if he fell. Bion turned in a flash and pulled her around the next stall. There was a crack from the pistol and an instant later she felt the bullet bite into her leg.

"Bastard!" she snapped, limping a few more steps before she crumpled. She tried to rise, but her leg refused to hold her weight.

"So you do know some curses." Bion pulled her behind a stall and lifted a finger to silence her.

Pain snaked along her calf, burning as hot as a fire poker. Bion pulled her behind some crates as she ground her teeth together to keep quiet.

"They can't be far," Aetos yelled.

Bion pushed her head down because every instinct she had wanted to fight. It was a sort of desperation and it was trying to take control of her. She fought it, needing her wits since she couldn't run.

But Bion could.

She looked at him, locking gazes, then she waved him away, motioning emphatically. Surprise flickered in his eyes, then they narrowed and he slowly shook his head. They glared at one another, neither one willing to give in until a soft step landed behind them in the stall.

Sophia lifted her head and shuddered when she saw Mr. Graves. He had a small crate in his hands and his lips were pressed into a hard line.

"Mr. Graves!" Aetos yelled. "Which way did my Navigators go? I hit one, so they can't be far."

The market was really bustling now, people crowding its paths. Mr. Graves put the crate down and pointed away from them. "That way, Captain. Saw it plain as day."

"Get moving!" Aetos barked at his men. There was the sound of people cursing as they were jostled and pushed aside.

But Mr. Graves stood still and looked down at them. "They're gone."

Sophia finally drew in a breath. She hadn't realized just how starved her lungs were for oxygen. She gulped like a freshly caught fish before mastering the urge to keep gasping. Once her need for breath was satisfied, the wound on her leg became excruciating, but she smiled.

"You make it hard to kill you, Mr. Graves." Bion looked through the crates to ensure that Aetos was gone before standing up to loom over their unexpected savior.

The sailor from the Soiled Dove shrugged, suddenly looking haggard. "I've done a fair number of things worthy of having my neck broken," he said, and ran a hand over his tired features. "All of them in the interest of living another day. I wasn't but a lad when I first ran afoul of them pirates. Life seemed too dear to give up, even if honor demanded it."

He closed his mouth, looking resigned to his fate. For the first time, Sophia found something in the man worthy of respect.

Bion looked like he was fighting off the urge to strike, but he finally nodded. "You'll have to face a Marshal."

Mr. Graves grunted. "You'll likely doubt me when I tell you I'm right pleased. See, I never held out much hope that I'd find my way onto land alive."

"That's a new way to look at it," Lykos offered as he appeared nearby. "I suppose I'll have to follow my comrade's example and decline to put a bullet through you. How very disappointing. After the chase I've had, I really want to shoot someone."

"By all means, go after Captain Aetos if it's blood-letting you crave," Sophia exclaimed with a big grin. "In fact, if you'd simply be so kind as to hand me that weapon—"

"We're getting out of here, Sophia." Bion stooped to flip her skirt back and inspect her wound, then gently pulled her to her feet. "Even if I agree with you."

Sweat popped out on her brow from the pain, but she managed to stay on her feet, firmly supported by Bion.

Lykos offered her a smirk. "Do my eyes deceive me? Is this not the second time I have discovered you bleeding from a limb?"

"I wanted matching scars," she shot back. For just a

moment, she enjoyed watching Bion's eyes narrow at her before she sighed. "Because once I am back in Britain, I plan to have a most normal and predictable life."

"Now that is something I agree with, Miss Stevenson." It wasn't the heartwarming admission she would have liked, but it was Bion Donkova. Her man of action, her pirate. He scooped her up and Lykos motioned them away from where Aetos had headed. He led them around the edge of a stall and back to where two horses were tied.

"The air station is a good day's ride," Lykos informed them as Bion helped her into the saddle. He tore a strip from her skirt and bound her leg, then held out a hand to Lykos.

Lykos hesitated before reaching into his vest and pulling out a small metal flask. "It's the last of my stash."

Bion unscrewed the cap, sniffed the contents, then took a swig. "High quality as usual. It certainly is nice to be back to normalcy."

He handed the flask up to Sophia and she took a long drink. When she lowered her chin, she smiled at the two men watching her with stunned expressions.

"Well now, don't you know an Irish gal can handle her liquor as well as any man? Even if my father insisted I keep that little skill for the kitchen, in the interests of maintaining appearances." She lifted the flask again because it was going to be a long ride and her leg ached. "But as an Illuminist, I won't be needing ladylike airs, so if you pass me the whiskey, expect me to enjoy it."

Bion smiled, his teeth flashing at her, and all he really lacked was a gold hoop dangling from his ear.

Lykos tossed a small purse to Bion. It jingled when he caught it. "Ride. I have to wait for Decima, but you two need to be gone immediately. We'll see you back in London."

Bion froze with one foot in the stirrup.

"Go, Captain. I can blend in. You and Miss Stevenson can't, and I would greatly appreciate you not placing me in the position of having to shoot you both when the prince's men surround us and we are completely outnumbered. I believe our luck is well and truly depleted."

"Agreed, but I do not like leaving you here."

"It is the best course of action with your eyes altered," Lykos insisted.

Bion's expression hardened, but he mounted. Lykos slapped Sophia's horse on the flank and the animal happily headed away from the noise of the market. But she pulled up, looking back at Lykos.

"He's right. We have to leave." Bion sounded disgusted as he pulled his purple-tinted glasses out and put them on. "He'll never leave Decima, and we're too easy to spot." He didn't like it, but he nodded and jerked his head toward the road. "Let's go home, Sophia."

She was sure four words had never sounded so sweet and at the same time so final. She gave the horse its freedom and soon they were leaving a trail of dust behind them. Prince Afanasi's house diminished as they rode hard toward the air station.

Yes, final. That was the feeling that settled over her. Like the ending of a book. The memories were grand and cheery, but reality was where one had to focus their attentions. Yes, reality—where Bion was her

Illuminist partner and pirate games became something relegated to the adventures of the past. Tears stung her eyes but she blinked them away. Bion was an Illuminist. He'd promised her nothing, and she needed to remember that he'd not been raised in her world.

You know you want more.

Maybe, but not if it was insincere. She was suddenly grateful for her future among the Illuminists, for it would save her from a marriage of convenience. It hurt to think of Bion offering for her when he had never spoken of love. She'd rather not have him under false circumstances.

But you love him.

Oh, do be quiet now.

Their adventure was over.

❦

Lykos wove through the market crowd with his hand tucked beneath his vest—it was comforting to feel the butt of his pistol. There was no way to see every face; there were just too many people. He searched for Decima, finally finding her.

He reached out and hooked her arm. She tensed, snapping her head around to see who had been so bold.

"I found Bion and Sophia—"

Pain exploded in his skull. It was blinding and too bright to escape. His knees buckled and the last thing he saw was Decima's green eyes filling with terror.

❦

Decima tightened her resolve. She fought the urge to test the rope binding her wrists again. It was tight enough to hold, and the sting of broken skin reminded her that she'd already tried to free herself. The room in the prince's home was lavish and clean, but it was less welcoming than the filthiest prison.

"Where are they?"

Decima simply stared back at Captain Aetos. Two of his men were nursing injuries; one of them wouldn't find his broken arm healing very soon.

"Do you think I have done my worst?" the captain continued. He walked in a circle around her, enjoying the sight of her nearly bare body. Her clothing was lying at her feet, shredded by the hands of his thugs. There were a few cuts in her chemise from their knives and the rope binding her hands above her head was very tight. The thin muslin undergarment floated freely but she wasn't going to squirm over modesty.

"Not at all," she answered calmly. "A man of your caliber is capable of much more."

Aetos grinned but stopped short of touching her. Something caught his eye and he bent down to sort through her ruined clothing. Her Illuminist pin with its Deep Earth Crystal and crossed sword emblem sparkled in the afternoon sun.

"You're a Guardian?" Aetos asked softly. "And a female. I've never encountered that combination before."

"Makes sense to me," one of his men spat out. "The bitch needs a lesson. Let me beat the location of those Navigators out of her."

"You will not gain what you seek," Decima responded in an even tone. "I promise you that."

"Well, I've got a promise for you—"

Aetos held up his hand and his man fell silent. He stared into Decima's eyes for a long moment.

"She doesn't know—that's why she's so certain," the captain shook his head. "You hit the other one too hard. The doctor tells me he doubts he'll live."

"In that case, it would be such a shame to destroy the perfection of this one."

Decima glanced over at the newcomer. He was a large man with dark hair and eyes. He studied her from head to toe, missing not a single inch of her.

She refused to feel exposed. She would not give into the urge because it would allow helplessness to seep past her defenses.

"I have never seen a female Guardian either."

Aetos shrugged. "She can't be any harder to break than any other woman."

"As I noticed, Captain Aetos, you fail to approach life as an admirer." The newcomer walked around Decima. "And you have not yet presented me with my gift. Did you tie her up for me? Excellent. I concede that a female Guardian is in fact the rarest of the rare. Adding her to my collection will be an extreme pleasure."

"If she'll satisfy our bargain, she's yours."

Decima lost some of her control over her emotions as the men shook hands. It shouldn't surprise her that men such as these would trade her like a commodity, and yet, her emotions came dangerously close to becoming involved. Aetos tossed her Illuminist pin to the other man and left the room, his men following.

"I am Jordon Camden." He slipped her pin into his pocket. When he locked gazes with her again, a flicker of challenge lit his dark eyes. "And you will be my pet."

His tone rung with certainty. Her belly tightened just a fraction before she controlled the response. She would give him nothing.

No matter what.

❦

"They cannot be far behind us," Bion insisted. But the captain of the Scarlet Dawn shook his head.

"You know the regulations, Captain Donkova. I must ensure your safety before all other concerns. I have already pushed the limits by waiting for two hours."

Bion leaned over the rail of the bridge, a pair of binoculars in his grip. The warning bell rang as the Scarlet Dawn made ready to leave the station. The escalator the captain had allowed to remain connected was retracted by large gears powered by steam. The sounds of metal meeting metal echoed through the bridge as the bell rang again and a crewman's voice came over the intercom.

"Ready to make sail, Captain!"

"Ten knots, Mr. Tailsman," the captain ordered in a smooth voice.

"Aye, Captain."

The engines hissed as steam billowed out of the twin smokestacks at the rear of the vessel, after they turned the turbines inside the engines. The airship accelerated smoothly, gaining altitude as the sun set. As much as Bion wanted to delay their departure, he couldn't ignore how delighted he was to feel the movement of the ship beneath his feet. It was like being home.

"I am sure the doctor has your companion patched up."

Bion bristled at the captain's words but had to concede defeat as far as Lykos and Decima were concerned. He didn't like leaving them behind, but the knowledge that Sophia was secure eased his mind. No man had it all, but at the moment, he felt richer than a king. He wove through the passageways, descending three flights of stairs until he found the medical facility.

It was a small cabin, like all those aboard the vessel. The Scarlet Dawn wasn't a passenger liner. She was built for cargo, precious cargo such as Deep Earth Crystals, and was constructed for maximum speed.

The doctor looked up as Bion entered and pointed to the narrow bunk Sophia lay on. Her eyes were closed, dark rings beneath them. But her chest rose and fell in a steady motion, and after a moment of assuring himself that she was finally safe, he felt fatigue ripping into him. He took off his protective glasses and rubbed his eyes, trying to remove the sting, but it only increased.

"You should join her," the doctor suggested as he handed Bion a clean compress. "Your eyes are in a delicate state."

Normally, he would have argued with anyone using the word "delicate" to describe him, but he simply didn't have the strength. For once, it didn't matter. Sophia was secure. That was all that mattered.

⤞⤝

"That one is going to die." The Russian doctor pointed an elderly woman toward a cot near the door of his clinic. The man's blond hair was stained with blood and his face was very pale. She motioned her companions forward, and they soon had him on the stretcher they had brought with them. They took him to a wagon and then on to the church at the end of town.

The woman sat down next to the bed they placed him in to wait for his death. It was a shame; he was a young, handsome man. It was her duty to pray for his soul, but she rose and brought back a basin of water. She wrung out a cloth and used it to clean the blood from the gash in his scalp.

"Why are you stitching him? The doctor said he would die," a younger woman said from her position next to an old woman who was drawing rattling breaths.

"It is good to practice and better to do so on those that will not live."

When she was finished, she stuck her needle back into the little book hanging from her belt. It was lined with a piece of felt wool to keep her needles from rusting. As the night hours passed, the man grew restless. She was tempted to use some of their painkillers to ease his thrashing, but it would have been a waste of resources. Her duty was to pray for him and tell the brothers of the religious order when he was ready to be buried. The prince provided a meager allotment to their order for their service to the dying who had no families to see to them. The doctor had more important things to do than care for those who were already lost.

So she gave him water, hoping it might ease his way into the next life. But when he was still drawing breath at sunrise, she gave him some of the weak broth the kitchen kept on hand for those in the next building who were expected to live. It had been a long time since one of her charges survived. If anyone might, it would be this man. There was something about him, something she sensed.

But the odds were not in his favor.

❧

London.

"You're enjoying this too much."

Bion raised an eyebrow innocently. Sophia glared at him and crossed her arms over her chest. He laughed at her, then adjusted the pillow beneath her leg. The bullet had hit the bone this time, leaving her with a lengthy recovery time.

"And you are not enjoying it enough, dear Miss Stevenson." He pressed a hand to the center of his chest. "My confidence in my nursing abilities is being cut to ribbons by your disgruntled looks."

"I doubt it."

He abandoned his innocent look and smiled at her, a slow twisting of his lips that betrayed just how much he was enjoying himself.

"Don't doubt it." He flattened his hands on either side of her. "I take a great deal of satisfaction in knowing exactly where you are and that you are in my bed."

She poked him in the middle of his chest. "You shouldn't talk like that. It's indecent."

And you like it a lot, missy.

But she really couldn't afford to. Her heart was already aching. She looked away because his gaze was just as keen as ever. It would be very un-Illuminist of her to inflict her emotions on him.

"It's honesty—a trait you'll just have to grow accustomed to." He cupped her chin and brought her attention back to his face. "Because I promise you, Sophia, I consider you my prize and like any self-respecting pirate, I intend to keep you secure."

"But—"

He sealed her protest with a kiss. It was hard and insistent, stirring her passion, but she winced when she moved her leg out of instinct.

Bion grumbled as he straightened up. "I suppose I will have to curtail my roguish ways until you heal."

"You know, I labeled you a pirate as an insult."

He laid his arm across his middle and bowed formally. "Yet a man of action makes the most of every situation."

She laughed, unable to resist his charm.

"Now I am wounded," he announced.

"Why?"

"Because you look surprised to hear me teasing you." His mocking attitude changed instantly. For a long moment, he watched her through the lenses of his glasses. But he turned back to the dressing mirror and finished buttoning his uniform coat. Every button gleamed from polishing, just like his boots and badge. He was every bit the captain, confirming their return to reality. She felt the tension in the room increasing until she found herself bracing for the moment it snapped.

She didn't have to wait long.

Bion returned to her bedside, taking a moment to stroke her cheeks. "Thank you for making sure I got the use of that Root Ball." The words sounded as if they were torn from his soul, but he didn't appear miserable. "That concludes our unfinished business."

"Does it?" she inquired sweetly.

"Yes, Miss Stevenson, it does. Which leaves us the opportunity to move on to new business." He reached into the front pocket of his uniform jacket and pulled something out. She didn't get a good look at it because he moved, shifting until he was poised on one knee next to the bed. Clasped tightly between his index finger and thumb was a gold band with a ruby set into it.

"Will you do me the extreme honor of becoming my wife?"

Once again, he flattened a hand over his heart, looking for all the world like a devoted suitor. But it was the torment in his eyes that drew her attention. There was a need there that mirrored her own and she blinked several times before daring to believe that it was real.

"But… well… I mean… why?"

His eyes narrowed. "Because I love you, Sophia Stevenson, and I think you love me, in spite of your efforts to conceal it."

"Well, you needn't act as if that's wrong of me," she sputtered.

One of his dark eyebrows rose. "At this moment, I consider it a travesty that you are not taking notice of just how gallant I am, sweetheart."

Her cheeks heated, and he gently wiggled the ring so that the light flashed on the facets of the stone.

"There is no one I've ever allowed to rescue me or anyone I've ever wanted to chain to my bed, and

I promise you, Sophia Grace O'Malley, you are the only woman I have ever respected enough to call my counterpart. You are going to be my wife."

"Am I now?"

He nodded, challenge flickering in his eyes. She laughed, unable to resist being amused by his arrogance while he was poised on his knee.

She nodded, her tongue stuck to the roof of her mouth. Bion blew out a long sigh and smiled as he pushed the ring onto her finger.

"I cannot believe you are on your knee," she confessed.

"Am I not gallant enough to shame even the aforementioned Jonathon Saddler?"

She laughed. "You are nothing like Jonathon Saddler, thank goodness. He bored me to tears and that's the honest truth." She sat up, reaching for him. "Yes, I do love you, Bion Donkova."

His face lit, joy mixing with the amber streaks in his eyes. He rose from his knee and flopped onto the foot of her bed, looking as if he'd just fought the fight of his life. Relief appeared on his face next, vexing her with just how tormented the man really was about making the proposal.

Honestly, she doubted she'd ever understand him. But that wouldn't stop her from doing her best to keep him guessing.

"Now you must go and ask my father for his blessing."

Bion raised his head, his forehead furrowed. Sophia crossed her arms over her chest.

"And don't think I will listen to a single word of argument, you rogue. Why, it's shameful, really, this rule that has prevented me from walking across the street to let my father know I am alive. He's suffered seven months of not knowing what's become of me. Well, since he is going to be your father-in-law, you can go and tell him what I cannot until I take my Oath of Allegiance."

"An excellent idea." Janette Lawley spoke from the doorway. Her husband was behind her and Bion groaned.

"You would pick now to visit."

Darius pushed the door wide for his wife and inclined his head toward Bion. "Of course, it took precise planning."

Janette sat on the side of Sophia's bed, peering at her new ring. Bion rolled over and onto his feet. He offered them a half bow before he retrieved his hat from the hat stand in the corner of the room.

"I can deny you nothing," he groused.

"A difficulty I know all too well," Darius commiserated.

Janette looked up, fixing her husband with a hard look. He laughed on his way out the door. Sophia listened to their footfalls in the outer room and simply couldn't keep from smiling. Everything was suddenly far better than perfect. Bion Donkova loved her and she intended to enjoy every second of their future together.

Read on for an excerpt from

A Lady Can Never Be Too Curious

Mary Wine

WITHIN MOMENTS, JANETTE STOOD ON THE OPPOSITE side of the street. The columns looked taller now. She climbed the steps, tipping her head back to investigate the construction of the roof. The portico was covered in brilliant paintings—perfect images of the solar system and other things she'd never seen before. But were the paintings of fact or fiction? Fact. She knew she was in the place of facts. Satisfaction filled her and left goose bumps along her arms because it was so intense.

Someone cleared his throat.

Janette jerked her attention down to discover a doorman standing inside the building with the door open for her.

"Good afternoon."

The doorman didn't even blink but remained at his post. He looked straight ahead, never focusing on her. Excitement renewed its grip on her. Janette wasn't sure if she forgot to draw breath or not, but she walked through the forbidden doorway.

The doorman shut the door behind her and walked

to a small booth. He stood there, facing the wall, but when she peered closer, she could see he was watching through some sort of window. It wasn't transparent, but she could clearly see outside.

Fascinating...

"The experiments have already begun."

She straightened abruptly as he spoke without looking at her.

"Yes, thank you."

It was difficult to turn her back on the window set into solid stone. She wanted to look through it and discover its secrets, but the doorman's words tempted her to see how much further she might go.

The hallway was lit, but instead of the green glow of gaslights, a muted white light glowed from behind frosted panes of glass. She reached out and touched one gently and found it cool. There was no smoke or soot either.

Astounding.

Voices drifted into the hallway from a large archway ahead. A few more steps and she could make sense of the conversation.

"So we know the conductive capabilities of Deep Earth Crystals..."

Janette entered under the arch and froze.

"We also know that Deep Earth Crystals respond to one another...It is this reaction that allows us to harness their energy...and produce steam for power..."

The lecturer was in the center of the room. A table stood behind him lit by huge panes of frosted glass that glowed brighter than a full moon. Each was held by a large copper stand with gears built into them so the light could be aimed in different directions. Like a lamp that might be moved to aim light in any direction.

But what was a Deep Earth Crystal? And how could it respond?

She took a step sideways into one of the rows of seats ringing the stage the lecturer stood on and sat down. Excitement gripped her as she leaned forward to hear the rest of the lecture. A sound rose from those watching as the man pulled a large crystal from a case.

"Impressive…yes…but remember…size does not dictate the potency of the conductive properties."

He set the crystal down and plucked what looked like a folded leather apron off the table. Once he flipped it open and pushed his hand into it, it was clear it was a glove, made of leather reinforced with sturdy canvas. Janette leaned forward, eager to see why he needed such protection from rocks. He lifted a dome such as she might expect to see on a breakfast service tray, and beneath it lay a small crystal.

It was no thicker than a broom handle and only about six inches long, but he handled it with great care, reaching out his gloved hand to pick it up while holding his head back, as though the crystal were molten metal.

"Here we have an excellent example of the true power of—"

The moment the smaller crystal came closer to the large one, the room filled with a sharp whine. The lecturer stiffened, fighting to maintain his grip on the smaller crystal. His assistants lunged forward to help him, but the smaller crystal broke his grip and went sailing up into the seats.

The whine decreased as it arced through the air and left the other crystal behind. The Illuminists watching in front of her ducked, and the crystal landed neatly in her lap.

Janette picked it up before thinking, and the pulse of electricity began shooting through her body. It was deeper, almost harmonic. She swore she could hear the delicate sounds of music, and the crystal itself felt warm against her palm. It felt completely correct to hold it, and satisfying in an unexpected way, as though she'd never truly been complete until this moment.

"Madam…*madam!*"

Janette was startled out of the strange euphoria by the lecturer's frantic voice. He'd rushed up the aisle but stood staring at her.

He suddenly smiled, and crinkles appeared near his eyes. "I wasn't informed we had a new handler in our midst. When did you arrive?"

The rest of the audience all stared at her.

"Well…just now." She stood, and those closest to her shifted back, their attention on the crystal she held. "Would you like me to place this somewhere for you?"

Four assistants were clustered around the lecturer. They wore leather overcoats and had leather hoods on their heads with a pair of goggles pushed up above their eyes. One of them leaned in and whispered in the lecturer's ear, pointing at Janette. The lecturer's eyebrows rose.

"You will need to come with me." A deep voice issued the command from behind her.

Janette felt a tingle race down her spine. The newcomer had a voice edged with steel, the solid sort of authority that announced a man who was accustomed to being obeyed. She turned to discover the owner of the voice standing only a single pace from her. She had to look up because he was tall with broad shoulders.

He was attired in a double-breasted vest and overcoat—just as proper as any gentleman—but there was something in his dark eyes that was very uncivilized. For all that they were surrounded by others, she felt like she was alone with him.

And that knowledge excited her.

Definitely wicked…

The sensation was unsettling, and for some odd reason, she sensed that he knew exactly how he affected her. It was in the narrowing of his eyes and the thinning of his lips—tiny little details she shouldn't have noticed but did.

"My apologies, Professor, for having your lecture interrupted by a trespasser," the newcomer said. "I will remove her."

"Mr. Lawley, she is still holding the crystal…If you touch her…the current…ah…" The lecturer's warning came too late. Janette barely felt the man close his grip around her upper arm when he growled and released her.

"I did warn you, Darius. That's a level-four sample she's holding. Because she's a Pure Spirit, the current is going straight—"

"Enough. She's heard too much already. She is not an Illuminist."

Darius Lawley offered the professor a frown. When he turned his head, Janette was treated to the view of some sort of device covering his ear. Several copper and silver gears were visible, and the men behind him wore similar devices. These men didn't look like the other Illuminists attending the lecture. They were burly, and their expressions, hard.

Like constables.

Darius jerked his head back toward her the moment she moved. There was sharpness in his eyes, but what she sensed most about him was the fact that he was dangerous. He was unlike any man she'd met. Her world had always been full of gentlemen whom she trusted to remain at a polite distance.

This man was nothing like that. He'd boldly touched her, and that brief connection felt somehow… intimate. Yet she wasn't offended. The surge of excitement was only growing stronger as she contemplated leaving with him.

"If you please, miss, give the crystal to Professor Yulric." His voice was deep and raspy, setting off a ripple of awareness that traveled down her length in spite of how perfectly polite his words were.

"Yes, quite right. Hand it here. It's quite volatile, you understand." The professor shuddered. He extended his hand with the protective glove still in place.

"I find the lecture quite amazing. I'd like to remain to learn more about the crystal."

"Illuminists only," Darius informed her. His expression tightened, his lips sealing into a hard line.

She sighed before turning her hand over so the crystal dropped into the professor's waiting palm.

"Clear a path…Clear the way…" Professor Yulric hurried down the aisle, and the crystal began to whine as he neared the other one. "Remove the male, for heaven's sake, or we'll have another uncontrollable reaction."

"The what? Did you say male? As in gender?" Janette asked, too curious to contain her question.

"Nothing," Darius informed her quietly. "You do not belong here."

He reached past her and grasped one of her shoulders and neatly turned her around so the sight of Professor Yulric was lost. It was done with such a light touch she stood slightly shocked.

"But I want to see—"

"I've no doubt you do, but you have snuck inside our chambers, which I cannot allow. Please come with me."

She really couldn't refuse; after all, he was correct. She followed him, and his men fell into step behind them.

Confusion needled her as they went right past the doorman. Her expectation that she would be tossed unceremoniously out onto the front steps vanished as Darius continued on, granting her the opportunity to see more of the forbidden building.

It should have alarmed her; instead, she felt another jolt of heat stab into her. She didn't care at all if the situation was proper, it was exciting.

"Where are you taking me?"

"To my office."

He lifted his hand to touch the device in his ear. Almost in the same instant there was a groan as a door ahead of them opened. Darius led her through it, and the door closed behind them with a solid sound.

About the Author

Mary Wine is a multipublished author in romantic suspense, fantasy, and Western romance. Her interest in historical reenactment and costuming also inspired her to turn her pen to historical romance with her popular Highlander series. She lives with her husband and sons in Southern California, where the whole family enjoys participating in historical reenactments.

Kiss of Steel

by Bec McMaster

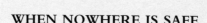

WHEN NOWHERE IS SAFE

Most people avoid the dreaded Whitechapel district. For Honoria Todd, it's the last safe haven. But at what price?

Blade is known as the master of the rookeries—no one dares cross him. It's been said he faced down the Echelon's army single-handedly, that ever since being infected by the blood-craving he's been quicker, stronger, almost immortal.

When Honoria shows up at his door, his tenuous control comes close to snapping.

She's so…innocent. He doesn't see her backbone of steel— or that she could be the very salvation he's been seeking.

"McMaster's wildly inventive plot deftly blends elements of steampunk and vampire romance with brilliantly successful results. Darkly atmospheric and delectably sexy…"—Booklist *Starred Review*

"A leading man as wicked as he is irresistible… Heart-wrenching, redemptive, and stirringly passionate…"—RT Book Reviews, *4.5 Stars*

For more Bec McMaster, visit:

www.sourcebooks.com

A Lady Can Never Be Too Curious

by Mary Wine

❧

**Beneath the surface of Victorian life
lies a very different world...**

Hated and feared by the upper classes, the Illuminists guard
their secrets with their lives. Janette Aston's insatiable quest
for answers brings her to their locked golden doors, where
she encounters the most formidable man she's ever met.

Darius Lawley's job is to eliminate would-be infiltrators, but
even he may be no match for Janette's cunning and charm...

❧

*"This fast-paced, unique steampunk story has
introduced me to a whole new world that I can't
wait to read more of."*—Night Owl Reviews

*"Filled with action, intrigue, and a small twist of
humor, A Lady Can Never Be Too Curious is for
the true lover of romance—some of the scenes are sure to
peel the wallpaper right off the walls."*—Book Loons

For more Mary Wine, visit:

www.sourcebooks.com

The Geek Girl and the Scandalous Earl

by Gina Lamm

❧

The stakes have never been higher...

An avid gamer, Jamie Marten loves to escape into online adventure. But when she falls through an antique mirror into a lavish bedchamber—200 years in the past!—she realizes she may have escaped a little too far.

Micah Axelby, Earl of Dunnington, has just kicked one mistress out of his bed and isn't looking to fill it with another—least of all this sassy, nearly naked woman who claims to be from the future. Yet something about her is undeniably enticing...

Jamie and Micah are worlds apart. He's a peer of the realm. She can barely make rent. He's horse-drawn. She's Wi-Fi. But in the game of love, these two will risk everything to win.

❧

"Lamm's wonderfully quirky romance brings fresh humor to a familiar trope, with snappy writing and characters who share a surprising, spicy chemistry."—RT Book Reviews

"A light romance with plenty of passion and conflict."—Historical Novels Review

For more Gina Lamm, visit:

www.sourcebooks.com

Geek Girls Don't Date Dukes

by Gina Lamm

---— ❧ —---

She's aiming to catch a duke.

Leah Ramsey has always loved historical romance novels and dressing in period costumes. So when she has a chance to experience the history for herself, she jumps at it—figuring it can't be too hard to catch the eye of a duke. After all, it happens all the time in her novels.

But sometimes a girl can do even better...

Avery Russell, valet and prize pugilist, reluctantly helps Leah gain a position in the Duke of Granville's household... as a maid. Domestic servitude wasn't exactly what she had in mind, but she's determined to win her happily ever after. Even if the hero isn't exactly who she's expecting...

---— ❧ —---

For more Gina Lamm, visit:

www.sourcebooks.com